LEAP OF FAITH

ELIZABETH JOHNS

CHAPTER 1

"What are we going to do?" Hope asked, twisting her black worsted wool skirt in her hands. The question had been asked a hundred times in the past day since they had received the solicitor's message that he was to call today.

Faith watched wearily as her sister made another frantic circuit across the Aubusson carpet in her oppressive black crêpe.

"We will be thrown out. I know we will!" She fretted.

Faith suspected the very same thing, but it would do no good to panic, she reminded herself.

"Let us see what he has to say. I have been saving as much as I can, and hopefully he will at least assist us in finding respectable positions." The four eldest sisters had been doing what they could to make money in genteel ways—teaching music, sewing, sitting with some of the elderly in the afternoons.

Joy, the youngest, began to cry, clinging to Faith's skirts.

"Hush, Joy. Crying will not help anything!" Patience scolded.

"Leave her be," Hope defended.

Grace stood quietly in the shadows of the thick, puce velvet curtains, looking out over the park as if it held the answers.

"I don't want us to be separated," Joy wailed.

"I know, dearest, but we must wait and see what Lady Halbury wished for us. Perhaps we will be allowed to remain here."

Patience scoffed.

"If not, then I will soon be of age. We will find a way," Faith said with an assurance she did not feel.

"What if we are sent to the workhouse?"

"Lady Halbury saved us from such a fate before. I cannot see that she would allow that to happen from the grave." Who knew what members of the aristocracy would do? By all accounts, everyone considered their guardian an eccentric for taking five girls in and raising them as her own. She had been their mother's old school friend. But none of them were related by blood to the new owner of Halbury Hall, and they had no family that would take them.

"How much longer?"

"It has only been five minutes since you last asked," Patience, the least patient of them all, remarked.

"I see a carriage." Grace did not turn around but watched the vehicle's progress. When they heard it stop, she finally turned to join the others. They sat soberly in their Queen Anne chairs from another generation placed in a half-circle facing the wall of windows overlooking Bath with its golden-stoned terraces and the abbey's pinnacled tower presiding over the valley.

When the door to the drawing room finally opened and Parkhurst announced the solicitor, all of them were at rigid attention in their unrelieved black.

"Mr. Browning to see you, Miss Whitford."

Faith indicated a chair for the thin, wiry, older man to sit in, then sat herself.

He looked a bit disconcerted by the lot of them, which was a common response to the uncommon appearance of five dark-haired, blue-eyed beauties of almost identical appearance. He cleared his throat. "Are you certain you wish everyone to be present, Miss Whitford?"

"Since what you say affects all of us, yes."

"Very well." He pulled open his leather satchel and extracted a sheaf of documents. He proceeded to flip through several pages before coming to the one he wanted. "Only a certain portion of the will pertains to you. I shall read only that."

Faith inclined her head.

He skimmed through some pages, muttering words as he read, then cleared his throat. "With regards to my wards, children of my heart: Faith, Hope, Patience, Grace, and Joy, I bequeath each 5000 pounds, to be kept invested until the time of their majority or marriage, whichever may come first."

A loud gasp resounded between them.

"That is very generous of her." Faith knew that was a gross understatement, but felt she had to say something. She had not expected anything so large. In fact, she had not known Lady Halbury to have such a vast fortune. "Since I will soon be of age, does this mean I am to receive the money then?"

"Indeed. But that is still some months away, and your guardian has the care of it until then. I suggest you discuss the matter with him."

"The new baronet? Her ladyship never mentioned the new heir."

"A distant cousin of her ladyship's dead husband. He has been in India these past years, but as Lady Halbury had a life tenancy in this house, it is likely she never thought to mention him. I wrote to him about you ladies, of course, but since he was not in the country, I allowed things to remain as they were until he gave further direction."

"And has he now?" Faith was afraid of the answer.

"He has returned from India, yes." There was hesitation in the man's voice.

"What is it, sir? Are we to lose our home?"

"Sir Reginald has returned with his family and wishes to take up residence here. Unfortunately, he has four young children of his own and does not wish to be encumbered with five more that are not relations."

Faith had known it was a likely outcome, yet it was still extremely difficult to hear that their home for the past decade or more was to be taken away. It was never really theirs to begin with, but still.

3

"Where are we to go, sir? Is there any hope that I might receive my portion a little sooner than my birthdate?"

"That is a question for your guardian. He might be prevailed upon to release the funds."

Why had Lady Halbury never mentioned a guardian? Faith looked warily at her sisters, who were equally dismayed. "Is Sir Reginald not our new guardian?"

"Indeed, no. I have contacted the gentleman on your behalf, but have received no response. The best I could convince Sir Reginald to do was to provide you with enough to see you on your way. A hundred pounds will hopefully see you comfortably to your guardian and then he may advise you from there." He slipped a piece of paper from the folio along with an envelope and handed it to Faith, who took them distractedly.

"How long do we have?" Hope asked.

"Sir Reginald will be here in a sennight and would like you to be gone by then."

"We are simply to arrive on our guardian's doorstep without any communication with him?" Faith was in shock.

"I am not certain how to advise you, Miss Whitford. I have done all I can."

"I cannot like haring off to London without any expectation of being received." It was not to be borne!

"A legal guardian can hardly refuse his wards. Perhaps you and Miss Hope could go and leave the others with someone in the village until matters are settled. It would certainly be easier for two of you to travel than five."

The man stood and made his way to the door, clearly ready to wash his hands of them. "Good day, Misses Whitford."

Faith watched him leave feeling oddly detached. It was hard to feel angry with Sir Reginald when he was only claiming his rights, but Faith could not help it. At least there was enough money to see them to London. But none of them had ever been to London, and she held no delusions that it would be a simple task to set up house there. She did not even want to set up house there. She knew her sisters would love to have a Season, but she also knew enough that they would have little success without funds or a sponsor. Her 5000 pounds would not last long in such an endeavour, let alone provide for her own future.

Her sisters were watching her, waiting for her reaction.

"Perhaps Hope and I should go and try to speak with our guardian before taking everyone to the city. It is not so far, and we would be back before the week is over. I am certain Vicar and Mrs. Carson would allow you to stay for a few days."

Grace and Patience were best friends with their eldest daughter, Louisa, and their younger daughter, Mary, was between Grace and Joy.

"Would you mind terribly?" She looked to her sisters. They had always made decisions together, even though she was more like a mother to them.

"If we may stay with the Carsons, that would be well enough," Joy said. She was the one that did not like Faith to be out of her sight.

Faith blew out a breath of resolution. "Very well. I will arrange it and plan on leaving first thing in the morning."

She gathered her sisters around her, and they all came together for a hug.

"I don't want everything to change," Grace said.

"Supposing our guardian is an ogre?" Joy asked.

"Supposing he's nice?" Patience countered.

"Supposing he won't let us have a Season?" Hope worried.

"We will resolve everything, I promise you. It is only a few more months until I come of age. At least now we know that we have some funds if we can survive for that long." Faith pulled back. "Now, we must pack and make arrangements."

"I wish we could all go," Grace bemoaned as they climbed the stairs to pack their trunks.

WHILE HIS FIVE newly acquired wards were plotting their imminent descent upon his peace unbeknownst to Dominic, Viscount Westwood, he was enjoying a reprieve with his old school friends and partners at his hunting box in Leicestershire.

It was completely devoid of any femininity, save Mrs. Barrett, the housekeeper, and it was perfect. The dark-panelled walls were lined with paintings of hunting scenes and trophies—no bright colours, gilt or floral patterns in sight. Scents of leather, smoke, and brandy wafted through the house, mixed with the roasting of game emanating from his chef's kitchen.

He and his oldest friends were enjoying glasses of brandy around the fire after a day of shooting pheasant while they waited for their supper from the renowned chef.

"What will your mother say when she realizes the guest of honour at her house party is a *ghost* of honour, Max?" Freddy snorted and laughed at his wit, which was anything but. Freddy Cunningham was too beautiful to be a man with his blond hair and green eyes. Too many silly females fawned and laughed at his ridiculous sense of humour.

"I do not care much what she says, though I can hear it in my head anyway. Devilish annoying to be set upon by matchmaking harpies. I will not dance to her tune no matter what schemes she concocts," Max, Lord Rotham said loftily. As the heir to a wealthy dukedom, he was constantly besieged.

"Better you than me, old fellow. Can't stand up to me mater for anything. She even threatens tears and I turn to mush," Freddy acknowledged.

"Well, we are all safe from females of any variety here." Dominic was himself tired of being hunted by the fairer sex, which was why he'd suggested removing here.

"Agreed, there's no chance of anyone finding us here. It's more off the beaten track than anywhere else I've ever been," Rotham agreed.

They all raised their glasses and drank to that.

"I'll remember that the next time I need a repairing lease," Montford murmured, having been uncommonly quiet. His dark eyes looked troubled.

"What's the matter, Monty?"

"I wish I could laugh about females. But the fact of the matter is I have to marry and soon."

One would have thought they'd just watched a comrade fall on the battlefield, so quiet and taciturn did the group fall in a matter of seconds. Truth be told, it was akin to losing a war, being the first man to fall to matrimony.

"Why?" Freddy asked.

"My father asked me. They want an heiress to replenish the family coffers and an heir, of course." He made a circle in the air with his fork.

They all made noises of sympathy. That was more than any of them could withstand.

"Any candidates yet?" Rotham asked.

Montford looked up with disgust. "My mother has made me a list. Two dozen of them and not a single one I can stomach the thought of being a tenant for life with."

"Does it have to be from the list?" Freddy scowled with distaste.

"I cannot see why it matters one way or the other. It is not like an eligible beauty is going to drop from the sky. Whichever way you look at it, I'll be leg-shackled."

They all took another drink and observed a moment of silence.

"At least we have a little while longer and the food is superb." Dominic did not wish to dwell on scheming females and marriage.

"Can we stay here forever, Dom? Good food, good drink, no matchmaking mamas or whey-faced chits."

"It matters not to me. I have no obligations at the moment and I intend to enjoy it."

"'Tis easy for you to say. You're as rich as Croesus."

Dominic could not argue that point.

Once they were well into an array of roast saddle of mutton, pheasant pie, civet of hare, prawns, and a fricassee of chicken served with asparagus in butter and spinach cakes, the distant sound of a rapper knocking on the door caused all of the gentlemen to look up.

"Who the devil could that be? Only my secretary knows where I am and he was instructed only to bother me under the direst of circumstances." Yet Dominic could not think of any dire circumstances. His mother and brother enjoyed the best of health, and were comfortably tucked up in their estates at the moment.

"Did any of you tell anyone where we would be?" Rotham asked scornfully, which was received with a series of rebuffs. All of them were equally desperate for privacy after Max had been recently chased down by a desperate mama and daughter, and had barely escaped the parson's noose.

Dominic heard the dreaded footfalls approaching the dining room, and Barrett entered the room.

"An urgent note from London, my lord. One of your grooms. He says he is to await a reply."

Satterlee had sent one of Dom's own men. It must be dire, indeed. He was conscious of all of his friends watching warily, and that they had ceased eating. He opened the missive in Satterlee's familiar script.

MY LORD,

FORGIVE THE INTRUSION, but I deemed this most urgent and felt you would agree. Two females have arrived on your doorstep, saying they are your wards and wish for your instruction on where they may reside. Apparently, they were taken in by the late Lady Halbury upon the death of their parents, who were missionaries. There are five of them, but only two are here at present. I have checked the validity of their claim with your solicitor, and it is unquestionably true. Even though I believe the intent was for your father to have been their guardian, it nevertheless falls to you. I am looking into any loopholes, of course, but what would you like me to do with them in the meantime? They are to be out of their present situation in less than five days' time.

YOUR OBEDIENT SERVANT,
    Charles Satterlee

. . .

DOMINIC STARED at the words on the page, but no matter how many times he read them, they did not change.

"What is it, Dom? You have me worried. Did someone die?" Freddy asked.

He sighed, then put the paper down. "No. Well, yes, someone died, but that is not the issue at present. It seems I have acquired five wards."

His friends stared at him, clearly as stupefied as he felt.

Then Freddy began to laugh. "He's funning with us."

"I assure you, my taste is not so poor as to fun about something like this."

"How old are they? Ship them off to school," Rotham recommended.

"Not a bad notion." He considered that suggestion for a moment. "I assume two of them are of age, since they arrived on my doorstep in London."

"Then your mother can handle them."

Dominic almost smiled because his friends were trying to be so helpful. He would do the same were the situation reversed. He shook his head as if trying to awaken from a dream. It still seemed too fantastic to be true. No one in their right mind would leave him five wards. Were they all female? He scanned the letter, and it did not say other than the two that had shown up at his door were of the fair sex.

"I beg you will excuse me. I must pen a letter to my secretary. Pray continue the meal. It is too fine to waste."

As he went to the study to seek pen and paper, the gravity of the situation disturbed him greatly. Rarely did anything disturb Dominic, but being saddled with young wards certainly was beyond inconvenient. If anyone could find a way out of the pickle, it was Satterlee. But likewise, it was not his wards' fault they'd all been placed in an impossible position. There was nothing for it but to make the best of things. Devilish inconvenient that they were at his London home, however. Certainly, they could not stay.

He wrote for his secretary to find them a place to live, and whatever servants were necessary for their comfort until he returned. He had no intention of curtailing his hunting trip for a pack of brats he knew nothing about. Hopefully by the time he returned, the mess would be sorted out. Dismissing any worry for the nonce, he returned to his friends.

"Billiards, anyone?"

CHAPTER 2

*L*ondon was like nothing Faith had ever seen—and she had thought Bath was large! As she looked out of the window of their hotel room, she felt like an insignificant speck of sand against a fathomless sea. Even though they overlooked Green Park, the constant flow of carts and pedestrians served as testimony they were not in their small city of Bath any longer.

"How long must we wait to hear?" Hope asked impatiently.

Faith did not bother to answer. She had been with Hope when Lord Westwood's secretary gave them the unfortunate news that his lordship was at his hunting box in Leicestershire and, to his knowledge, was unaware of the guardianship. He had promptly sent them to the Pulteney Hotel with their maid, Gibson, promising to send a message to Lord Westwood post haste. That was over four-and-twenty hours ago.

"We have wasted two days, and now only have five left!" Where Faith was the practical, responsible one, Hope was equally a dreamer, and she had spent much time dreaming of a London Season.

"I am well aware of our situation, but what else are we to do? Our sisters are safe at the vicarage, and the Carsons understand our predicament. Our belongings are already packed, so there can be no problem with Sir Reginald's return."

"But are we expected to sit here until his lordship bothers to answer us? Our funds will only last so long. Why did Mr. Satterlee tell us not to go anywhere?" Hope paced the room. "Perhaps he thinks we need someone older to lend us countenance?"

"Fustian! I am almost of age and have had responsibility for all of you since Lady Halbury died." Truthfully, since their parents had died.

"Like an older matron would do?"

Faith scowled at Hope.

"I was only trying to think of why he would not want us to leave. Perhaps our clothing is embarrassing?"

"It may not be of the latest mode, but it is hardly an embarrassment!"

"Then I cannot imagine what may be the stumbling block. He may leave us a note and then we might call on him as soon as we return," she decided.

"I suppose we could visit a few attractions whilst we are here, but I would feel guilty doing so without our sisters."

"We can always bring them back another time," Hope reasoned. "I will simply go mad if I have to stay in these rooms a moment longer, knowing all of London is outside that window, awaiting us. I will go mad!"

"Very well. What do you wish to see?" Faith was beginning to feel a bit imprisoned herself.

"Everything!"

Faith gave her sister a look of derision.

"Perhaps we could start with a walk through Hyde Park. The Society page is always discussing that the most fashionable people go there."

"We can hardly consort with the most fashionable," Faith argued. She had seen enough in their short foray through Mayfair to know they were far from the mode.

"I only want to look."

"Surely there could be no harm in taking some fresh air at the nearby park. Let Gibson know, then let's gather our bonnets and pelisses." Faith was tired of looking at the walls, even though they were nice walls with a lovely floral pattern woven into some vines. To girls who were used to walking miles over the Bath countryside, this was a great change. "Maybe he will have an answer by the time we return. I must say it is most vexing to have a guardian when I am almost of age! We have done quite well without one for the past year!" she continued, simply to justify defying their guardian's secretary's edict.

They made their way down the stairs, stopping to ask for directions, and then began to walk along Piccadilly towards Hyde Park. Green Park was closer, but no, it must be Hyde Park for Hope. "I have read so many times about it that I can picture it perfectly!"

"I pray only that it does not disappoint."

"I do not see how it could if Green Park is anything to go by." Green Park was situated just across from the hotel, and was across the street that they walked along towards Hyde Park. It was indeed a pleasant prospect.

When they entered the gate, they stopped to get their bearings and looked around.

"I thought it would be more crowded," Hope said in a tone Faith knew to be disappointment. She looked around and noticed some gentlemen on horseback, riding upon a nearby path. Across the grassy area, there were children playing with their nurses.

"That must be Rotten Row!" Hope exclaimed, noticing the horsemen. "The Serpentine must be up that way." She pointed to the right of them.

Faith was glad that Hope wasn't to remain disappointed. They walked along a gravelled path through some beds of flowers towards the Serpentine. It was an unexpectedly large lake near the park adjoining Kensington Gardens, and the cool breeze plastered their skirts to their legs, whilst they had to hold on to their bonnets to keep them from flying back.

"Is it not marvellous?" Hope asked with a radiant smile.

Faith thought it was pretty, but not more so than Bath. They walked on near the water's edge when they came upon a group of small children feeding the ducks.

"Look at the ducklings!" Hope exclaimed, pointing to where little balls of fluff swam in a row behind their mother.

The older two boys of the group were lying on their stomachs, trying to reach the babies, while the youngest pointed with one hand, at the same time sucking on the fingers of the other. "Want! Want!"

A harried nursemaid was trying to correct all of them at once, and such a task was clearly beyond her capabilities.

Faith and Hope may not have known the children, but with several younger siblings, it was without thought that they moved closer. Soon, one of the boys was half in the water, trying to reach a duckling. The mother duck took issue and began to peck at the boy and chaos ensued.

The children shrieked and screamed. The other boy jumped in to save his brother—or at least not miss the fun—whereupon the nurse-maid had a fit of the vapours.

"That will never do!" Faith turned to Hope. "Deal with the nurse. I shall deal with the boys."

As she turned back to the water, she heard a resounding slap across the nurse's face. "Well, that is one way," she muttered, then quickly discerned the boys had now taken to splashing and playing in the water and the ducks were swimming away.

She lifted her skirts and stepped into the water and plucked the first young offender out and deposited him on the bank.

"Boys!" A voice of authority called from behind just as she took hold of the second offender. They scrambled to attention and out of the water with haste.

Faith turned to see a beautiful lady who looked straight out of a fashion plate from *La Belle Assemblée*. "I left you with Nurse for ten minutes while I spoke to an acquaintance and this is how you behave?"

"Sorry, Mama."

"I should say so. Look at what you have done to Nurse, and these two young ladies had to come to your assistance. You shall walk home and I will think of a proper punishment by the time you arrive there."

"Forgive me, my lady," the nurse said. Having regained her senses, she gathered the other children and began leading the boys away. Faith and Hope remained there, watching the scene. Faith desperately hoped the woman would leave so she might return to the hotel and exchange her soaking boots for some dry ones. Instead, the lady turned a moment later to survey them. Faith tried not to squirm under the scrutiny.

"I must thank you for your assistance. Our other nursemaid fell ill, and I was but a poor substitute." She flushed an apologetic smile that indicated she knew precisely what had occurred. "I do not believe we have met. Perhaps under the circumstances, we may forgo the formalities. I am Lady Sarah Jersey."

Faith and Hope bobbed proper curtsies. "I am Faith Whitford and this is my sister, Hope, my lady. We are new to Town."

"May I ask where you live, so that I may call and thank your mother?"

"Actually, our parents are deceased. We are only visiting whilst waiting to meet our new guardian, so he can tell us where we may live."

"May I ask who your guardian is?"

Faith, knowing nothing about with whom she spoke, answered quite readily. "Lord Westwood. He is apparently hunting in Leicestershire."

"Westwood you say?" The lady looked as though she had heard a juicy bit of gossip. Perhaps she had.

"Indeed. We have never met him, but Lady Halbury appointed him our guardian."

"Lady Halbury..." she appeared to be searching her memory for the name. "I do not believe I have had the pleasure."

"Oh, no, my lady. She never ventured from Bath," Hope added.

"And are you staying at Westwood's home now?"

"No. His secretary sent us to the Pulteney while he sent word to Lord Westwood."

15

"Well, I do hope you will call on me so I may thank you properly should you stay in London."

"Thank you, my lady, but we left our three younger siblings in Bath with the vicar's family. We will be returning to them as soon as we hear from our guardian."

"Ah, a pity. I was very much looking forward to the storm." She smiled and left.

"What did she mean by the storm?" Faith asked with a frown as they began walking back towards the hotel.

"I have no idea. She was very grand but friendly. Oh, look. Is that Mr. Satterlee?" The staid secretary was hurrying towards them.

"I believe it is. I would dearly like to change my boots, but I suppose that will have to wait." They walked forward to greet him.

"Good morning," Faith said as he neared. He looked a bit hurried and flustered, though he still bowed when he reached them.

"Have you news from my guardian, Mr. Satterlee?" Hope asked.

"What are you doing in the park? I thought I made it clear you were to stay at the hotel until I received instructions from Lord Westwood."

Faith bristled at his reproach. "We are country girls, Mr. Satterlee. We did not think we were being imprisoned and might take a little air in the park. Now, what has our guardian had to say?"

"He desires me to find you a house and a chaperone where you may reside until he returns."

"Did he say where he desires this occurrence? And for how long?"

"In London, of course."

"I am afraid that will never do. Our other sisters are in Bath and we wish to remain in Bath."

"That will require me to send another letter to his lordship. He might be quite agreeable, but he did not give me implicit instructions to do otherwise." He held the response from Lord Westwood in his hand, waving it about. Faith took the missive and read it.

"I believe it would be more efficient to speak with his lordship ourselves," Faith argued.

"I am afraid that is quite impossible." He looked horrified, which only made Faith think it was just the thing to do.

"As long as he is alive on this earth, it is possible. He is only in Leicestershire."

"But you may not disturb him there. He left implicit instructions that he is not to be bothered."

"Unfortunately for us, we are his wards. He will have to be bothered. It will only take a few moments of his time."

"You do not understand, miss. I cannot allow it."

"Fortunately for you, I will make certain he knows you did not allow it, but I will go to Leicestershire."

"You will never find it without directions," he said with a hint of smugness.

"Oh, but I have the direction." She held up the letter in her hand, then placed it in the pocket of her gown so that he would not try to take it from her. "Come on, Hope, let us go to Leicestershire."

They began walking back to the hotel, Mr. Satterlee hot on their heels trying to talk her out of it.

He paused when they reached the door, clearly debating a public confrontation.

"If you would be so good as to arrange our transportation and settle our bill, I am certain our guardian would wish it." Faith turned and left him at the door, hoping he would comply.

Dominic was feeling quite pleased with himself. They'd had perfect weather and had bagged several brace of pheasants, and were now relaxing around the fire after a fine meal and brandy.

The fact that he had five new wards never crossed his mind again after he sent the directions back to Satterlee.

"Excuse me, my lord, but there are two females requesting a word with you," Barrett said.

"What the devil?" He was startled.

"Two females? Only two?" Freddy whined.

"Not that kind of female," Barrett corrected.

"What do they want?" Dominic asked with a sinking feeling. Any lady who had tracked him down at this location only wanted one thing and that was a noose around his neck.

"They only requested a word and said it was most urgent."

"What is it this time? Lost? A broken axle?" Rotham teased.

"I bet you a monkey they are alone and unchaperoned," Freddy added most helpfully.

"I never bet against a sure thing," Montford drawled.

Dominic sighed and rose, very much resenting the disturbance of his peace. "I will see them in the study."

"You cannot be such a spoilsport as to see them without us!" Freddy objected.

"Oh, can I not?" He raised an imperious brow that normally made people quiver. Unfortunately, all of them had been boys at Eton together, and only laughed at his expression. "I tell you what, if I am not returned in half an hour, you may come to my rescue."

"Leave the doors open," Rotham called as Dominic left.

His mood did not improve in the steps it took to reach the study and thus his wards' first glimpse of him was with a forbidding scowl. His first impression was in another vein entirely.

Nothing much surprised Lord Westwood, who had become cynical after years of being one of the biggest prizes on the marriage mart. He was toadied to, his opinion sought, and a person's success often rode on whether or not he approved of them. But even he was surprised at the visions standing before him. There were not one, but two identical beauties of which the *ton* had not seen in his reign. Suddenly, his interest was willing to be piqued.

"Miss Whitford, and Miss Hope Whitford, my lord," Barrett announced.

They curtsied and openly surveyed him, which was no new occurrence to one such as he. He returned the scrutiny, but with more subtlety. Their clothes were quality, but immediately marked them as being from the country. However, their hair was like ebony silk and their eyes shades of blue he had only seen in the waters of the

Mediterranean. Neither was tall, but their carriage bore them proud and the equal of any *ton* matron.

"Lord Westwood?" Miss Whitford stepped forward. "As your secretary informed you, we are your new wards. While I am certain neither of us is pleased by this unforeseen circumstance, you need not be alarmed, for I will be of age in but a few months."

"You are certain of my feelings?"

"Well, why would you be pleased having the responsibility of five unknown females thrust upon you?" she countered without withering as many a female was wont to do.

"Indeed."

"Your secretary said you intended to house us in London, but that will never do, sir."

"And pray tell, why not?" He was growing more amused by the minute. He had not been anything but bored since he could not recall when, and the eldest beauty was even more enchanting by her animation.

"We have been happy in Bath. When I come of age, I intend to settle there and raise my sisters. What would be even better would be if you could see your way clear to releasing my portion to me now and thus be rid of what must be an unwelcome burden."

By this point, Dominic had glanced at the other sister, who, by her facial expressions, did not seem to agree with her sister's sentiment.

"And what of you, Miss Hope Whitford? Do you share the same desire to remain in Bath forever and raise your sisters?"

She seemed taken aback that he had sought her opinion. "Well, my lord, I would not mind some time in London."

He nodded absently, but said nothing to her reply. He returned his attention to Miss Whitford. "And where are your other sisters? There are three more, are there not?"

"We left them in Bath with the vicar and his family, sir."

"And the new Lord Halbury?"

"He is a baronet. Sir Reginald Halbury. He has asked us to be removed from Halbury Hall by Saturday. As it is now Wednesday, we have a little time to find a new place to live. He did offer us the use of his carriage and one hundred pounds to come to London and find you."

"How very gracious of him." The sardonic curl to his lip indicated his thoughts on Sir Reginald Halbury. "You seem to have found me." Satterlee had much to answer for, that was certain.

"You have a chaperone arranged for at this home in Bath?" If they had an elder matron to give them countenance, he was perfectly willing to consider the matter.

"Of course, I do not. If we had anyone, we would not be here!"

Before he could expound in his mind on his intended plan, his friends had decided he needed saving. All he needed was his three very eligible friends seeing his new wards to set flame to the kindling that had already begun to spark with their very unwise and unexpected decision to arrive there.

He heard the collective intake of breath from his friends once they caught sight of the beauties. "Are you not going to introduce us, Dom?" Rotham drawled.

"Certainly not."

Miss Whitford frowned at him. "I am Miss Whitford, and this is my sister."

Rotham smiled knowingly and walked over to take her hand. "Rotham at your service." He took her hand and bowed over it. Dominic would have called him out had he kissed that hand. A great show was made of all the men introducing themselves and bowing regally over both ladies' hands. It became increasingly clear that Dominic would not be able to simply take a peripheral part in these girls' lives. He was not certain if he was pleased or disgusted by that fact.

After the introductions, it was growing late and nothing had been decided. He ushered his protesting friends back out and closed the door behind them.

"May we return to Bath and seek lodgings there?" Miss Whitford persisted.

"Where do you intend to stay tonight?" he asked.

"Our maid has taken our carriage and is arranging accommodations. They were to return for us in one hour."

"You set off across country with no chaperone, and you intend to stay at a public inn with only a maid?" His tone was quiet but dangerous to those who knew him well.

"What choice did we have? Your secretary put us at a hotel in London," she argued.

"The Pulteney, I assume? It is hardly a common coaching inn. Any manner of person could see you unaccompanied at the latter and consider you fair game."

There was only one thing to be done. "You will have to stay here for the night. My guests and I will stay at the inn, then we will escort you back to Town tomorrow."

"There is really no need, my lord. As I was saying, if you would but release my portion to me now, we may set up household and not bother you again. In a matter of months, I will be of age."

Dominic opened the door to his study and called for Barrett. "Please inform my guests that we will be removing to the village inn. Have Mrs. Barrett prepare rooms for the Misses Whitford."

"Yes, my lord."

Dominic was already regretting an uncomfortable night at the Cork and Barrel with visions of straw mattresses and fleas, but he eased his discomfort somewhat by the thought that his friends would be made to suffer along with him.

Dominic turned back to the ladies to see Miss Whitford's eyes flashing fire.

"Is it common practice amongst the *ton* not to answer questions put to them?"

"You did not ask a question, but made a statement." He began to leave the room, but she called out to him.

"When may we finish this discussion?"

He turned slightly. "Nothing shall occur until we are returned to Town and I have read the will."

"I cannot leave my sisters indefinitely!"

"No, I suppose not. I will have Satterlee send for them."

"Well!" He thought she also then muttered, "Insufferable, odious, high-handed ogre!"

Had she seen his answering smile, he mused, she likely would have thrown something at his head. It was probably criminal how much he was enjoying baiting her, but nevertheless, no decisions could be made until he knew what his obligations were.

He and his friends were soon packed and mounted and on their way to the village inn.

"You are going to have your hands full, Dom, with beauties like that. And two of 'em!" Freddy remarked wistfully.

Didn't he know it.

"I say, Dom, it's not very sporting of you to make us go to the inn. Someone should be there to protect them," Montford added.

"There are at least a dozen servants. You know dashed well their reputations would not withstand being under the roof with the four of us."

"Who would tell? And you are their guardian," Rotham, the most dangerous of all, remarked unhelpfully.

"Will you bring them out?"

"There are three more, you say?"

"Do they have dowries?"

Dominic did not bother to answer the questions they peppered him with. He was too preoccupied with his own conflicting thoughts on the Misses Whitford.

CHAPTER 3

*W*ell! The insufferable, odious, high-handed ogre!" Faith muttered as Lord Westwood left the room.

"Did you see Mr. Cunningham? Was he not the most beautiful gentleman you have ever beheld? What beautiful blond curls he has! And Lord Rotham! He is dark and dangerous and promises roguish delights. And Montford, such presence! Not to mention our guardian is also very handsome, but he is more intimidating. The four of them together are quite arresting!"

"Do be serious, Hope. What if Lord Westwood forces us to go to London?" Faith did not hide her annoyance with her sister. All she could think about was the gentlemen's appearance when their future was at stake!

"What would be so terrible about that? It would not be forever."

"I know you have always dreamed about a Season, Hope, but I must think about what is best for everyone."

"Forgive me. I did not mean to discount what you do for our family, but perhaps you take too much responsibility on your shoulders. Why not let our guardian help us?"

"You wish to be beholden to a man like...like that?" She pointed towards the door he had just walked through as though he had left a trail of fire behind him.

"Like what? He seemed very capable. He certainly managed you with very few words." Hope did not realize the thin ice she was skating on with her words, doubtless because of the truth in them.

"What can I do until I convince him to give me my portion and let us manage for ourselves?"

"Precisely. Why not enjoy someone else being responsible for once?"

"But we know nothing about him!" Faith could not believe her sister was so willing to trust a handsome face.

"We know he is honourable. Why else would he remove himself and his friends but to protect our reputations?"

Faith crossed her arms and tapped her foot. "I suppose there is some merit in what you say."

"There is nothing to do tonight but to rest."

Mrs. Barrett knocked on the door. She was a plump, grandmotherly sort with white hair tucked neatly beneath a cap. "Ladies, I should be pleased to show you to your chamber, but have you dined yet? The gentlemen left before the second course, and there is plenty of food prepared. It would be a shame to waste it."

"You are very kind. Dinner would be most welcome. Thank you, Mrs. Barrett."

When the first course was brought in, Faith wondered if the King had been set to dine with them. She had never seen such luxury or richness at a table in her life. She smiled to herself, wondering what Lord Westwood thought about trading this feast for the common fare they would likely be served at the inn. Lady Halbury had held peculiar ideas about food, so their diets had been somewhat restrictive—for their health, of course. Soup, vegetables, and a small portion of meat were all they were used to, so after their onion soup was removed, the crab cakes, roasted pheasant, side of venison in bechamel, vegetables, and syllabub were more than either young lady could fathom doing justice to. And there was another course to come!

"The gentlemen must have hearty appetites! I do not think I could eat another bite!" Hope said as Barrett began to remove the dishes from the first course.

"Oh, yes, miss. Only the best will do for Lord Westwood. He is famous for his chef and his table."

"Perhaps you might send the next course to him at the village inn? It would be a shame to waste such a fine meal," Faith suggested.

Barrett smiled. "Aye, miss. That would be just the thing. I will see to it at once and let Mrs. Barrett help you ready yourselves for the night."

Mrs. Barrett bustled in to usher them up to a luxurious chamber. Dark wooden panels covered the walls, with mahogany furniture tastefully arranged. The windows and bed curtains were draped with thick dark green hangings. It was clearly a masculine haunt, and Faith felt her intrusion more acutely. But what else could she have done? She refused to sit idly in London at Lord Westwood's convenience. She had never before been separated from her sisters and did not intend to remain so a day longer than necessary!

"I thought you might wish to remain together, but if you prefer, I can have another room made up for you," Mrs. Barrett said as she followed them inside.

"Together is perfect. I apologize for the inconvenience we have caused," Faith said.

"Well, miss, I cannot say as I ever remember another female being in the house, not that it is not a pleasure to have you here."

"How kind of you to say." Hope smiled brilliantly and instantly made a conquest out of the elderly woman.

"It is hard to imagine Master Dominic with two wards, though I do think it will do him much good," she said in a familiar way that Faith and Hope enjoyed with their own servants at Halbury Hall and thought nothing about it being too forward.

"Oh, there are three more sisters in Bath," Faith corrected the kindly, elder woman who looked suitably shocked, then laughed. "But what I would not enjoy watching him handle that!"

"Watching what? Is he of a foul disposition?"

She clicked her tongue. "He is a wonderful boy, but is too much used to having everything his own way."

Faith had no intention of letting Lord Westwood have his way this time if his way meant dictating how she should care for her sisters.

"But no, he is not of a foul temper. A better master would be impossible to find."

Faith certainly hoped so for their sake. But thus far, she could only think he was high-handed and disagreeable.

The next morning, Faith and Hope were eager to be on their way not long after sunrise, but it was some time before the gentlemen joined them with their carriage and coachmen.

As soon as they heard the cavalcade on the drive, Faith and Hope went outside.

"Well, this is a change, having ladies wait on us!" Rotham said as he reined in a beautiful grey gelding, dismounting smoothly and bowing before them.

"Then, sir, clearly you have been in company with the wrong ladies!" Hope teased.

"I shall let my mama know that," he said, with a wink at Hope. Faith wanted to groan aloud. The last thing she needed was for Hope to set up a flirtation with some Town-bronzed rogue.

"I trust you passed a pleasant evening, Miss Whitford?" Lord Westwood asked politely, somehow coming to stand next to her without her realizing it.

"Yes, my lord. Mr. and Mrs. Barrett took excellent care of us."

"It was kind of you to send the rest of dinner on to us." His eyes somehow seemed to be twinkling with amusement, which made him look sinful.

"Not at all. It was intended for you, after all. You certainly could have stayed long enough to dine!"

"I do not think it would have been wise. In fact, if you are not opposed to the idea, we will drive straight through, stopping only to change horses. It would not do to be spending the night at an inn with us either. I asked Mrs. Barrett to pack enough refreshments for the journey."

"I am amenable to the suggestion, sir. Anything that reunites us with our sisters quickly will be acceptable."

"I have seen to it. You shall be with them by the week's end."

"Thank you, my lord." She acknowledged she might have perhaps misjudged him a bit harshly, and they had surprised him yesterday. Hopefully, it meant he would allow her to remain in charge of the children and have her portion so they may set up house. "I do apologize for intruding upon you, but the sooner we have this resolved, the sooner we may both go follow our own inclinations."

"Just so."

Faith and Hope settled into the carriage with Gibson, Faith feeling confused by his lordship. He was a mixture of arrogance and entitlement and occasional glimpses of kindness.

She watched him walk away towards his horse, and she forced her attention to her surroundings. Mrs. Barrett had packed several hampers of food for their journey, which took up the extra space inside the carriage.

The gentlemen were all mounted on horseback and, together, presented such a stunning picture that Faith and Hope spent a great deal of time watching the magnificent view instead of noticing the countryside pass by.

"Could we not stay in London just for the Season, Faith? Imagine, dancing with those gentlemen!" Her voice was just a bit too dreamy for Faith's peace of mind. Hope was beautiful, of course, but such gentlemen like that would not be interested in country misses like themselves, with only respectable portions.

"I would prefer to return to Bath, but perhaps whilst we must be in London, you may attend a few entertainments of which our guardian approves." Much though it galled her to cede any authority to him.

Hope's face lit up. "Do you think he will allow it? I should like that above all things!"

"I THOUGHT I was dreaming yesterday, but they are still easily the prettiest pair I have ever seen. Either one of them alone is a vision, but together..." Montford wore a look of pure infatuation on his face.

"I doubt either of them has a large enough dowry to qualify for an heiress, Montford." Dominic knew full well he was being petulant in the extreme.

"I do not need an heiress," Freddy pointed out.

"Nor I," Rotham added.

"What's this? None of you were considering leg-shackles yesterday —and what is more, you were mourning my impending fate!" Montford protested.

"If you have to be leg-shackled, having one of them to look at every morning across the breakfast table would help soften the blow," Freddy reasoned.

"You do realize you would need my permission to wed one of them, do you not?" Dominic was becoming annoyed, even though he would've been enjoying himself hugely were the situations reversed.

The three of his friends burst into fits of laughter.

"I will have you know that Miss Whitford wishes to return to Bath immediately." Dominic took devilish pleasure in their astonishment.

"No! It would be a travesty! May I try to convince her otherwise?" Rotham had a gleam in his eyes.

Dominic looked back towards the carriage. "Be my guest." He expected to be greatly amused by Rotham's efforts. It would help alleviate the boredom of the trip. He still had not yet determined what to do with the chits, though he would have to leave them with his mother for the time being. He rather thought his mother might enjoy bringing the ladies out. She had always wished for daughters.

The foursome slowed back to ride beside the carriage, of which the window was subsequently lowered to speak with them.

"How do you do?" Miss Hope asked with a brilliant smile as though she'd been waiting for that very thing.

"We just heard some appalling news, Miss Whitford," Rotham said, addressing Faith.

"Oh, dear! What has happened?"

"We heard you intend to return to Bath!"

Dominic could see her face stiffen.

"What is so appalling about that?"

She really was beautiful when she was on her mettle, Dominic reflected. He was going to enjoy watching gentlemen of the *ton* fall at her feet.

"Why, we will not be there!" Rotham said, with a hand over his heart. Truly, he had missed his calling in life.

"The answer to that is simple. You may visit us in Bath!" she retorted.

"The two of you are wasted on the elderly and infirm!" Freddy said in all earnestness. "Would be the Season's Incomparables! Two of 'em!"

"That does not sound very nice," Hope said hesitantly.

"Oh, but it is the highest honour a débutante can receive," Freddy reassured her. "I've never seen any women as beautiful as the pair of you," he said to each of them with open admiration.

"Thank you, but Lady Halbury says vanity is a sin."

"It ain't vanity if it's the truth, is it?" he reasoned.

Dominic could see that the younger sister was perplexed by the question, especially coming from one as Adonis-like as Freddy.

"Forget beauty," Montford said. "Think of all the delights of London. Museums, shopping, Vauxhall Gardens…"

"Is that where they have the fireworks, sir?" Hope asked.

"Fireworks, acrobats, concerts, dancing, and it all takes place under beautiful lanterns and stars. It's magical. Then there is Astley's Amphitheatre—the young ones would like that especially. All manner of tricks are performed on horseback."

"Oh, Faith, do say we may go! Our sisters would adore it!"

"At the moment, dearest, it would appear the say is no longer mine." She looked away from him, likely trying to maintain her composure, and Dominic realized he did not wish to take control from her. Yet, it would be a shame for them to return to Bath and hide away there.

"Perhaps Miss Whitford and I may discuss the situation further when we reach London. I believe there must be a satisfactory arrangement for all parties."

She looked sharply back at him, eyes searching for sincerity in his words. Dominic had no wish to play the fool and become sentimental over a pair of pretty blue eyes. He was an excellent card player and she would find little meaning in his expression when she looked.

"Shall we stop for a while? It appears to be an excellent location for a picnic and to stretch our legs a bit," he suggested.

"Picnic? Capital idea!" Freddy announced.

Soon, they had pulled off the road where they could be private while the footmen quickly unloaded the feast that had been prepared.

Dominic noticed Miss Whitford walking away from the group—whether to stretch her legs or remove herself from the company, he could not say. Meanwhile, Miss Hope was quickly surrounded by his friends, though just waiting to be adored.

Miss Whitford was going to be a prickly one, and he rather thought he was going to enjoy crossing swords with her.

"May I join you?" He saw her startle and almost laughed.

"Yes, of course. I thought to stretch my legs a bit."

He almost offered her his arm, but was not quite ready to annoy her further.

They walked a little way in silence. Dominic had little to say, but he suspected there was a great deal she would like to rail at him for. He did not have to wait long.

"You seem amused by all of this, my lord."

"I can choose either to be amused or annoyed, but it changes nothing. Would you prefer me to be the latter?"

"No, of course not. I would not think you would be pleased by having five females thrust upon you."

Dominic raised an eyebrow but only smiled.

"We are not used to *ton* ways, my lord. Lady Halbury was very odd in her habits."

"Be that as it may, do you not wish for your sisters to make good matches?"

"Of course I do!" Her eyes flashed and her cheeks pinkened as he had known they would.

"Do you expect to find these matches in Bath?"

"I do not see why not." Her chin lifted, and her eyes met his. What a fierce little tiger she was. He felt his interest stir but had no intention of succumbing.

"What do you mean to do with us, then, sir?"

"As I said before, I intend to read the will for myself."

"There was very little to read with regards to us, I am afraid."

"You have read it yourself?"

"No, but Lady Halbury's solicitor read it to us. There was only a short portion stating she set aside 5000 pounds for each of us in the funds, and that you were named our guardian. The solution seems simple to me! I have been caring for my sisters alone this past twelve-month. I am very happy to continue doing so. If you would but release my funds to me, we may set up a household and manage quite comfortably."

"And you have a great knowledge of what it takes to run such an establishment?"

"Lady Halbury taught me to manage Halbury Hall."

"Admirable. And how many months remain until you are of age?"

"Six."

"And do you realize it could very well take longer than that to arrange what you ask?"

He could see that she did not realize. He softened his tone. "Would a short stay in London be so terrible? Your sister could make a great match. She already has the three most eligible bachelors in the palm of her hand." Quite literally, Dominic noticed, as they looked over to where his friends, who would normally run as far as their feet would take them from an eligible miss, were at her feet fawning over her and handing her food.

"I have little doubt Hope would be a success," Faith said. "However, the expense of a Season would consume my entire portion. Then where would we be when six months has passed?"

"Where, indeed?" They turned to walk back towards the others.

"What of yourself, Miss Whitford? Will you be a martyr for the cause of your sisters?"

"I would hardly call it martyrdom! They are everything to me."

"And when they are married and gone?" He held up his hand. "You will have your cottage in Bath." She had no idea how she would herself be besieged. He suspected she would next think she could chaperone her sister and watch from the dowager's seats. If Satterlee had followed his instructions this time, his plan had already been set into motion. Miss Whitford would meet her match in his mama.

He smiled as she stepped over to where the repast had been spread out on a blanket. His friends stood and made a great show of seating her and preparing a plate of food for her.

Dominic made up a plate for himself and ate in contemplative silence. Miss Whitford had no idea just how unwelcome his guardianship of her was.

CHAPTER 4

*I*t was very late by the time they reached London, and even though she had read, played chess and cards, napped, and been idle in a carriage for the entire day, Faith was still exhausted and ready to seek her bed. To her surprise, however, they pulled up at an unknown house instead of the Pulteney.

They pulled to a stop, and a footman opened the door, but Lord Westwood was there to hand them down. Faith hesitated, but took his hand, very conscious of how the touch of him made her feel very odd. She looked up into his meadow-green eyes, with cheeks and a jaw that looked chiselled by a master sculptor. His lips were pursed in a habitual, careless irreverence.

"Where are we?"

"Westwood House. My mother resides here. I have arranged for you to stay with her whilst you are in London instead of a hotel."

Faith stopped. "We could never impose so!"

He raised a questioning brow at her, and she was reminded of how she'd unwittingly done that very thing to him. She felt heat rise to her face and neck.

"You will be more comfortable here than in a hotel, I assure you. I wonder why Satterlee didn't think of it. Come! Let me introduce you to my mother. She is expecting us."

Faith paused while he handed Hope out as well, and stood looking in wonder at the magnificent house before them. It was a square mansion of Portland stone several storeys high, with large columns supporting it and a pediment bearing a coat of arms surrounded by intricate carvings.

"Where are your friends?" Hope asked, looking around to see if they were out of sight.

"They have departed to seek their own homes. They bid me wish you adieu, and will call on you soon."

"You do not live here as well?"

Lord Westwood glanced at her, baffled. "I prefer to keep my own house." Without further elaboration on the subject, he escorted them into the house. The door was opened by an imposing-looking butler who clearly felt his own consequence. "Welcome, my lord."

"Hartley," his lordship acknowledged. "This is Miss Whitford and Miss Hope."

He bowed. "Her ladyship awaits you in the saloon."

"We will show ourselves up."

"Very good, my lord."

Lord Westwood led them up a beautiful marble staircase, the walls of which were adorned with statues and paintings that glowed by candlelight, then through a beautifully carved wooden door into a room that was quite the opposite of what had graced his lordship's hunting box. The walls were white panelled with gilt, and groupings of cream upholstered chairs surrounded low tables. Marble fireplaces at either end of the room held a blazing fire, and next to one of them, in a high-backed chair, sat a handsome woman not above perhaps five and forty years, who was surveying their entrance critically.

Lord Westwood released them and bent over his mother and kissed her cheek dutifully. "Mother, may I present Miss Whitford and Miss Hope Whitford?"

They curtsied deeply.

"Come here and let me have a good look at you."

34

Faith very much disliked being brought out like a horse before auction, but since she was at the woman's mercy, who in all likelihood had also been told, not asked, what to do, she complied.

The lady looked to her son. "There will be riots, you understand quite well, do you not?"

Faith and Hope glanced at each other with confusion.

"Perfectly," he replied, and the lady smiled at him.

"I suppose that was your plan. And there are three more, Satterlee tells me? What are their ages?" The latter was addressed to Faith.

"Patience is eighteen, my lady. Grace is seventeen next month, and Joy is fifteen."

"You are almost one and twenty?"

"Yes, ma'am, and Hope is nineteen."

"And not a boy amongst you!"

"No, my lady."

"Are your sisters as beautiful as you?"

"I am often told we all favour each other greatly." Faith set little store in her beauty, though she could acknowledge that her sisters were uncommonly pretty.

"You will be deemed the virtues, no doubt."

"We have been referred to in such terms before. Our parents were missionaries, my lady."

She sniffed, making clear what she thought of such occupations. "And how come you to be my son's wards?"

"I do not know, my lady. The guardianship was stipulated in Lady Halbury's will."

"Ah. Then the blame is likely to be laid at my door."

"You knew Lady Halbury?"

"Not as well as you would think, but my husband and I did make her acquaintance on a visit to Bath. I recall one conversation in particular about her childless state and how, in the same situation, I thought I might likely adopt one. My husband, a kind man, professed his agreement with me. I see she thought it qualified us to be your guardians."

"But the duty has fallen to your son."

"It appears it has, though he seems very willing to share the duty with me." She looked at her son with undisguised amusement.

"Was I wrong to think you would be unwilling?" he asked.

"No, Dominic, but four are ready to be brought out now!"

"Perhaps three," Faith intervened. "I have no need of a Season, and Grace can certainly wait until Joy is of age and they may be brought out together. However, I would prefer to return to Bath and bring them out there myself!"

"Nonsense, child! You have little hope of making them eligible matches in such a place. Unless, of course, your fancy them marrying men old enough to be their fathers?"

"Of course not," Faith said. "But neither do they need to make grand marriages. They have a respectable portion, thanks to Lady Halbury. But nothing enough to tempt fortune hunters."

"Nothing will be resolved tonight, however, and it grows late. I will speak with my solicitor in the morning then call afterwards," Lord Westwood said.

Faith was relieved to pause the conversation. She was too tired to fence with those that were used to having their every word obeyed without question.

Lord Westwood went immediately to his mother's side to help her rise from her chair. "I am not an invalid, Dominic," she scolded with affection.

"Surely a mother does not scold her son for gentlemanliness? I only wished to kiss you good night."

She offered him her cheek.

"Besides, would I bring a pack of young ladies to you if I believed you an incapable invalid?"

Faith knew she should not be listening to this private exchange, but she could not help herself and knew not where to go. She turned slightly and pretended to study a painting on the wall. It was heartening to see this man had a good relationship with his mother. Thus far, he had seemed nothing more than an autocratic lord with no redeeming qualities other than a handsome face.

"Dominic, you are a rascal of the first order, but I will do it!"

"I knew you would not fail me," he said quietly in her ear.

"I only hope you know what you are about," she warned.

"Dashed if I do!"

He made a proper bow to them, then stopped near Faith and whispered, "As you've seen and experienced with all in my acquaintance thus far, there is no one here to hurt you or your sisters. We are only thinking of your family and what is best for you. You may want to think on that instead of argue and gainsay every suggestion."

He left before giving her the chance to reply, leaving her burning with shame for there was truth in his statement. Yet, to take all of their choices away from them as though he knew them—it was unfair, and she was losing control of the situation entirely.

Faith and Hope followed Lady Westwood to their chambers, feeling as though their world had been upended even more than Faith had when the solicitor had broken the news of a guardian to them. Never could she have imagined this.

How had life changed so much in less than a week? Never before had she even considered her sisters' fate would be taken from her hands. She did not think it was at all what Lady Halbury would have wished for them, yet she felt powerless to stop it. She supposed a few months in London would not be so terrible, but what would she be left with to live on once her sisters were fired off? She knew it would be horribly expensive. But most of all, what she could not determine was why a Town Buck of the first stare would not want to be rid of the lot of them when he had the chance. Why ever would he wish to trouble himself with five females? Three of which he had yet to meet! Although to give proper due, it seemed as though he was going to fob that duty off to his mother.

Faith could not put her mind at ease at all about the situation she now found herself in. Never would she begrudge her sisters anything, including Seasons and good marriages. However, she did have the future to think of beyond. Resolution returned to anger and she finally drifted off to sleep, determined to put her foot down with the high-handed lord who was now their insufferable guardian!

THERE WAS nothing unexpected in what the solicitor had to say to Dominic. He had combed through the will and, unfortunately, even though the intended guardian had probably been his father, as he shared his name, it was difficult to prove. Possibly, it could be revoked in the courts, but as Dominic had suspected, it would take longer than the remaining six months of Miss Whitford's guardianship—and involve a great deal of bother—in Miss Whitford's guardianship to see such a task done.

Dominic sat thoughtfully for a long time after the solicitor left, wondering why he felt the need to force Miss Whitford to remain in London for that time. Was it because he knew she thought to sacrifice herself on her sisters' behalves, or because he was bored, and this would amuse him? Certainly, he enjoyed fencing and flirting with her.

True, it would also require him to bestir himself at events he normally avoided, but he would dance with each of his wards then escape. He need not spend more than an hour at such insipid doings.

He glanced at the ormolu clock on the mantel and rose. It was just about time for Satterlee to be returning from Bath. When the coach and four bearing his secretary appeared at his door, however, Dominic was more than surprised by the vision that alighted.

Three almost identical—except for height—visions in black crepe and black bonnets with bright blue eyes stepped into the street and could well have caused traffic to come to a halt had there been any to witness such an event. Once combined with their siblings, they would turn London on its ear. Certainly, there would be a storm the like of which London had ever seen. Beyond the shock that Lord Westwood was a guardian to five beauties.

A devilish grin crossed his face as he left his study to greet them. They were looking around and above them at his entrance hall.

"Ladies, allow me to introduce myself. I am Viscount Westwood." He bowed.

"Our guardian?"

"Indeed. Would you like some refreshments before I take you to your sisters? I believe my chef has bestirred himself to prepare something for you."

"That would be grand, sir!" the youngest said with an impish smile.

"You must be Joy."

She bobbed a curtsy. "I am the easy one. Can you name the others?"

"Joy!" One of them whispered harshly with an elbow to her side.

"What? It was a perfectly valid question."

Dominic tried to hide his amusement.

"But it is proper to be introduced, not ask a person to guess!"

"But he knew my name!" she persisted.

"I do believe you must be Grace, but I confess I would be guessing if I were to try to attempt to distinguish between all five of you at once."

Grace bobbed a curtsy.

"Patience is the impatient one," the little imp advised confidingly, "but she gets angry if anyone says so. She is anything but, according to Lady Halbury."

"That is quite enough, Joy," Patience intervened.

Dominic studied the girls and noted a slight difference in their mannerisms but keeping them correctly apportioned would be another thing altogether.

"Shall we have some of my chef's cakes and tarts before we leave? I am certain you must be tired of being cooped up in the carriage!"

"That would be pleasant, my lord," the eldest answered.

"But is it proper? Lady Halbury always said a young lady may never be alone with a gentleman," Grace recited.

"Indeed that is correct. You will meet your chaperone shortly, but as you are together and I am your guardian, I believe we can enjoy a quick tête-à-tête so I may know you a little."

His chef had outdone himself. Dominic, never one to appreciate any pudding or sweet, was clearly unappreciative of his genius. And now to have three young ladies with which to create masterpieces for! Before them was an array of delicacies fit for the King and Queen to visit.

"Does everyone eat like this with their tea?" Joy asked with wide-eyed wonder.

"No. In fact, I have hardly experienced such glories myself," he muttered.

"Can your chef make us these every day?"

Dominic smiled. "You will be staying with my mother. She has her own cook, who I am certain will be delighted to make such pastries for you."

"Why did you bring us here, then, Lord Westwood?"

He thought it was Patience who asked.

"Because I wished to meet you first."

She frowned prettily.

He had never explained himself before, but found he was doing so now. "I wished to meet you away from under the watchful eyes of your sister. She has a notion that she would like to return you all to Bath and set up house there. I rather think it would do no harm to present the four eldest of you and have my mother bring you out."

The sisters glanced at each other with, no doubt, a full conversation communicated in those looks.

"If you all prefer to return to Bath and marry an aging military man or an infirmed widower, then far be it from me to go against all of your wishes!"

"Oh, no! We would like to stay in London!" Joy answered for all of them.

Dominic looked at the others with a raised brow.

"I would love to see London, my lord," Grace answered.

"We would wish to have a Season above all things," Patience answered.

"As I thought. Then you would do well to help me convince Miss Whitford."

They all seem to recoil a bit from this. Were they terrified of her?

"Are you afraid to talk to your sister?" he felt compelled to ask after their unexpected reactions.

"It is not that," Patience hesitated.

"Someone please enlighten me. I would prefer not to be at daggers drawn with her."

"We owe everything to Faith. She found a way to keep us together when our parents died, and she has been taking care of us ever since—especially this past year."

"I do find it odd that Lady Halbury did not wish me to be notified of her demise until mourning was ended. What would you have done if something had happened?"

"She did not wish for Sir Reginald to remove us from our home, I presume," Patience remarked.

"So, you would rather I be the dictatorial dragon and force her?"

"Oh, would you, my lord?"

"But you would rather her not know your wishes? Surely if she knew you all wished for a stay in London..."

"Not if it would hurt her feelings."

Dominic did not respond, but was impressed with the loyalty. The eldest Whitford sister had inspired these girls despite her own young age.

As he contemplated his next move, he noticed all of the cakes, tarts, biscuits, and sandwiches had been consumed. These were no little dainty *ton* misses and he liked them the better for it.

"I'll tell you what we will do. We will contrive to keep Miss Whitford here without her realizing what is happening."

"Perhaps we might help a little," Patience suggested. "If we presented it more in the manner of a holiday rather than a permanent situation, she will never deny us a treat."

"As she reaches her majority in six months, it could hardly be permanent," Grace pointed out.

"And I have installed you at my mother's house instead of setting up house here, as you phrased it, so we shall present it as a prolonged visit. And if the four eldest of you happen to attend some balls and make some connections whilst you are here, then all the better. Shall I take you now to my mother and your sisters?"

They put their bonnets and pelisses back on as Dominic gathered his own hat. They stepped outside, but the carriage had gone.

Seeing the confusion on their faces, Dominic explained. "We shall walk. I understood country-bred girls prefer it. Especially since my mother's house is not far."

"Yes, certainly," they agreed.

As they strolled from Berkeley Square over to Charles Street, Dominic was secretly hoping they would not see any acquaintances yet. He wanted all five of them together at once, and to be outfitted in the latest mode and no longer in mourning blacks. The luck was not to be with him. One of his neighbours was coming down her front steps as they neared Westwood House.

"Unfortunately, ladies, we must greet this lady and placate her. Allow me to do the talking."

"Westwood. I had been hoping to run into you."

"And why is that, Sally?" He made a proper bow.

"Why, I made the acquaintance of two of your wards the other day. And are these the delightful sisters they told me about? Are you not going to introduce me?"

"Of course. These are the Misses Whitford: Patience, Grace, and Joy. They have just now arrived and will be joining their sisters."

Dominic was trying to think of what disastrous things Faith or Hope might have done to put themselves in the way of Lady Sally Jersey, the most notorious gossip, yet arguably the most powerful lady in the *ton*. She had a twinkle in her eyes that he did not trust.

"A pleasure to meet you, girls. I understood Miss Whitford to say they were returning to Bath?"

"Oh, I intend to keep them here for a little while."

"Excellent! Then I will be certain to send them vouchers if you will promise to cross our hallowed threshold."

'Hoist with his own petard' yet again. At least Faith and Hope had not offended her, though he had little doubt foisting these beauties on the astonished *ton* would amuse her as much as he.

"I must consult my valet to see if I own any knee breeches."

She smiled knowingly at him. "I know of a tailor. I will send him your way." She turned to leave, then turned back. "By the by, do you intend to bring all of them out at once?"

"Oh, no, my lady, I am too young, so Grace and I will wait," Joy said, with a smile that never failed to charm.

"One of my nieces is about your age. Perhaps you could become acquainted while your sisters are making their debuts."

"I would like that very much, my lady!" Joy curtsied very properly.

"I will send over the vouchers, Westwood."

"You may send them to Westwood House. They will be under my mother's chaperonage."

She smiled and went to her awaiting carriage. Dominic knew the news would be all over Town by the supper hour.

CHAPTER 5

*I*t was quite apparent which way the wind was blowing as soon as Lord Westwood arrived with her sisters. Faith had little doubt that Lord Westwood had already charmed them and filled their heads with promises of dresses and balls, and any number of grand amusements from the theatre to Astley's.

Nevertheless, she was delighted to see them. Never before had they been separated so much as a day.

However, before Joy could race into her arms and Lady Westwood think her lacking all proper teaching and decorum, Faith stepped forward. "Lady Westwood, may I present to you my sisters: Patience, Grace, and Joy. Make your bows, sisters."

She looked up and caught Lord Westwood's gaze, which was watching her with undisguised amusement.

"We have just had the most splendid treat at Lord Westwood's, Faith! His chef made it special for us!" she exclaimed.

Joy must have put on quite a show for him already! It served him right.

"Lord Westwood." She curtsied to him, and he returned it with a bow.

Lady Westwood was already exclaiming over the younger girls. It

44

happened nearly every time they were seen together. She was rhapsodizing over the plans she had already made for them. How quickly she had taken to this notion! A dressmaker had already been arranged to attend them, and Faith felt powerless to stop this extravagance. What she could not understand was why it was happening. She needed to speak with his lordship, but every time she began, he seemed to anticipate her intent, and was talking with someone else or fetching a paper from the study.

Was he avoiding conversation with her for some reason?

"Your trunks will be taken to your chambers, and the dressmaker will be here shortly to take your measurements and begin some new gowns for you," Lady Westwood announced.

"That is a certain sign for me to take my leave," Lord Westwood proclaimed.

"When will we see you again, sir?" Joy asked. "Will you take me to see the animals at the Exeter Exchange I have read about in Ackermann's Repository?"

"Joy!" Faith scolded. "You should not impose upon his lordship in such a manner."

"But I am certain he would wish to see them, and who better to take me?" she asked with such innocent guile that even Faith paused to consider.

"Who, indeed, little imp?" Lord Westwood teased and ruffled her hair.

"Perhaps we can invite Lady Jersey's niece as well," Joy added.

Lady Westwood looked up at that. "Lady Jersey? Do you know Sally?" she asked Joy.

"Oh, yes. We met her this morning, and she mentioned she had also made Faith and Hope's acquaintance, and would be pleased to send them vouchers."

"My goodness! I am happy to know it will not be necessary to seek the patronesses' favour!" her ladyship exclaimed.

"What are these vouchers?" Grace asked.

"Why, they are one of the most coveted tokens of approval a young lady may aspire to—tickets to a subscription ball at Almack's

Assembly Rooms. They are most exclusive to obtain. May I ask how you became acquainted with Lady Jersey?"

"Oh, we helped to fish her sons out of the Serpentine during a walk. Their nursemaid was quite overcome. They are much too exuberant for one nurse! The other nursemaid was laid up with a toothache or some such malady, and her ladyship had been conversing with someone and the children had gone on to the lake in order to feed the ducks."

"Extraordinary!"

Faith looked at Lord Westwood, who looked as though he were choking back a laugh.

"Well, I am certainly glad the dressmaker is coming! Let us not keep her waiting." Lady Westwood began ushering Faith's sisters from the room and she saw Lord Westwood trying to escape.

"My lord, may I have a word with you?"

He stopped and inclined his head. "Of course. Will here suffice or would you prefer a turn about the garden?"

Was he deliberately trying to distract her? "The garden, I believe." There, she would not feel the need to restrain herself.

He led her through the entrance hall beyond the dining room and the library—outside to a brick pathway that wound throughout the garden. The air was thick with the sweet smell of flowers and blossoms. Faith instantly recognizing the familiar scents of lavender, roses, and jasmine. At the back of the garden was a small gazebo and pond with water lilies, where a solitary bench sat beneath lush trees. He indicated for her to take a seat, which she refused.

"What did you wish to speak about?"

"Well, to begin with, you said you would consult your solicitor and review the will. Is there any hope for breaking this guardianship?"

"Unfortunately, there does not appear to be any question that my name is writ upon the will. It was also my father's name, but as to which viscount was intended, there were no specifications. Furthermore, the cost and time of objecting to the guardianship would, as I suspected, take longer than it will for you to attain your majority."

"And what of my sisters? Will they be under my care after my majority?"

"Unfortunately not. But let us cross that bridge once we are closer to your time. I do not mean to be a tyrant."

"But you do mean to keep us in London!"

"Your sisters all seemed very pleased by the prospect," he said gently.

"You have turned them up sweet, have you not?" she accused.

"I merely asked them what they would wish to do," he said with infuriating calm. "What is the harm in them enjoying a few months in Town?"

"Harm? I do not have unlimited resources, as you must know, my lord."

"No, but I do."

"I will not be beholden to you any more than we already are! Why would you take this upon yourself?" She looked up at him when he did not answer, and his eyes were twinkling down at her. The urge to wring his neck was very strong. "Well?" She barely resisted the urge to tap her foot. "Can you tell me that a determined bachelor with a reputation such as yours wants to squire five provincial ladies about Town?"

"Why not?"

She narrowed her gaze. "Is this some gentlemanly code of honour that compels you to perform this unwanted obligation?"

"I cannot deny some truth in that, but simply, it amuses me."

Faith was aghast. A burst of anger so strong and unsurprising that she had to check herself. "Amuses you, my lord?"

"Indeed. Town has been sadly flat of late."

"So against my wishes, we are to provide entertainment for you?"

"Most ladies of quality would be thrilled. I daresay most gentlemen would consider it my duty to see you well settled. But, yes, thrusting five young beauties—even just three of them at once—on the *ton* will cause me no undue amount of satisfaction."

"So much so that you are willing to foot the bill?" It would serve him right if she went on a spending spree!

"My mother would say it a much better use of my funds than many other ways I could spend it!"

Faith could only imagine his spendthrift ways. Despite their sheltered upbringing, she'd still heard of the ways gentlemen of fashion wasted their blunt: gambling, sporting pursuits, hunting, women. "Just so," she replied tartly, not approving in the least of imagining him with the latter!

"Are you concerned you all might enjoy yourselves? Or that you or your sisters might make excellent matches? You are very becoming when in a rage."

"You need not practice your flirtations on me, my lord, if that is your intent."

"When I flirt with you, you will not doubt it."

Her face burned with mortification while he looked amused and wicked. How did she always come off worse in all of these arguments, and he made it seem like he was being perfectly reasonable?

He was determined to make her lose her composure. Well, she would not give him the satisfaction! To make matters worse, he moved disconcertingly close to where she would be obliged to look up at him, but she stared at his neck cloth instead. He took her chin and gently forced it upwards, looking into his fathomless green eyes.

"Pax, my dear. It will not be so terrible, you know."

A pithy retort had been on the tip of her tongue, but Faith had never been so near to a man in her life. Her body betrayed her. Her ears started to pound, and her heart started to thrum and flutter in her chest, while her brain and voice ceased to function. All she could do was stare at him, dumbstruck.

He smiled down at her, which transformed his already too handsome face into something otherworldly. Apparently, he was not as affected as she, which was a very good thing, she tried to convince herself. For he was able to speak with annoying calm.

"Does your silence mean you agree? I think you'll find it very agreeable. Stop fidgeting so much about taking care of your sisters, and allow me to bear the responsibility for you. You are not so old, you know."

He stepped back leaving her head in a whirl.

"Enjoy your dress fittings. I would think shades of blue and lavender would suit you very well. I will call soon to see how you go on."

With that impertinence, he made her a bow and left. Faith stood there, slowly regathering her wits and thinking of all the clever things she should have said to him.

~

DOMINIC FELT a strong need to distance himself from this overwhelming amount of femininity before he was drawn into something he did not wish to be.

A masculine endeavour would be just the thing. His friends were most likely to be found at a club or Jackson's Saloon this time of day, so he first stopped at the club since it was nearest his house.

He entered and handed his hat and cape to the majordomo, then sauntered through the morning room, greeting those holding court at the bow window, but fending off deeper conversations of politics and the next vote in the House. Looking through the room full of tables and leather chairs, he discovered his friends were not to be seen. He climbed the stairs and found them in the coffee room, seated on a large, red-leathered sofa with a low table in front of them.

"Where have you been?" Montford asked. "We have been waiting for you at least two hours since you did not show your face in the park for our morning ride."

Dominic sat in a chair across from them and casually crossed his legs before bothering to answer. "I was seeing the remainder of my wards settled at Westwood House." A waiter placed a cup of coffee before him, and Dominic shook his head as he waited for further requests.

"You have brought all of them to Town?" Rotham asked.

"Why would I not?" Dominic responded, then sipped at the bitter brew and inhaled the deep aroma.

"Why would you want schoolroom chits underfoot?" Rotham retorted.

"Technically, they are at my mother's house, and only one of them is still in the school room, although the second youngest will not be brought out yet."

"You mean to bring three out at once?" Montford asked.

Dominic felt a mischievous smile take over his face.

"Are the rest of them pretty?" Freddy asked.

"Most assuredly," Dominic agreed.

"You are enjoying this a little too much," Rotham groaned.

"I confess I am. After watching the three of you make fools of yourselves on the ride back to London, providing me with no end of entertainment, I knew it would be just the thing."

"You have run mad!" Montford scolded.

"Quite likely," he agreed with unruffled affability. "It will not be long before bets are made, though. We came across Sally Jersey this morning as we walked through Berkeley Square."

"Remember who your oldest and dearest friends are," Montford reminded Dominic.

"This following you saying I am mad," he retorted.

"Kindly forget the first statement."

Dominic shook his head. It was just as he had prophesied.

"Are you certain you don't plan to steal a march on all of us?" Montford could not help but ask.

"I am certain you do not wish to be insulting, but I can hardly woo one of my own wards even if I were so inclined, which I am not. I have a perfectly healthy brother as my heir, and any number of excellent male cousins in line thereafter."

"Wouldn't be the thing!" Freddy chimed in.

"You have no need to be threatened by Dom," Rotham added. "He has earned his reputation as a confirmed bachelor."

"There have never been beauties tempting enough to rival his wards, either!" Montford argued.

"Where will they make their first public appearance?" Rotham asked, thankfully drawing the conversation onto another avenue.

"That will depend on when their new wardrobes are completed, though I have a feeling the youngest will do her best to convince me to take her to Astley's, the 'Change or the Tower before the week is out!"

"You mean to squire them about?" Freddy asked with disbelief.

"Some."

His three friends stared at him as though he'd sprouted horns.

"What about the widow Taylor? She won't like any attention being diverted from her," Montford pointed out about Dominic's latest flirt.

"She won't mind if she knows what's good for her," Rotham said, knowing how much Dominic loathed female tantrums.

"Jealousy is a dead bore," he agreed.

"But every man in Town is after her. She won't like it," Freddy prophesied.

"Then she may have her congé. There are always other flirts to be had."

The looks on his friends' faces were priceless. He managed to keep a straight face. Jemima Taylor was a buxom beauty, but she wanted marriage. And Dominic believed that her beauty did not compensate for her bird-witted intellect. "Would you have me shirk my duty? Of course, it is not convenient to be in such a situation, but I am in honour bound to do the best for them."

"Yes, yes, certainly," they agreed, though seemed to think differently.

"Perhaps we should help you with them," Freddy said.

"You just want a head start on everyone else!" Montford scowled.

"There are plenty to go around!" Rotham assured them.

"This grows tedious! I, for one, do not intend to allow them to affect my normal pursuits. Since I missed my ride this morning, would anyone be in the mood for a bit of sparring?" Dominic intended to do something besides discuss his wards.

"As long as you're not angry," Freddy said, rubbing his jaw. "I can still feel that last left hook from weeks ago!"

"You have to learn to feint, my boy," Rotham remarked and then grimaced.

"What is it?"

"Sir Julian Wright. But there is no time for escape."

The leader of the pinks of the *ton* pranced over in his dashing primrose pantaloons, Damask waistcoat with saucer-sized gold buttons, high shirt points, and white-topped Hessians with fringed tassels.

"Lord Westwood, is it true?"

"Be so good as to inform me as to what you refer?"

"Beauties! I heard you inherited a whole gaggle of them."

"I do have some wards," he said carefully, wondering why Sir Julian cared.

"When will they be introduced?"

"When Lady Westwood sees fit to do so." Dominic stood. He had no intention of obliging this fool with any fodder for gossip or whatever it was he was fishing for. "Excuse us, we were just on our way out."

They gathered their hats and capes and began walking towards Jackson's, but stopped on the pavement.

"Why do you think the popinjay is interested in your wards?" Montford asked.

"I cannot begin to fathom."

"Beauty!" Freddy said. "Obsessed with it. Used to make me uncomfortable with the way he stared. Never heard of him being in the petticoat line, though."

"He is very well to pass, so he is not looking for a fortune," Rotham interjected.

"He would not find it with them, anyway, though they have a respectable portion." Dominic wondered if the spectacle of five beautiful ladies would have unforeseen consequences. "Help me to keep an eye on Sir Julian. I've never known him to cross the line besides in his dress, but if he is so preoccupied with beautiful things, who knows what five of them might do to his sensibilities!"

"My guess is he wants to place a bet on them," Rotham prophesied.

"Perhaps that is all it is. It is bound to happen, regardless of who starts it."

"Let us go before anyone else waylays you!" Montford insisted.

Soon they were at Jackson's Saloon, perfecting their punishing rights, menacing left hooks, and swift one-twos. Before long, the thought of his wards and the sight of a pair of pretty blue eyes and an impudent countenance were forgotten.

CHAPTER 6

*T*hey had seen neither hide nor hair of Lord Westwood in four days. Faith didn't know whether to be glad or annoyed, but if her mood was anything to go by, it was the latter. They'd heard a great deal about him, however.

He was a Corinthian, all the go, Top-o'-the-Trees, a first-rate whip, and other names Faith did not fully understand, but all of this she had gleaned from servants who clearly thought much of their master's prowess and popularity. It was clear all of them were besotted.

Faith had only been guessing when she had thrown accusations at him before based on Lady Halbury's descriptions of a Town Buck. It made it even more perplexing why he wished to keep the five of them in Town! Then to completely abandon them to his mother? It was vexing in the extreme!

Several extraordinary gowns had arrived for each of them that morning, and her sisters were in raptures. Even Faith had to admit she'd never owned anything so fine. As a missionary child, she had learned to sew out of necessity. And while Lady Halbury had not been a miser, she had encouraged the girls to continue making their own gowns unless they were going to a special event. In her later years, they never went to special events.

It was something indeed to see her sisters outfitted in colours again. They looked like a veritable rainbow in pastels of soft primrose, peach, pale green, lilac, rose, and celestial blue. They were sitting on a sofa after breaking their fast, when Lord Westwood walked in.

"Perfection!" he exclaimed in an approving manner. "Pretty as a picture!"

They stood and made their curtsies.

"Have you come to take us somewhere?" Joy asked without preamble.

"Maybe I have, little imp," he said, tweaking her cheek.

Faith watched with a little pang of jealousy, wishing she could be so open with a gentleman while also trying not to feel piqued that he had ignored them for several days.

"Where are we going?"

"Perhaps it should be a surprise," he said with a devilish grin.

"I love surprises! Except I also want to know." Joy frowned at her own fickleness.

"Then I shall keep mum. Our escorts should be here any moment."

"Escorts?" Hope asked.

"As all of us do not fit into one vehicle, I asked my friends to come to our aid."

Faith would never have admitted it, but she was a little bit excited to see some of the amusements in Town. When his friends arrived, there was a great deal of exclamation and adoration of the sisters. The gentlemen had yet to see them all together.

"Where are we taking them?"

"To the 'Change to see the animals first. After that, I thought they would enjoy Gunter's."

"If you are planning on taking them anywhere fashionable, you will need to bring smelling salts," Rotham warned.

The girls laughed at the absurdity. They were shown outside to where four very smart vehicles were lined up with their tigers holding the horses' heads.

"How very dashing!" Hope exclaimed.

"But there are four vehicles, sir. Are some of us to ride alone?" Joy asked, of course noticing such a thing.

"That or make Freddy drive himself."

"I will ride with him!" Joy announced kindly. "What a bang-up pair you have, sir!"

Faith tried to smother her groan. Joy had spent more time in the stables than was good for her vocabulary.

Freddy apparently did not notice, and if he was disappointed not to be driving one of the elder sisters, he did not show it as if his young charge knew the way to his heart was admiration of his horses. "Much obliged! I would be delighted to drive you."

"May I handle the ribbons?" Faith heard Joy ask as soon as she was handed up.

Lord Westwood chuckled. "Freddy will have his hands full."

Indeed, Faith thought as Joy was already discussing the merits of matched teams, broad chests, and well-set hocks.

Faith watched as Hope sat with Grace in Lord Rotham's vehicle, while Patience went with Lord Montford. Which left her alone with Lord Westwood.

He handed Faith into his curricle. She had never touched a man thus before, and she was suddenly very conscious of his large body against hers from shoulder to thigh. He smelled very different from her sisters, with a mixture of starch, leather, and cologne of which she could not identify the foreign scents.

He took the reins from his tiger and masterfully set the spirited bays in motion.

"It will be a parade of the virtues!" Rotham teased as they passed by.

"Good God!" Lord Westwood said, apparently appalled at the very thought.

They drove through the streets and Faith was so amused by listening to Lord Westwood's description of Town—pointing out a particular *tulip* that resembled a *peacock* accompanied by his poodle, hence earning the nickname Poodle Byng. She scarcely noticed all the people who stopped and turned their heads to stare at them.

When they reached the Strand, they alighted, and left the vehicles to the offices of the tigers.

"Is it not funny that your groom is called a tiger when we are going to a menagerie?" Joy asked Freddy.

"I do not think there are tigers here," Freddy remarked, missing the irony entirely. Faith and Lord Westwood barely smothered their laughter.

"Oh, but there is a Bengal tiger!" Joy informed him.

"Capital!" Freddy replied.

"I say, shouldn't we have a chaperone or two on this outing?" she asked.

"It is perfectly acceptable for a lady to ride in an open carriage with a gentleman. But Westwood is your guardian, so you need not worry."

They made their way up to the exhibit, smelling it before they reached it, which was more pungent than the stables. Joy was walking exuberantly as they all trailed indecorously behind.

The group walked past a rather impressive collection of beasts: a hyena, a lion, a jaguar, a sloth, a camel, monkeys, an ostrich and some other exotic birds, elks, kangaroos, and antelopes.

They stopped before a very ugly creature labelled a rhinoceros.

"What is that, Joy?" Faith asked.

Joy had commentary on each species, on the authority of Acker-mann's Repository, and quoted of the rhinoceros:

WHERE IT INHABITS *it is a dread to the human race, as well as to all beasts of the forest, being in strength inferior to none, and so protected, by nature, with his coat of mail, as to be capable of resisting the attacks of any other animal, and even the force of a musket-ball.*

"THAT IS BOTH ASTONISHING AND FRIGHTENING," Lord Westwood remarked.

Faith gave an apologetic glance. "We have had little other way to learn about the world other than through reading. Thankfully, Lady Halbury did not deny us periodicals."

"Most young ladies quote the Bible or poetry."

"She can do that as well."

As they stood before the hippopotamus, Freddy frowned. "What is it, Mr. Cunningham?"

"I heard Byron likened this fellow to Lord Liverpool. By Jove, I believe I do see the resemblance!"

At the end was a creature known as an elephant named Chunee.

"Chunee does not sound like a bold enough name for such a large creature," Lord Westwood remarked as they watched the enormous grey beast toying with Lord Rotham's hat, much to her sisters' amusement. "You are quiet. What do you make of this?"

"A mixture of fascination between seeing the exotic creatures, and disliking the small cages to which they are confined," Faith replied.

"Rather more humane than my thoughts," he answered.

After they had seen every animal at the menagerie, they wandered back through some of the shops at the arcade below, but Joy was immediately drawn away. Before Faith realized what was happening, Joy was sitting on the dirty pavement with several kittens on her lap.

"Look, Faith!" She held up one with stripes like a tiger.

"Tigers seem to be the theme of the day. I suppose this was destined to be," Lord Westwood murmured.

Soon, all of her sisters were holding one, cooing and fawning over the little beasts.

"Please say we may have one!" Joy pleaded before Faith could tell her it was impossible.

"We do not have a home of our own, dearest. Perhaps, when we remove to the country again, we may have a mouser as we did at Halbury Hall."

"But I will be so lonely while you are at your entertainments! Surely we could have at least one?" Faith could see Joy's eyes filling with tears and her lower lip beginning to protrude.

"Come along now, we cannot bring kittens to Lady Westwood's home!"

Joy allowed herself to be brought to her feet and Faith watched as her sisters handed the kittens back to the boy who was trying to sell them for a shilling apiece. What she did not see was Mr. Cunningham's heartstrings being pulled by the little imp, and giving her the shilling to pay for the miniature tiger, then telling her to hide it under her pelisse.

~

DOMINIC FOUND he was enjoying himself. At first, he thought it would be amusing, but he was surprised that none of his wards were simpering misses. Equally, none of them seemed the least bit affected or aware of the attention they were drawing.

However, he realized they would need a great deal of entertainment until they were brought out. Apparently, country girls were not used to being confined indoors.

They rode from the Strand to Berkeley Square, where the famous Gunter's happened to be near his Town residence. He suspected during his wards' stay in London there would be a great many visits to the confectionery. While he did not care for sweetmeats himself, it was a rare lady that did not.

The square was crowded in the late afternoon and he prepared himself for an invasion. He was not to be disappointed. No sooner had they drawn up their vehicles, and the waiters had come to take their selections, than a barrage of people made their way over for introductions on the slimmest of pretences.

"Everyone in Town is certainly friendlier than I expected," Faith remarked in a small pause between visitors.

"Curious, more like."

"I will never remember all of their names."

"Think of some silly things to help you. Poodle Byng is easy, of course, because he always has that silly dog with him. But I find there are often idiosyncrasies with everyone if you can but find them. Take your new acquaintance, Lady Jersey, for instance. Her nickname is Silence because she never stops talking."

"Oh, that is too cruel!" Faith protested.

"That is too true," he countered, making her laugh.

"Tell me some more," she begged as a waiter brought their ices. He had selected the Gruyère for her and could not wait to see what she thought of it.

"My, how dainty these are!" she said, looking at the little dish with a mound of creamed ice and a tiny silver spoon in it.

"It is best to taste them before they melt, you know. They are not only to be admired for their looks."

She glanced remonstratively at him before she thought better of it but did scoop a bite and tasted it. The look on her face hid nothing of her feelings. He wondered if she realized how expressive she was. His inner voice told him he'd like to put that look on her face himself, but then he quickly told it to be quiet. While he was conversing with himself, Joy's head appeared over the side of the curricle.

"What flavour do you have, Faith? I have the lavender. Would you like to taste it?"

Soon, they were all on the ground. Hope had the lemon, Patience the vanilla, and Grace the pineapple.

Dominic, Rotham, Freddy, and Montford stood watching them as they shared and delighted in the treats in their unguarded innocence.

"Your peace has ended, Dom." Rotham watched with undisguised admiration.

"Don't I know it." Rotham only knew the half of it.

"A crowd is beginning to gather," Montford remarked. Dominic was well aware, but he knew it would happen. Even if the Whitford ladies did nothing more than exist.

"There is Lady Wilton and her two fusby-faced girls. She must be livid!" Freddy laughed. "Serves her right for all the times she's put her daughters forward as though it's our duty to admire them."

"I would not call Lady Agatha fusby-faced," Montford argued.

"It's difficult to see past her remarkable personality," Dominic agreed with no little sarcasm.

"It does not look as though she intends to be introduced." Rotham lifted a hand to wave at the countess, knowing full well as a duke's heir, she would not snub him. She did incline her head, and looked as though she was warring with her better judgement, but clearly not wishing to be introduced to Lord Westwood's beauties won out.

"That must have been a difficult decision," Rotham reflected. "She has intended me for Lady Agatha since I was in short pants."

"Won't it rankle when she hears they've already received vouchers?" Dominic asked.

"They have? However did you achieve such a thing before they've been introduced?" Montford asked.

"Apparently, Miss Whitford and Miss Hope saved one of Lady Jersey's little rapscallions from the Serpentine."

"How fortuitous."

"Indeed. Here comes Brosner. This is better than any play I have seen recently," Rotham reflected.

"I had a feeling it would be. Are his pockets still to let?" Dominic asked as they watched the handsome Marquess approach. Dominic did not particularly have anything against him, but as a guardian he had to be awake on all fronts.

"As rumour has it," Montford said, "but he's probably no worse off than I am. He does still like a good wager."

Freddy had wandered off to help Joy with something. Dominic could not help but laugh. She would run circles around him if he let her. It did not seem as though it would do any harm. As long as Freddy was amused by the chit.

"Westwood," Brosner said by way of greeting. "I see the rumours are true. God must have a wicked sense of humour."

"Certainly something," Dominic agreed coldly.

"Think you can fire all of them off in one Season?"

"Very likely, but I do not intend to."

"No?"

"The youngest is not yet sixteen."

"Pity. How many of them, then?" he asked, with a gleam in his eyes that Dominic did not like.

"The three eldest. You are not thinking to wager on my wards, are you, Brosner?"

"Can Westwood remain impervious? It certainly sounds like a good wager to me." Brosner looked smug.

"You impugn my honour when you say such things."

"Nonsense. The eldest cannot be too far from her majority." He waved his hand in a dismissive gesture.

"I think you had best move along, Brosner," Rotham warned.

"Before an introduction?"

"Most certainly," Montford agreed. "Remember, they are not of age."

Dominic smiled sweetly. The marquess walked away with a scowl.

"He did not play that well."

"Not at all. He must be desperate," Montford agreed.

"What the devil is Freddy doing with the youngest?" Rotham asked, looking over towards a large plane tree.

Dominic squinted to try to see better. "Is he climbing the tree?"

"If that doesn't beat all," Montford said. "Do you think she dared him?"

"Do not look now, but it appears she is going up after him."

The other sisters must have noticed as well because they scurried en masse towards the tree.

"That is not going to make it any less conspicuous," Rotham observed unhelpfully.

"Shall we go see what possessed Freddy to revert to a twelve-year-old?"

"I am not certain he ever progressed, actually," Dominic reflected.

Nevertheless, they walked as casually as they could over to where the sisters had gathered beneath the tree.

Joy was stretched out on one limb, and Freddy was on the one just above.

"Here, kitty, kitty," Freddy called, trying to coax the little tiger into coming to him.

"You didn't," Dominic scolded.

"I am quite certain he could not say no to a pair of pretty blue eyes," Rotham reflected.

"I think I should have drawn your cork at Jackson's. I would be happy to oblige when this charming display is over."

While they considered ways to coax the miniature tiger down, from walking over to his townhouse to grab a ladder to throwing a sheet over the branch, Miss Whitford had taken some stones and was tossing them around the kitten, causing the branch to shake and the little fellow mewed with displeasure.

"Will that not make the little monster go higher?" Patience asked.

It did not. A little ball of fluff jumped—or fell—down into Grace's waiting arms.

"That was unexpected," Montford reflected.

"Come on down, Joy. I will catch you if needs be." Dominic held up his arms.

But Joy needed no such help. Lithe as a cat herself, she climbed down and landed on her feet as though this was a common pastime for her. Very likely it was.

"Will you catch me if I need it?" Freddy looked down with a huge grin.

"You may rot in the tree for that caper," he retorted. "I hope you intend to keep the creature with you, because there is no possibility of my mother allowing it in her house!"

Freddy swung himself down from the tree without incident

"You would think a schoolroom miss would bore him," Rotham remarked.

"On the contrary. A schoolroom miss suits him perfectly!"

"I shall name him Freddy Tiger after you," Joy announced with a beaming smile at Freddy, which caused his friends to go into peals of laughter.

CHAPTER 7

*S*urprisingly, Lady Westwood had not minded Joy having a kitten, after all, when they presented the young feline to her upon their return. Faith was mortified at the imposition, but her ladyship had thought it would be just the thing to keep Joy occupied while her elder sisters were out and about.

"The two of them will get into mischief together, I have no doubt," Lady Westwood said with a twinkle in her eyes that greatly resembled the one her son often had.

Even Mr. Cunningham had been to visit his namesake twice, though Faith did wonder if it was merely an excuse to visit her sisters. There was no denying that he had taken to little Joy like an older brother would.

The day after the escapade with the kitten in Berkeley Square, the sisters were sitting in the drawing room with Lady Westwood before they went out for the day. Hope was reading the gossip columns and gasped with excitement. "Listen to this!"

DOES anyone else see the delicious irony in Lord W—having five beautiful wards? Alas, will he himself—London's most determined bachelor—be able to withstand the unearthly beauty that has been placed before him like the forbidden fruit in the Garden of Eden?

INSTEAD OF REMARKING on the hoydenish behaviour that had prompted Joy to climb the tree in front of half the *ton* taking ices at Gunter's, they remarked upon Mr. Cunningham's heroism at rescuing her kitten.

"I tossed the rock which caused him to jump down," Faith muttered peevishly.

Joy was delighted to be famous.

Had it only been two weeks since their lives had been turned upside down?

"Girls, I have been debating how best to present you to the *ton*. Since matters have progressed rather more rapidly than I anticipated..." She slid a glance to the newspaper, which they had just been reading aloud. "What do you think about holding a ball here?"

"A real ball?" Joy asked with delight.

"We must do something to present you. The Queen is not well, and is not expected to hold her débutantes' ball or any drawing rooms for the foreseeable future, so we will make do."

Faith was very relieved to hear it, though she did not wish the Queen unwell. After the awful tragedy of losing the princess only a year ago, it would have been more odd if the Queen did hold any parties.

She had also heard of the gowns required for court presentations, and was very relieved not to bear the expense of something so ostentatious that would never be worn again.

But a ball in their honour? It also sounded very extravagant. She could not fathom why Lord Westwood would choose or wish to bear the expense and still meant to repay him what she could when she received her portion. It was vexatious not to understand. Was it out of the goodness of his heart or was there another unknown motive? It was irksome not to know why he was doing this...especially for girls that were supposed to be his father's wards.

"You must not think a ball necessary, my lady. We are happy enough to attend some small entertainments."

"Nonsense!" she protested. "I host a ball every Season, only we must hold it quite soon. I suspect with the three eldest of you here, it will be a sad crush!"

"Perhaps you should have a Season now, Grace," Joy said thoughtfully. "It does not seem fair for you to have to wait two more years for me! The Town already knows about you, anyway."

Faith looked at Grace. "Joy is probably right. What do you think, Lady Westwood?"

"Indeed, I had thought there must be some good reason, but if not, then most certainly she should make her come-out with the rest of you! We will engage a governess-companion for Joy so she will not be neglected."

"But I have Freddy Tiger for that!"

"But little Freddy cannot take you to visit museums and parks and other adventures that are to be had while in Town," her ladyship coaxed with great cunning.

"But Mr. Cunningham and Lord Westwood will take me."

"Of course they will when they can, but they will be attending many of the same entertainments your sisters will be at."

"Oh." A frown formed on her face. "I had not considered that."

"But do not fret. We will make certain we find you someone you can like. No stuffy old matron for you!"

Faith was relieved. It had been her main concern about having Grace presented with the rest of them, but Joy would wilt under a strict duenna.

"Would you like to help us plan the ball as well, Joy?"

"Me?" No one had ever asked her such a thing.

"Oh, yes. Balls in London are spectacles," she said, as if confiding a great secret. "Some, of course, are mundane, but a superior hostess does something special that leaves her guests treasuring the memories for Seasons to come. Lady Ashbury, who is a great friend of mine, does something original every year. She has three identical triplet daughters, who I dare say may be the only group of sisters to ever have rivalled you. When she presented them at a ball, her theme was a night with Beethoven, and her ballroom had been transformed into a replica of Vienna! There was a miniature Hofburg Palace, the Rathaus, St. Stephen's Cathedral, and an actual water feature of the Donau River running through the 'city'!

The girls gasped trying to imagine such a thing.

"Then, to present the girls, the building, shaped like the Viennese Opera House, began to rotate. On the other side of the building were the triplets, one behind a pianoforte, another sitting behind a cello, and the third held a violin! There was even an enormous cake shaped like a pianoforte."

Her sisters gasped in astonishment.

"Needless to say, I welcome your fresh ideas. I will have my secretary review the social calendars and decide upon a date as soon as possible because *we must not wait*. Therefore, I need all of you to help with this. Consider the matter, if you will, while I speak with Jones." Lady Westwood left the room.

"How exciting!" Hope exclaimed. "What could we do to rival the Ashbury ball?"

"Make it into a garden?"

"Make it into a starry night?"

"An enchanted forest?"

"A masquerade?"

"I have a feeling all of those will have been done before," Faith remarked, "but I have no better ideas myself."

"How about the Exeter Exchange and everyone can dress as their favourite animal?" Joy said, brimming with excitement. "Or the Tower of London, and the gentlemen can dress as Henry the Eighth and we can dress as one of his wives."

"Before or after he had them beheaded?" Patience asked dryly.

"Either, of course," Joy replied.

"What a bloodthirsty wench you are, imp," Lord Westwood said, strolling into the room in moulded buff pantaloons, a well-fitted blue jacket, and riding boots, looking very modish. "Why are we discussing our unfortunate monarch who had a predilection for beheading?"

"We are trying to think of a theme for our ball!"

"Of course, a ball," he said with aplomb. "My mother has left you to think of a thing to rival Lady Ashbury, I gather?" he asked rhetorically, as he took a seat in a chair next to Faith and crossed his legs.

They told him their other ideas, and he assured them they had all been done—except for Henry the Eighth's wives.

"There must be something besides the Tower of London, though it would be original, and require every carpenter in London to pull it off," Westwood pointed out.

"Is there any story that has five females?" Hope asked.

They all wrinkled their brows in thought.

"Henry the Eighth did have six wives," Joy said, clinging to the idea. "Lady Westwood could be Catherine of Aragon."

"That is not how I want my sisters to be remembered for years to come, thank you! I cannot believe we are discussing it as a serious option," Faith said in exasperation.

"I apologize, Faith," Joy sounded disappointed.

"No, no. I beg your pardon. I did not mean to snap at you."

"Here is an idea. You could all be different goddesses and make the ballroom up to be the heavens with clouds and harps and such—what do you say? I cannot think that has been done in my recent memory, anyway."

"Would you be Cupid, shooting arrows at us?" Grace asked with a devilish smile.

"No, I will not prance about in my unmentionables with wings strapped to my back. We could be fallen angels, me and my friends, though."

"Not so far from the truth," Faith muttered to herself, but Lord Westwood must have heard.

"Baggage," he leaned over and said appreciatively.

"There is always Shakespeare. We could transform the ballroom into the woods and grotto from *A Midsummer Night's Dream*," Patience suggested.

"It has been done, I am afraid."

"Certainly not Julius Caesar or Romeo and Juliet," Grace shuddered. "No tragedies."

"What about a jungle?" Joy asked as she stroked Freddy Tiger's head. "Or something exotic like China? They have the most exquisite dolls we could dress as!"

"You would have to paint your faces white and I would not think anything to hide your natural beauty would be the thing to introduce you to the *ton*. They will have heard about you by now and will be wanting a glimpse," Lord Westwood reasoned.

"Then we might as well do the Exeter Exchange and put us in display cages!" Patience moaned.

"That's the ticket!" Westwood said ironically.

"Let us see what Lady Westwood thinks," Faith put in hurriedly before the discussion dived any deeper into the ridiculous.

DOMINIC GLANCED up as his mother glided back in the room, looking more excited than he had seen her in years.

"Two weeks!" she announced. "Oh, there you are, Dominic. Have you helped the girls decide what our theme will be?"

He rose and placed a kiss on his mother's proffered cheek. "Certainly. They would like to be animals in cages on display like at the 'Change."

She gasped as he knew she would.

"Besides the options of Henry the Eighth's wives or goddesses in the heavens, we are at a loss," Miss Whitford said sheepishly.

Dominic wished he had a portrait of his mother's face in that moment.

"What about a carnival or Astley's Amphitheatre?" Joy persisted. "We are all very good horsewomen," she said with modest innocence.

"Joy, you do not say such things about yourself," Faith quietly scolded.

"But it is true. I miss Nightingale."

"Was Nightingale your mare?" Dominic asked.

69

"Yes, but we had to leave all our horses behind. Faith did not think they were truly ours to take, but I've had her since she was a foal!"

Dominic could see he would either need to speak with Sir Reginald or visit Tattersalls very soon. Unless Sir Reginald was intending on keeping the girls' horses for his own offspring, he might appreciate them being taken off his hands instead of eating their heads off in the stables.

Meanwhile, his mother was still fretting about the theme, and was growing more horrified with each suggestion made to her.

"Shall I send Satterlee to you, Mother, and take these ladies for an airing in the park?" Surely offering his best of secretaries would appease her.

"May we please go to Astley's?" Joy asked without hesitation.

"Joy, we have discussed the impropriety of imposing on Lord Westwood," Faith reminded the youngest, who they were going to be hard-pressed to keep in the school room.

"There is no showing today, imp, but I will take you soon." Whatever was happening to him? He'd been brought to heel by a fifteen-year-old slip of a girl.

"A walk in the park would be just the thing, my lord," Faith said.

Fortunately, the country girls did not take long to ready themselves, and soon they were gathered with their bonnets and cloaks about to set out when there was a knock upon the door.

"Freddy. We were just about to walk in the park. Would you care to join us?"

"Certainly! It will be just the thing! I have brought a lead for my namesake."

Joy squealed with delight as Dominic looked on with horror.

Freddy pulled out a little bejewelled black collar and a matching lead.

Joy held up Freddy Tiger and Freddy clasped the collar round his little neck.

He then proceeded to stroke the kitten behind the ears. "This way he will not escape up into a tree again. Will you?" he said in that annoying little voice that people talked to babies with.

"You unman me, Freddy!" Dominic said acidly.

Freddy, who was by now allowing the kitten to rub its chin all over his, merely grinned at Dominic.

"Not so amused now?" Miss Whitford asked knowingly.

"Certainly not bored!" he retorted and held out his arm to her.

She laughed for the first time he could remember. The low, musical lilt affected him in ways even her beauty had not. She needed to laugh more, he decided.

They began their procession two by two with Freddy and Joy leading the way trying to convince little Freddy Tiger to walk on the lead. Thus far it had only managed to become tangled in Joy's skirts.

"I believe Freddy is in danger of becoming another Poodle Byng."

"Oh, but a kitten is much more dashing! Perhaps we should return to the Strand and select one for you as well," Miss Whitford said with a smile that quite transformed her face.

Dominic pretended to shudder which made her laugh again.

"Come now, I have heard anything Lord Westwood does is certain to take."

"Who is filling your ears with such nonsense?" he protested.

"Your servants think very highly of you, and we read the Society pages."

"Unfortunately, when retainers have known you since birth, there is little threat you can make to them," he replied ruefully.

Thankfully, Green Park was neither as crowded nor as occupied with members of the *ton* intent on socializing as Hyde Park. The park was instead full of playing children and merchants going about their business.

They entered through the gate near Bath House and walked along the row of stately homes in the Palladian fashion similar to Westwood House.

"Are those cows?" Miss Whitford asked, squinting towards the far corner of the park.

"Yes, indeed. I had forgotten about them. Would any of you care for some fresh milk?"

"They have milch cows in the middle of the park in London? How curious!"

"No one can ever say you were deprived in London. Not only do we have milk, but fresh and warm, straight from the cow!"

The others had by this time noticed the herd and were wandering closer with curiosity, while Joy and Freddy still struggled to teach little Freddy Tiger to use his lead. Currently, he was climbing Freddy's glossy Hessians much to his dismay, resulting in a blistering scold to his junior. Once he had divested Hoby's masterpiece of the feline, Freddy Tiger then began attacking his lead.

Dominic could only shake his head. He paid the attendant for five warm glasses of milk, thinking himself rather magnanimous for considering Freddy Tiger.

He placed the cup down on the ground, and the cat eagerly helped himself.

"Do you wish for some, Freddy...the great? Senior? It is a bit confusing to know what to call each of you when you're together."

"I don't care for milk myself, reminds me of my old nurse. Look at him go!" he said as if he were responsible for providing the creature with milk and his ability to drink it.

Several of the sisters were watching adoringly.

Dominic turned away from the spectacle his friend was making of himself, only to see that Joy was watching the maids milk the cows with fascination.

She was right next to one of the girls, asking questions and was now bending down to watch closely. It was almost like watching an accident in slow motion. The milkmaid stood up and helped Joy sit on her stool, then proceeded to show her how to squeeze and draw milk from the giant black and white cow.

"Why is my ward milking a cow?" He began to move forward, but felt a staying hand on his arm.

"At this point, it would be best to let her finish. If you scare the cow, it might hurt her."

"Again, I ask, why would she do such a thing?"

"I would think you know Joy well enough by now that she is infinitely curious about everything."

"I see. It is educational."

She smiled at him as though pleased with his understanding. "Why, yes. But I do not think there is any harm in it. In the country, she was not restricted perhaps as much as girls are in the city."

Dominic had no doubt of that assertion whatsoever. It did not seem as if she'd had any restrictions at all. "There may not be any harm to her, but think of me!"

"I believe your reputation will withstand such an assault."

"Not at this rate! What next? You will have me sewing samplers!"

"Shall we retire to Bath after all, my lord?" she taunted, a devilish twinkle in her eyes.

"Baggage!"

CHAPTER 8

Faith had never planned a party or a ball, but she knew it must be a great deal of work. When they had returned from the outing in the park, it seemed the servants had multiplied into an army and were turning the house inside out in the process of cleaning, polishing, and rearranging.

Lady Westwood was still undecided on a theme. She called to Faith on her way in the door while her sisters and the gentlemen somehow managed to escape.

Her ladyship had already set the servants upon preparing the ballroom and had her chef and Lord Westwood's conferring over menus. "We must decide on the theme now. If we do the heavens, I fear people will try to name each of you as goddesses, which could have devastating implications. You cannot all be Aphrodite!"

"Very true," Faith agreed, not knowing why it mattered or what else to say.

"But it is certainly easy to decorate for. Since we have so little time, I do not think we could recreate Paris or anywhere to rival Vienna. The ballroom already has statues in its alcoves, and it is simple enough to have cherubs playing harps in clouds."

It didn't sound simple to Faith at all. "What if we were angels instead of goddesses? If we need to be anything at all."

"Why, of course you do! You are the main attractions!"

She watched Lady Westwood's face as she considered. "It might be the very thing," she said, looking very pleased with herself. "It is not every day that five almost identical beauties come along at once. But do we dress you all in white so that you are indistinguishable? Or do we give you each your own pale colour like a rainbow?"

"Rainbows are biblical," Faith replied noncommittally.

Lady Westwood was not attending. She was already off in her own world, dreaming of heaven and how to replicate it in her ballroom. "Pastels, I think. With your colouring, it does nothing to diminish your beauty. But I do not care for wings protruding from your back. It would be vulgar!"

Faith tried not to laugh.

"We can have actors dressed in white with wings hanging from the ceiling, perhaps. And harps. Several harps! We must have the ceiling transformed into the sky, but do you think fabric or paint would be better?"

"It will take a great deal of fabric, but it would cover everything and not be permanent," Faith reasoned.

"Indeed." She looked at the two secretaries who were sitting, taking furious notes. "Jones, send someone as soon as possible to the silk warehouses! It will take an act of God to find enough fabric in time!"

Lord Westwood's secretary left immediately on that task. Faith would have gladly gone in his stead.

"Now for the clouds. Perhaps the entire floor should not be covered because there must be dancing."

"What about having tables around the room decorated as clouds with fountains?" Jones suggested.

"Fountains! Yes! I had forgotten about fountains. I do think we should have a river as well, for even though Lady Ashbury did it several years ago, what would heaven be without a River of Life?"

Faith could see there would be no point in pleading with Lady

Westwood not to be extravagant on their account. It did not seem as though this was much about them, after all.

"Now for flowers. What kind of flowers would they have in heaven? Lots and lots of them, I think." She held one finger in the air. "We should have a Tree of Life to go with our River of Life! It must be very large and at the centre of the room, I think, and covered in fruit! Did you take note of that, Jones?"

Faith bit her lip to keep from laughing. Was it not the Tree of Life that caused Adam and Eve to sin and be cast out? Though perhaps, on second thought, that was a different tree from the Garden of Eden. As long as she did not insist on a serpent...Faith would have to object to *that*.

Lady Westwood and her secretary were conversing about the logic of putting the tree in the centre of the room. Jones insisted it would inhibit the dancing.

"Has my mother completely lost her mind yet? When she realizes reality does not match her dreams, I fear there may be the devil to pay."

How had he sneaked in behind her?

Faith felt laughter bubbling up inside.

"Don't hold back on my account!" he said, his eyes brimming with mischief. "Ridiculous, is it not? But look how happy she is."

Faith sighed loudly before she realized it.

"You do not care for any of it, do you?"

"If it makes her happy and sees my sisters well established, then I suppose it will have been worth it. I cannot like the extravagance on our accounts. You must know I can never repay you."

"But what of you, Miss Whitford? Do you have no thoughts for yourself?"

"Why should I? They are my responsibility so, of course, I must think of them!"

"I thought we had established that I am now their guardian."

She shook her head. "I have been more like a mother than a sister to them for more than ten years. Lady Halbury was kind enough to take us in, but we had already been on our own for some time while trying to return to England and they have always looked to me."

"Poor Miss Whitford! My shoulders are big enough to bear some of this responsibility for you."

"They are no burden. We may be your wards in name, but the rest..."

"Yes, I know! I forced you to London!" His eyes twinkled down at her.

"Well, yes, you did!" she rejoined.

"Would it not be easier for you to marry and allow a husband to help you?" he asked more gently.

"A guardian is more than enough to deal with for now."

"Do you know how to dance?" He wisely changed the subject.

"You can dance, Miss Whitford?" It took Faith a moment to realize that the second question had been addressed to her by Lady Westwood, who had overheard Lord Westwood's query.

"A little, ma'am."

"You have been to assemblies?"

"No, but we were permitted to attend some private dinners where there was some dancing afterwards."

Lady Westwood began fanning herself.

"Now is not the time for the vapours, Mother," Lord Westwood teased. "We will simply hire a dancing master to make sure they are up to snuff."

"Now is not a time to speak in such a vulgar manner, Dominic! You cannot imagine Monsieur Dubois will have any availability at this time?"

"I generally find that for the right sum anyone has availability," he mumbled wryly.

"You and your friends will make yourselves useful. In fact, gather them now, and we will begin today!"

"You should have kept your thoughts to yourself, my lord." Faith was definitely trying to smother laughter now, but it tumbled out.

"Do you think my friends will make themselves available at a moment's notice?" he asked.

"I find that for the right sum anyone can be available!" His mother intoned his own words back at him.

He barked an appreciative laugh. "Touché. Very well, I will round 'em up!"

~

DOMINIC SHOULD HAVE FORESEEN something like this. He had fallen right into that trap. Nothing could be more tedious than dancing lessons. But first, he would have Satterlee contact the dancing master, and send him to wait upon Lady Westwood. His mother was wrong. Everyone, including Monsieur Dubois, could be bought.

Now, how to find suitable partners? He doubted if there were any, but at least his friends could be trusted not to step over the line. They were neither ones to bother young innocents nor on the lookout for *eligible partis*.

Besides, he never asked for favours, and he knew they liked the sisters. Montford was predictably at White's. Sometimes, Dominic wondered if he had been forced to let the family Town residence, but it was more likely that he was avoiding his mother and sisters who were there.

"Dancing? You know I'm not over-fond of the past time, Dom."

"Neither am I, old chap, but if you asked me to help because your sisters were in desperate straits for a ball in a fortnight, I would oblige you."

Montford scowled. "At least your wards are a dashed sight prettier than my sisters," he said with brutal frankness. But he came along anyway.

Freddy was at home and only too delighted to help.

It was another thing to track Rotham down. Dominic finally found him at Tattersalls.

"We need one more. Perhaps I could send for Ashley, but he has Guard duty." Dominic's younger brother was always a favourite with the ladies, but he hated to trouble him for such a tedious matter.

Therefore, the last partner proved to be more difficult to find.

They stood admiring some black horses being led around the ring while contemplating. Dominic had not heard back from Sir Reginald about the girls' mounts. What a sight they would be on black horses...

"What about Worth?" Rotham asked, interrupting Dom's machinations.

"Too high in the instep, not to mention old." Dominic dismissed the suggestion.

"Sudley was at White's," Montford said.

"Isn't that Carew over there?" Freddy asked.

"The Irish rogue?" Dominic lifted his brows at Freddy. Though Dominic had no issue with their old friend from school, he was hardly one to dance attendance on débutantes. Mamas hid their young from his devastating charm. Freddy had already hailed him over.

"Carew, are you engaged this afternoon? Westwood has five new wards that need help learning to dance."

Dominic attempted chagrin to keep Carew from taking the bait. As long as Freddy didn't...

"Five great beauties. Will set the *ton* by storm."

"Five, eh?" Carew pretended to consider while Dominic smothered a groan.

The Whitford sisters were a vision even in their mourning dresses. The girls were standing in formation and performing the steps without partners, Monsieur Dubois circling them with a critical eye, adjusting postures and calling out corrections.

They danced like graceful swans. It was quite a sight to behold. Carew was evidently not prepared for the sight.

"The devil!" Carew exclaimed.

"By Jove!" Freddy added, even though he had seen them.

"Just so," Dominic agreed. "I cannot ask just anyone for this favour."

"I should say not. I do not envy you this task, though I fully intend to stay and watch now."

"Far be it for me to overturn your plans, Carew."

"Not at all."

His mother exclaimed with delight when he strode in, not only with five dancing partners, but having secured the most sought after master in London.

"I will not ask how you made this happen so quickly, but I knew you would not fail me!"

He dutifully kissed her cheek, followed by bows from each of his friends.

"And you will all be on your best behaviour!" she warned his friends with a twinkle in her eyes as she returned to her sofa to watch. Many a school holiday had been spent at their country estate, Taywards, in their youth.

"Perhaps you could create a sensation by having them simply dance for everyone," Rotham said, with an appreciative gleam in his eyes.

"Not a bad notion, but I fear there are not enough smelling salts for that combined with my mother's mad notions."

"Ah. A theme?"

"A theme," Dominic confirmed.

"My sympathies."

The song they were dancing to ended, and the ladies noticed they had an audience.

Charming blushes bloomed across their cheeks.

"It's a shame to see them spoiled by the *ton*. I suppose it must be done."

"Ladies, may I make known to you Lord Carew. We are here to partner you."

"Carew, perhaps you could partner Miss Joy?"

"Oh, I already promised myself to Miss Joy," Freddy interrupted.

"Very well then. Perhaps Miss Grace?" Grace stepped forward and curtsied. "This is an old school friend, Lord Carew."

When Dominic turned around, the others had paired themselves off.

"I suppose no further introductions are necessary?" he asked Faith, who was awaiting him.

"None at all, but I fear you are forced to suffer my company again," she said.

"I shall contrive, ma'am," he said with a severe bow.

"You mock me, sir!"

"Only a little," he confessed as he took his place before her.

"I thought you might choose one of my sisters, who…"

The music began, and she ceased speaking immediately.

Dominic performed the steps without thinking about them, so long ago had it become second nature to him, while he waited for her to finish her sentence.

"Why should I prefer one of your sisters?" he prompted.

She hushed him.

That was something he could not say a lady had ever done to him before. "As you wish."

"I must listen to the music or I will make a hash of my steps," she said during a brief pause.

"Naturally," he agreed, finding her little nose wrinkled, her eyes narrowed, and her lips pursed as she concentrated.

He looked around at the sisters, who all wore similar expressions of concentration, and then to his friends, leading them about the room with looks of adoration. How the mighty were falling! He chuckled out loud.

"What is it?" Faith asked, almost stumbling as she did so. He redirected her back on the right path.

"The whole scene is amusing. Never would I have thought to spend an afternoon at dancing lessons once I reached my majority, but also to witness my friends…"

"I am glad we are fulfilling your hopes for amusement, my lord," she said primly.

When her cheeks were flushed and her eyes flashed, was when her beauty arrested him. However, she was also distracted and not missing her steps. She had not noticed that fact.

Rotham had charmed Hope into smiling. Patience was talking in animated fashion with Montford, who looked smitten. Dominic already dreaded the horrible poetry he was likely to write. Grace, it seemed, was trying not to look above Carew's neckcloth, while

Freddy and Joy were distracted in their steps by something. He did not know what had their attentions.

Unfortunately, they bumped into Dominic and Faith.

All sense of decorum was lost, much to Monsieur Dubois' dismay. Joy giggled. Freddy Tiger, who had apparently been a stowaway in a pocket, leapt to the floor and towards the dancing master, who shrieked and pranced about screaming 'rodent,' which caused all of them to go into whoops of laughter.

Instead of catching their wayward pet, Freddy and Joy were doubled over in their hysterics, tears streaming down their faces, which Monsieur Dubois took exception to.

Faith went over and captured the little beast while Dominic led the sensitive Frenchman to a bench, and Lady Westwood hurried to waft her smelling salts beneath his nose.

"It is only a kitten," his mother tried to explain, but Dubois' nerves would not be soothed.

"I cannot perform in such conditions!"

"We will make certain the kitten is put away before our next lesson," she soothed.

He shook his head in the Gallic fashion. "Non, non, non, there will not be ze next time!"

No controlling or bribing would convince him. His nerves! His delicate sensibilities! Everything was offended! He was the most sought after dancing master in all of England!

By that point, Dominic was ready to throw him out by his powdered wig.

Once he was gone, the girls seemed to feel the weight of what had happened.

"What a horrible little man!" Joy exclaimed as she stroked Freddy Tiger.

"We are very sorry, my lord. We were not laughing at him, precisely," Grace said.

"Come now, it was deliciously amusing!" However, Dominic knew it consigned him—and his friends—to finish their dancing lessons. They were nowhere near ready to perform in front of Society.

CHAPTER 9

*F*aith and her sisters quickly discovered that they were *de trop* when it came to preparations for the ball, and learned to stay out of the way. Lord and Lady Westwood's secretaries had everything in hand, so that the only thing the girls could do was learn the dances and try to prepare for the idiosyncrasies of the *ton*.

Lord Westwood and his friends had literally danced attendance on them every afternoon to make certain no one could fault their abilities in a ballroom. All had promised the opening set to them as well, so they could be comfortable with their first partners and have no fears of being wallflowers—not that Faith thought her sisters were in danger of that fate.

It would be ungrateful if Faith were to admit how much she wished this dratted ball over with. Having been forced into a London Season was one thing, but it seemed they had no time to themselves and, therefore, no peace whatsoever.

It was almost as if Lord Westwood could read her mind when he arrived that morning before they had breakfasted.

Faith was in the garden, seeking a small measure of quiet before the day's chaos began.

"Miss Whitford."

She jumped at his voice. He always managed to startle her.

"Forgive me for intruding."

"Not at all, my lord, I was far away with my thoughts."

"I was wondering if you and your sisters would care for a ride in the park this morning?"

"Do you mean on horseback?"

"What other way is there?"

For a moment, she tried to assimilate his finding five horses for them to ride, but she could not.

"What is it, my beauty?"

She frowned at the endearment. With his reputation, he probably called many women that—and not all ladies. "You should not call me that."

"Likely not," he said unperturbed. "Could you perhaps rouse your sisters to put on their riding habits? The horses are waiting."

"Yes, of course." She hurried back into the house and upstairs to their chambers.

Her sisters were awake—it was hard to break country ways—and quickly changed into their smart new riding habits they had not yet had a chance to wear. All were in shades of blue—Faith had never known there were so many, from celestial to azure to Saxon to Prussian to indigo. Hers was of the latter to match her eyes, with a skirt and bodice joined in a single dress with narrowed sleeves and a trained skirt with gold trim. A small, peaked hat with a gold ribbon finished her toilette.

"Me, also?" Joy asked, obviously wondering if this was the beginning of her being left out of such entertainments. The new governess had been hired and was to begin in time for the ball—probably not a moment too soon, Faith reflected fondly.

"I should think you may still ride with us. Perhaps you can look out and see how many horses Lord Westwood has brought?" Faith suggested, hoping dearly that he had not excluded Joy. She might not be out of the schoolroom, but they had always ridden together.

A loud screech of excitement answered the question quickly.

"I presume there are enough?"

Joy jumped up and down. "Look!"

All the sisters hurried to the window and looked down at the street to where their own mounts from home stood magnificently in a row, waiting with grooms holding them.

All of the horses bred from the same sire, with gleaming ebony coats except for a small white patch on them—some their noses, some their legs.

"I do not believe it!" Hope exclaimed.

"Lord Westwood has outdone himself," Patience agreed.

He had, indeed. "I hate to think of how indebted we are to him for this."

"He would not have done it if he did not wish to, Faith," Grace reasoned.

Joy and Grace raced down the stairs, followed by recriminations from Faith not to act like hoydens.

The others followed at a hurried but decorous pace, only to see Joy exclaim and hug Lord Westwood quickly before hurrying to greet Nightingale.

The horses were magnificent, standing there in a row, just as pleased to see their mistresses. They were greeted with nickering, tossing their heads, and pawing at the ground.

"I do not know how you contrived this, but it must have been at great expense to you. We are in your debt yet again, Lord Westwood."

"You do not wish to become a bore, Miss Whitford. I was hoping you would tell me how delighted you are to see your mount."

"I would be lying were I to say otherwise. It was with great sorrow that we parted from them, not expecting to see them again."

"If it sets your mind at ease, Sir Reginald was only too happy to have them off his hands instead of 'eating their heads off' in his stables as he put it."

It did relieve her mind a little to know that, but still the expense of stabling them in London must be great!

"Besides," he continued as he boosted her up into her saddle, "the picture you present is too great a temptation to resist. Shall we go, ladies? No more than a canter in the park, Miss Joy," he warned as she was already urging her horse forward.

"None of my sisters will embarrass you in the saddle, my lord," Faith said, noticing him as he watched them intently.

"I see that." He nodded with approval.

Once inside the park, the group of them set out at the prescribed canter when they reached the bridle-path.

"Do we really create such a spectacle, my lord?" Faith asked as she noticed several gentlemen stopping to stare.

"Indeed, you do. I imagine most of them are trying to determine if their bachelorhood is worth holding onto at this juncture."

Faith laughed. "Your absurdity knows no bounds!"

"To be sure," he agreed complacently.

Faith could only wonder when he would grow bored of them.

"This way!" he called to her sisters and led them over to where his friends were waiting.

"Well met!" Freddy said in cheerful appreciation as they approached.

Rotham whistled. "Five well-matched mounts. However, did you find them, Dom?"

"I cannot take the credit," he confessed.

"These are our mounts from Halbury Hall," Faith said. "They are all brothers and sisters from the same sire. Daily rides were our favourite past time during our time of mourning. There was little else to do."

"I can see we will need to plan some rides out to the country. Perhaps two days from now? After your highly anticipated debut ball?" Lord Westwood suggested.

Faith smiled. "I would like nothing more. The city is closing in around me—although I must admit this helps a great deal. I appreciate what you have done for us."

"No longer an ogre?"

Before she could defend herself, she saw a group of soldiers ahead on the path. One of them hailed Lord Westwood.

"Forgive me, I believe I see my brother!"

Faith watched as he rode over to meet the group.

"Where did he go?" Hope wheeled her mount back to ask with Rotham by her side.

"He said he thought he saw his brother."

"Very likely. He is part of the household cavalry, after all," Rotham explained.

"I did not know he had a brother," Grace remarked, as they looked towards the group of soldiers.

"They look magnificent!" Patience said breathlessly. "Look, they are coming!"

Her sisters turned their horses about and lined up next to her, whether consciously or not.

A handsome gentleman in a uniform approached with Lord West-wood. "Ladies, against my better judgement, may I introduce my scamp of a brother, Major Ashley Stuart?"

Major Stuart took off his hat and bowed from the waist. "The plea-sure is mine. I had heard the rumours, but they do not do you justice!"

"This is Miss Faith Whitford and her sisters, Miss Hope, Miss Patience, Miss Grace, and Miss Joy Whitford."

Faith watched with pride as her sisters inclined their heads and smiled.

"When Mother said you'd inherited five wards and were bringing them out, I'll admit I had a good laugh, Dom, but this beats all!"

Where Lord Westwood was inclined to appear bored and cynical, his brother was all friendliness and amiability. Faith liked him imme-diately. Where Lord Westwood's hair was golden, Major Stuart's was sandy. He had a dimpled smile and looked very handsome.

Faith could see that if there were five of these brothers, how easily there might be a rebellion amongst the ladies.

"Did the devil get into you, Dom?" Major Stuart teased.

"No more than usual," he answered with a half-smirk that made Faith feel funny inside.

"I think you're in for a deal of pother, big brother."

"Think what you like. No, Joy, you may not jump the seats in the park!"

~

Before they even left Hyde Park, there was a plan in place to ride out to Richmond the next day for a proper gallop, followed by a picnic instead of after the ball.

Dominic should have expected something of the sort, and being conscientious enough not to overtax his secretary when he was currently at Lady Westwood's beck and call, he sent a groom out to the Star and Garter at Richmond to bespeak a picnic luncheon for the morrow.

He would say one thing for the ladies Whitford, he was not yet bored. One would think five unmarried females might drive a hardened bachelor to distraction, but fortunately, they were not like most Society misses. They were punctual, and they did not simper. Had they been, would he have still brought them to London?

In all likelihood, he would have done, but he would have left them entirely in his mother's capable hands.

His friends gathered at his stables, and they each led one of the Whitford ladies' horses to Charles Street. The sisters were already ready and came down the front steps at their arrival.

"I don't believe it!" his brother exclaimed. "I've never known a female not to keep one waiting above half an hour!"

"You have been around the wrong females, then!" Miss Whitford replied.

"Apparently so," he agreed.

"May we go now?" Joy asked impatiently.

"Why the hurry, imp?" Dominic asked.

"I want to ride, of course,"

"There will be time for that."

"But there is also Hampton Court Palace and a maze to see!"

"Easy, sprite. We have all the time in the world for the other amusements!" Though he had no intention of gallivanting all over the country for her pleasure. He tweaked her cheek then boosted her into her saddle. It was not long before she left his side and found her way to Freddy. They both seemed to be of the same mind, and considered each other great guns in addition to sharing an affinity for the little cat. Dominic had little doubt the beast was somewhere hidden on Joy's person, and could only hope there were no misadventures in that quarter.

He spent some time alongside each of his wards, but Grace did not talk much to him. The only one she seemed comfortable with was Montford. Carew was flirting outrageously with Miss Whitford—or attempting to, Dominic noticed with amusement. Miss Whitford was not much of a flirt, thus a greater challenge, which was likely why Carew was doing it. While Patience and his brother were wholly engrossed and Rotham was equally monopolizing Hope, he fell in alongside Grace in attempt to draw her out.

"Are you enjoying London, Grace?"

"Yes, my lord. More so now that we have our own horses, regardless of what Faith may say."

"And what does Faith say?"

"That we will be more beholden to you." She coloured a little as though she shouldn't have said as much.

"She said the very thing to me, but I see it as a prudent move."

"You do?"

"It will keep the five of you occupied at least part of the day."

"Oh, I see. Yes. And exercise is good for the constitution."

"Precisely. What else would you like to do while you're in London? Joy and Faith often seem to choose for everyone."

"I do not mind because they make good choices."

"Come now, is there not one thing you should like to do?" he coaxed.

"Hampton Court Palace would be interesting, but I confess I would like to climb the steps of Saint Paul's."

"Then Saint Paul's it shall be. You are certain you don't mind being thrust into this Season so unexpectedly?"

"No, Faith says it is likely to be our only opportunity, so it makes sense."

"Are you always so practical, Grace?"

"If it makes sense," she answered with a twinkle in her eyes.

"We have passed the city, shall we gallop? It makes sense."

She laughed, then was already off and the others followed in rapid pursuit.

He laughed, then gave Maximus his head. The horse lengthened his stride, gaining on the others with ease. Were there any spectators to the event, they might have assumed they were riding to hounds, since they rode in a tight pack as though giving chase.

They crossed Richmond Park and pulled up at a hill overlooking the Thames, all pink-cheeked and breathing heavily from the exertion, yet smiling with laughter.

Who was racing whom and who won was a matter of great debate, as they left their horses at an inn to rest and be cared for while they enjoyed their picnic.

"I won by a length!" Joy exclaimed.

"Not so!" Dominic argued.

"Maybe by just the length a nose, but I did win," she insisted.

"I wish we had wagered on it and had someone to measure," Freddy said mournfully.

"Next time." Then they were back to cordial terms like children would be.

A place had already been set for them in the shade of some large oak trees overlooking the water.

"An idyllic setting," Rotham remarked in his usual sardonic tone.

"It is rather," Dominic agreed.

"Although it is altogether unlike you to be entertaining a nursery party."

"They may be younger than my usual set, but hardly in the nursery. They are all, with the exception of Joy, of marriageable age."

"Even worse! How long do you mean to dance attendance on them?"

"The ball is fast approaching."

"And just like that?"

"Until it ceases to be amusing."

"You have been spending a good deal of time with Miss Whitford."

Dominic gave his friend an icy glare that froze most people from more impertinence. Rotham laughed.

"For that matter, you have been favouring Miss Hope."

"I have, haven't I?" he agreed with an unrepentant grin.

"Careful, Rotham. I am their guardian. I expect you to help me protect their reputations."

"You realize once the gates are open after the ball, it will be an endless flood of proposals?"

"Am I to expect one from you?"

Rotham didn't answer. Dominic knew what his friend said to be true, but he would make it very clear that he would not entertain fortune hunters or rogues.

They turned their attention towards the luncheon spread out before them, which was a feast of fried chicken, cold meats, egg salad, fresh bread, and fruits with some jam tarts and elderflower wine.

Dominic watched dispassionately as his friends charmed his wards. Perhaps it had not been wise to allow practiced rakes and rogues to be their first experience with the opposite sex, but on the other hand, they would have friends and a little bit of practice conversing. So long as that was all they learned, he thought with a frown, but it was too late to recriminate with himself now.

A deep, rich laugh startled Dominic out of his musings, and he was surprised to find Miss Whitford laughing at Carew. What precisely was he about?

Did Dominic care? That was an interesting thought—not one he cared to reflect too much upon. Very little moved him beyond himself, his family, or his close friends. He had been pursued and courted by every beauty and noble house with an eligible daughter this past decade or so, yet none of them had ever stirred more than a passing acknowledgement of their charms. Certainly there was never any desire to make a permanent connection or bestir himself to give up the comforts of bachelorhood—for there were many that would be forfeited upon such an occasion as wedlock. Miss Whitford certainly held allure, but her beauty could not be enough to provoke this feeling within his breast. So what emotion did he feel now if it was not affection? Jealousy? Even pique?

Pique was certainly more comfortable than either of the other feelings, he decided. Perhaps it was only that Miss Whitford was indifferent to the rank and fortune that drew the other females of his acquaintance like ants to honey. He liked her better for it, but realized it did not reflect well on him that he had come to expect it as his due. As her guardian, he had no right to claim her attentions for himself. It was only the novelty of a female's indifference, was all. Having satisfied himself with these revelations, he determined that it did not matter one whit.

CHAPTER 10

*F*aith was relieved that the day of the ball had arrived and yet, was terrified to face the *ton*. They'd had an informal introduction to members of Society through their activities with their guardian, but Faith had little confidence that they were truly prepared for what they were to face. The sensation they created was made greater by their number, but at least they had each other—equally a blessing and a curse.

After debating ad nauseum, Lady Westwood had decided they should be gowned in white after all since they were supposed to be angels. She had decided their colour would be in their jewels. Lord Westwood presented them with tiaras encircled with different coloured jewels which would be their halos—diamonds for Faith, pale rubies for Hope, emeralds for Patience, and pearls for Grace. He'd even had one of aquamarines made for Joy so she would not feel left out. Faith prayed they were paste but was too afraid to ask.

The gowns were similarly clever—the front was designed like that of a Grecian goddess, tied over their shoulders with a dipped neckline, the delicate material flowing from just below the bodices from beneath a golden belt. The backs were designed with pieces of fabric at different lengths, which looked as though they had wings when they walked. Faith was not certain how that feat of sewing had been accomplished, but she appreciated it, nevertheless. Their gowns alone would create a sensation if the girls inside them did not.

Lady Westwood did not have them attend the dinner held before-hand—she wanted their presentation to be a complete surprise. Personally, Faith would have preferred to meet the smaller group of thirty or so distinguished guests first.

They were sent their dinners on trays, but most of them could do little more than pick at the food, so excited as they were.

Joy had no such qualms. She attacked the meal with all of the gusto of the girl still growing to her maturity.

They watched from the upstairs windows as the guests began to arrive, speculating on who each of them might be.

"It is too far to see well," Hope complained.

Matrons with turbans, bedecked in fortunes of jewels, and their portly elder husbands arrived first.

"I hope the guest list does not consist only of old frumps!"

"You know our particular friends will be here, at least. They are promised the first set with us, and you know it is not fashionable to be early!" Patience said.

Joy sat curled up in the window seat stroking Freddy Tiger, who was purring almost as loud as the orchestra tuning their instruments below.

The new governess had arrived that day, a Miss Hillier, but she would not begin her official duties until the morrow. Joy wanted to be with them whilst they waited anyway.

"Will you be terribly sad you cannot join us?" Faith asked.

"I have Freddy here to keep me company. I can watch from the gallery if I wish. Besides, Mr. Cunningham said he might sneak up there and dance with me.

Faith smiled. It really was good of Mr. Cunningham to dote on Joy the way he did.

There was a knock on the door, which made them all jump. Faith opened it herself to see Lord Westwood standing there, looking precisely how she would have imagined Lucifer the Tempter to look.

Unostentatious by *ton* standards, she could not imagine anyone more handsome. All in black save his crisp, white neckcloth tied in the Mathematical fashion, no fobs or seals or large buttons were needed to proclaim his elegance. He bowed deeply. "Ladies, you are positively ethereal. But that was the point, was it not? I do believe my mother has equalled, if not surpassed her rival's creation."

Faith and her sisters laughed. "Flatterer!"

He smiled with deviltry, and the wicked gleam in his eyes melted her insides. She needed to guard her heart. The more she was in his company, the more she allowed her thoughts to consider him, and that would never do. That way led only to heartache.

"Are you ready to go? Your audience awaits."

Faith turned to survey her sisters, including Joy, who wanted to watch the procession, and sent each one of them through the door as she approved, tucking a loose curl up or straightening a glove.

"But what of you?" Lord Westwood asked as she was about to pass by him through the door.

He placed his hands on her nearly bare shoulders, and that simple touch was like fire. He examined her critically, but his gaze was warm and approving. He lifted one hand and trailed a light fingertip down her cheek.

"Perfection," he whispered.

A shivering warmth passed through her body, rendering her tongue-tied as her gaze joined with his. It was intimate and disturbing and she both relished and hated in equal measure that he was affecting her so.

"Are you coming?" Hope interrupted, recalling Faith back from her reflections.

They descended the stairs to the ballroom, and entered when they were announced. They were surrounding Lord Westwood, with Faith and Hope on each arm.

First, there was silence, followed by loud murmuring. She was too overwhelmed with trying not to miss a step as they descended, and also with the transformation of the ballroom before them. Lady West-wood had not allowed them to peek.

The ceiling was draped with sky-blue silk, and angels swung on swings above the ballroom. There were fountains and harp players on clouds on dais' so well disguised that they looked like they were floating in the air. A very large tree with colourful fruit graced one corner, surrounded by a flowing river with a waterfall.

"It's magical," she whispered.

"It is impressive," Lord Westwood conceded. "And now the *pièce de résistance!*"

Lord Rotham stepped forward to claim Hope's hand, Major Stuart for Patience, and Montford claimed Grace. This had been scripted by Lady Westwood as well as every other detail.

Lord Westwood took Faith's hand and led her onto the ballroom floor, which had been chalked white to appear as if they were on clouds.

The four couples lined up for a set of the minuet as the stringed orchestra began to play.

Faith finally noticed the crowd surrounding them, and the people staring.

"Heed them not. Keep your eyes on mine," Lord Westwood said as her gaze wavered.

"There are so many of them."

"Yes, a proper crush. My mother will dine on this for years to come."

The note struck signalling the beginning of the dance, and he bowed to her and she curtsied.

Keeping her eyes on him, which was no great imposition, she followed his lead and managed to perform the steps creditably, she felt.

"Now you must smile, as if you are happy to be here. Whether you are or not." His eyes twinkled.

"I am grateful you practiced with me, or I would certainly be stumbling over my feet. How will I dance with another partner?"

"For now, there is only me," he replied.

They met in the centre of the line. Their hands touched palm to palm and they circled each other. It was intimate and heady having his full attention centred on her.

Her breath felt tight in her chest while she also felt as if she were floating on air. She would forever remember this dance and wondered if all others would be a disappointment henceforth.

She permitted herself to forget there was anyone else in the room watching, and made the mistake of allowing herself to imagine things she had long ago decided were not possible for her.

However, she need not dream of them with Lord Westwood, whom she knew to be impossible with his reputation. It was dangerous enough for him to awaken the possibilities in her. Why had she allowed him to? She had warned her heart from the beginning, yet felt a crack in the armour she'd carefully shielded herself with.

Yet the moment was perfect.

Only until the dance is over, she allowed.

"Do you still hate me for forcing you into this?" Lord Westwood asked with a bow as the dance ended.

"Never hate, but you are most definitely still an ogre."

"Perhaps that will change, Faith," he whispered in her ear as he released her.

DOMINIC DID NOT DANCE AGAIN that night. For one, he was behaving abominably with Miss Whitford, and he needed to decide what he was about. For two, there was no need—he was mobbed for introductions the moment he stepped off the ballroom floor with her. For three, he did not want to set any kind of precedent. He could have danced with his other wards, but it was quite unnecessary as they were successfully launched.

He made his way around the ballroom, greeting each of his guests.

Those with no daughters to launch congratulated him on their success. Those with maidens of a marriageable age barely restrained their angst while simultaneously trying to convince him to dance. He quickly excused himself to mingle, sidestepping matchmaking mamas with a decade of experience in polite indifference.

He may have been talking, but he was observing. Each of the sisters already seemed to have a following. Strange how like seemed to attract like. Young Grace was surrounded with mostly those recently down from university. Patience was surrounded by a sea of red regimentals, and Hope was occupied with more of the outspoken, politically minded. But where was Faith? She would not abandon her sisters—he knew she carefully kept watch over each of them while holding her own court of admirers, despite knowing his mother was chaperoning them. Faith had danced every dance—despite her belief that she was nearly on the shelf. Silly girl!

His eyes scanned the crowd for a second time before they alighted upon her. Carew was leading her onto the floor for the supper dance. Was that not his second dance with her? Dominic frowned. Carew was the least likely of them to succumb to a pretty face, and no one would convince Dominic that Miss Whitford's hand had not been solicited by others. Had she made a conquest of the Irish rogue? He would bear watching. Dominic would not waste emotion on jealousy when he could not make up his own mind.

Dominic caught a glimpse of some mischievous blue eyes looking down from the gallery, then noticed Freddy leave towards the stairs. Was he going to spend the supper dance with the little imp? Dominic would not put it past her to request such a thing of him! But Freddy was a grown man, even if young at heart, and could handle his own affairs. He posed no danger to little Joy.

As Dominic entered the card room, where a dozen tables were full of games, a hush fell, and instantly his eyes fell on Sir Julian, who flushed. Dominic acted as though he had not noticed, but he would need to see what the devil the fop was about this time. It could only be a wager, but he was certain his wards had done nothing thus far beyond being beautiful to cause rampant speculation.

He chose a seat next to his father's closest friend, Sir Walter Hornsby, and the room resumed its chatter.

"Have your hands full?" Sir Walter asked.

"In a manner of speaking."

"If I were you, I would find them a chaperone apiece, and I don't mean your friends!"

"That would be very tiresome," Dominic drawled. And it would. However, if it became necessary to take such drastic measures, he would—or send them back to Bath. "Has Sir Julian begun some foolishness?"

Sir Walter leaned closer and said just above a whisper, "Aye, he's begun his own private wagers on each of the girls. You won't find them in the books at the clubs."

"It is not terribly private of him to discuss such goings-on in my own home at their debut ball."

"I do not know what the coxcomb is about."

Nor did Dominic, but he would root it out. "You will send me word if you hear of anything specific?"

He nodded. "That I will."

Dominic stood and greeted a few more of his father's set before escaping, his thoughts more consumed with his wards. Perhaps he was becoming a nursery maid! Yet he had taken them on, and he must protect them. A devilish notion.

He would have to bestir himself to discover Sir Julian's wager, and find a way to thrust a spoke into that wheel.

There was no doubt part of the wager involved secrecy from Dominic, but with Rotham, Montford, Freddy, Carew, and his brother, someone was bound to slip in front of them. The Whitford sisters already had an army of chaperones, even though all of them would scoff to be labelled as such. Perhaps knights errant. The thought made Dominic smile, and that was the expression he was wearing when he re-entered the ballroom and almost ran into Miss Whitford and Carew as they headed to the supper room.

His first impulse was to join them to sniff out his old friend's motives, then he checked himself. It was not like him to pay attention to one female overly much. It would draw more attention to her and only increase speculation and wagers. He looked around. Perhaps continuing his flirtation with Jemima Taylor would be the best thing to divert his attention, but she did not truly interest him, and it would be tiresome. She was waving her fan in a come-hither signal, and Dominic was toying with approaching her when his mother hailed him. With some relief that he had resisted his odd impulses, he went to his mother's side. She was standing between a fountain of champagne and—was that chocolate? Dominic shook his head.

"Congratulations, Mother. You have achieved a sad crush by anyone's standards!"

"I should say so!" She was wafting the fan he had given her to mark the occasion—a painted scene of heaven much like that of Verrio's *Beautimous*. "The girls have all danced every dance, and with some very promising suitors."

"I had noticed."

"But what of Carew? I cannot think what he means by dancing with Faith twice. I believe he is a more devoted bachelor even than you, which is saying much. I think you should warn him away."

"When he has done nothing more than dance with her twice?"

"He has never done so with any other innocent maiden before."

Dominic could not argue the truth of that. However, he had no intention of interfering at this point.

"And then there is Freddy Cunningham, making up to a chit still in the schoolroom, engaging though she may be."

"There is no harm in Freddy. Besides, she needs occupation."

"Hopefully, the new governess will have the necessary energy."

"Anyone else you wish to censure? Ashley perhaps?"

She waved her hand in a dismissive gesture. "That is a harmless flirtation. He has years before he is ready to settle down."

"Unnatural, Mother! He is your best hope for grandchildren."

"At least I do not tease you about your own single state."

"It would do no good if you did."

"Do I not know it. Will you not dance with anyone else?" she asked. "Other than Mrs. Taylor, who is making herself look ridiculous."

"There is no need for me to dance attendance on the Whitford ladies. As you pointed out, the girls have danced every set."

"I thought certain one of them, Miss Whitford perhaps, would set her cap at you." She seemed to ponder this notion. "It's something else to see a female who has no designs on you—quite the opposite, in fact! You seem to have little effect on her."

"Lowering indeed! I do not think it has occurred to her that anyone might have designs on anyone but her sisters."

Dominic saw Miss Whitford laugh at something clever Carew had said, so he left his mother's side and went to Jemima Taylor.

CHAPTER 11

The next day was almost equally overwhelming. Faith was hoping for a day to relax, but apparently it was as important as the ball itself.

As they had been used to do at home, her sisters all made their way into her chambers when they awoke, and either climbed into her bed or lounged on the chaise or window seat.

Her maid brought in chocolate and rolls and they set to discussing who they had each danced with and favoured.

"It was better than I could have ever dreamed!" Hope exclaimed.

"It was crushing," Grace contended. "I need a week in the corner of the library with a stack of novels in order to recover."

"Oh, I thought it was heavenly." Patience smiled at her pun.

"Did you dance with anyone not wearing a red coat?" Faith asked her.

"There might have been a blue one!" She laughed. "It was a perfect evening."

"At least the war with Bonaparte is over, but are not the officers all on the half-pay?"

"Not the Life Guards! This is their regular duty."

"I suppose that is acceptable, then. I would not think it very comfortable to support a wife on half-pay."

"I would not mind following the drum if it meant being with the man that I loved in support of our country."

Faith smiled fondly. Patience meant every word.

"And Grace, did you not enjoy yourself even a little?"

"It was a bit tedious. Most of my partners were still silly boys not long down from school."

"Surely you exaggerate?"

She shook her head. "I do not think one of them could grow a beard and they either spouted nonsense about my blue eyes and celestial beauty, or they talked about nothing but cockfights and mills." She made a face of disgust. "I would have given my eyeteeth for a dance with a more seasoned, elegant gentleman. Just one!"

They all laughed.

"What of you, Faith? You were the only one Lord Westwood danced with. I heard it remarked upon more than once," Hope said.

"He only danced with me because he is our guardian."

"Be that as it may, apparently he is so confirmed a bachelor that he avoids dancing altogether—at least with unmarried misses."

Faith tried to keep her thoughts impassive, but it was hard to hide anything from her sisters. She almost wished she had not danced with him. The rest of the dances paled in comparison, but she knew he had meant nothing by it more than to launch her and her sisters into their Season. He had rather made a point of proclaiming his disinterest by ignoring them the rest of the night. Even though he had not danced again, she had seen him flirting with a dashing widow. That had deflated any silly notions she'd been spinning about him.

"Lord Carew is divine," Grace said. "I think it most unfair that he danced with you twice and yet did not take a single turn with me. You can tell by the look in his eyes that you would never grow bored with him." She wagged her eyebrows.

"Grace! Perhaps we should postpone your debut," Faith said with mock severity.

"It is too late to close the stable door now. Although, if I am to be allowed to dance only with silly boys, perhaps I should retire from Society for now." She thrust the back of her hand to her forehead and pretended to swoon back against the pillows.

"I told you that you should have waited," Joy said with much self-importance. "I had a grand time."

"Watching from the gallery?" Hope asked doubtfully.

"I watched a little bit, yes. But not very much."

"Then what did you do?"

A mischievous smile spread across her face. Before she could answer, Lady Westwood swept into the room.

"Good morning, ladies!" She made rising movements with her arms. "Up, up, up! We mustn't delay! There will be callers here soon! Hurry now!" And with that proclamation, she was gone again.

"My feet doth protesteth!" Grace said with vehemence.

Faith wanted to plead a headache and stay in her room all day, but she forced a smile on her face when she saw Hope's and Patience's excitement. They roused themselves to dress and made their way to the drawing room.

Everyone that had danced with them had sent flowers—the drawing room and the library were overflowing even into the ball-room, which was still full with flowers from the evening before.

Callers were already being entertained by Lady Westwood when the sisters arrived downstairs. Some of the matrons Faith had met the evening before, but most of the callers were young gentlemen unknown to her.

Soon, some familiar faces made the time more pleasant—Lord Carew, Lord Rotham, Major Stuart, and Mr. Cunningham—but strangely, no Lord Westwood.

An extremely garish-looking gentleman—one Faith believed what was called a tulip—arrived wearing primrose-coloured pantaloons with a blue waistcoat with yellow stripes and tasselled Hessians so highly polished as to rival the shine on a looking glass.

She was certain it was of the latest stare, but she was unused to seeing gentlemen in such bright colours. He was handsome, once she looked beyond the clothes. "Who is that?" she leaned over and whispered to Hope.

"Sir Julian Wright. I was introduced to him last night. Is he not handsome?"

"If you do not mind being outshone by him," Faith retorted.

"Come now, he is all the crack!"

Faith could only laugh and shake her head at her sister's cant, then found herself the centre of his attention.

Lady Westwood beckoned to her. "Faith, my dear, there is someone who would like to be introduced to you."

Faith could only hope her expression was polite, but she would much rather not entertain suitors. Once her sisters were married, she still had Joy to consider.

However, she did allow Sir Julian to be introduced to her. She could hardly refuse. Then Lady Westwood turned back to her friends.

"Miss Whitford." He made her an extravagant leg. It was all she could do to keep her face straight. This was not a promising start.

"I had been hoping for an introduction last night, but you were positively swarmed! I was hoping I might beg you to take a turn around the park with me this afternoon before someone else has the opportunity to steal you away."

Faith racked her brains quickly for an excuse—any excuse—but she could think of none. "I would be delighted. Thank you, sir."

This seemed to satisfy him, and he left her to greet others.

However, when the time for morning calls was ending, he had not forgotten as she had hoped, and was standing by the door of the drawing room, waiting for her.

Once she had fetched her bonnet, she was unfortunately not surprised to discover his curricle was as obtrusive as his clothing. Not only was the vehicle a bright yellow, it was drawn by matched white horses with their own livery with yellow trim to coordinate.

It was on the tip of her tongue to ask if he changed the horses' outfits to match his own, but she decided against it.

He assisted her into the vehicle and then set the horses in motion towards the park, tooling the ribbons with unconscious ease. One thing she could say for him was that he was no mere whipster. He handled the horses very well, and at least she need not worry herself on that score.

"How do you like London so far, Miss Whitford?"

"It has been diverting in its own way, sir."

"But you prefer the country?" He sounded shocked.

"I confess I do. However, we were brought up just outside of Bath, so not completely devoid of amusements should we wish for them."

He made a choking sound.

"I gather you think Bath is only for the infirm and elderly?"

"You must confess, ma'am, they do tend to congregate there."

"I cannot argue it, but Bath does enjoy elegant assemblies and the theatre." Not that Lady Halbury ever took them to such enter-tainments.

"I wish that I were so easily amused," he said indulgently, as though she were a small child.

Had they continued on in this manner, she would have been fully disgusted and written Sir Julian off as a ridiculous nonentity. However, one of the first people they saw was Lord Westwood.

He did not look in the least bit pleased to see them when Sir Julian hailed him.

Lord Westwood pulled up alongside in his own elegant, but unas-suming black curricle with matched bays, making the contrast between the two gentlemen all the more apparent.

He inclined his head to Sir Julian. "Miss Whitford. There appears to have been a misunderstanding."

"And what is that?" Sir Julian asked.

"It is customary to ask a guardian for permission to drive in the park or court a young lady, is it not?"

"Of course, but in your absence, your mother made the introduc-tions and made no objections."

Faith could not understand why Lord Westwood was being so rude. They were in an open carriage in the park and while Lady West-wood had not consented in so many words, she had introduced them, so Faith had thought him an acceptable parti.

Lord Westwood ordered his tiger to take the reins, then climbed down and held out his hand to her.

Faith stared at it and wondered what would happen if she objected.

"Do not try me in this, Miss Whitford," he said in quiet command, but she heard. She cast an apologetic glance at Sir Julian. Lord Westwood handed her down into his curricle and then mounted into it himself.

As soon as she was seated, Westwood snapped the reins, but instead of driving home, he turned back towards the park.

"May I ask what this is about? Is Sir Julian a bad person?"

At first, she did not think he would answer. He greeted a few acquaintances as though she did not exist. She even contemplated climbing down when they had slowed enough to do so.

"Sir Julian is accepted in Society, but he is not to be trifled with."

"He seemed perfectly polite to me."

"That is doing it a bit too brown, my girl!"

"He is a bit ridiculous," she conceded, "but there was no civil way for me to reject his offer."

"Well, now you have one. I forbid it."

"For no reason other than he is a fop?" she argued.

"Did I say so?"

"Not precisely in those words, no."

"You must trust me on this. You are still very green when it comes to London ways."

"And I am here against my wishes."

"I suppose I deserve that. Despite being an ogre, I will not deliberately put you or your sisters in harm's way."

With that, Faith had to be satisfied, because Lord Westwood said no more on the matter. Except she was not satisfied in the least, and she had to swallow her spleen at his high-handed treatment.

DOMINIC CURSED himself for losing his temper, but Sir Julian had completely caught him by surprise. Never before had Sir Julian made an attempt to court a respectable young lady, so why should Dominic have expected that would be his attack? And what did he mean by it?

He had deliberately stayed away from his mother's drawing room that day, because he had little interest in such things. However, Sir Julian meant mischief, and he knew how to force Dominic's hand.

He needed to consult his friends and alert them to the danger. The one thing he was certain of was that there would be nothing respectable in the wager Sir Julian had instigated.

His mother was to escort the ladies to a recital that night, and Dominic was fairly confident that Sir Julian would not demean himself for such an event, even for the sake of a wager. However, he would also warn his mother. Of first importance was to send notes to his friends for an impromptu dinner and then he would consult them on the matter.

His friends would not fail him. No one would decline a dinner made by his Italian chef, Marco.

Dominic went personally to convince the chef what a treat it would be to prepare a specialty for his guests at the last minute.

Rotham was the first to arrive that evening. "I could kiss you, Dominic. My mother was blackmailing me into attending the opera."

"You are most welcome." He poured his old friend a glass of brandy and handed it to him. Rotham raised his glass in salute before taking a drink.

Next was Montford. "You saved me from a night with the mater and sisters. Much obliged." He was handed his own glass of brandy while they waited for Carew and Cunningham.

They were all relaxed with their restoratives before Dominic broached the topic. "You may have wondered why I called you here on such short notice."

"Are we creating our own secret counsel? I rather like the idea," Rotham said.

"Of a sort," Dominic conceded.

"I gather this is about your charges? Already more than you can handle, are they?" Carew looked very amused.

"If you do not wish to assist, then by all means, you may leave." Dominic waved his hand towards the door.

"No, no. I am vastly amused. However, I imagine they are more than you bargained for when you first set out to turn the *ton* on its ear."

"What is the problem?" Freddy asked.

"Sir Julian. He means some kind of mischief. When I went into the card room at the ball, the room fell silent, and his face said everything. When I enquired of Sir Walter, he knew of nothing specific, but had overheard that Sir Julian had created his own secret betting books and wagers involving the Whitford sisters. I have no doubt they involve keeping them secret from me. I need each of you to do what you can to discover the details."

"Everyone knows of our ties to you," Montford remarked.

"But you are not me, at least, and the more of us who are trying to ferret things out, the more likely someone will slip."

"Of course, we will do what we can," Rotham agreed.

Dinner was announced, so they made their way into the dining room where Marco had outdone himself with a spectacular array of Italian dishes. Dominic would be sure to reward him, as if his exorbitant wages were not reward enough. Their discussions had moved on to the races through the first course of cioppino soup with exotic spices of fennel and saffron, mussels in lemon juice, salad with olives, cucumber and tomato, and fresh bread with a dipping sauce of olive oil and vinegar.

"Either you need to hold dinners more often or at least let me borrow your chef on occasion," Freddy said appreciatively.

"By Jove, I would never dine out if I had Marco at home," Carew remarked as the second course of meats and pastas with creamy garlic sauces and rich tomato-based ones were laid before them.

"There is one more thing. Sir Julian invited Miss Whitford out for a drive in the park today," Dominic mentioned.

That silenced the room. His reputation was well known.

"That isn't playing fair," Freddy pointed out with a frown.

"Indeed. It is why I grew concerned and called you here tonight."

Rotham blew a low whistle. "The blackguard, to indulge in such foul play. There must be a lot at stake."

"Indeed. But what? It caught me by surprise, and I may have made a fatal mistake. I pulled up my bays alongside his curricle and required Miss Whitford to join me."

"In the middle of the park?" Rotham asked in disbelief.

"It was not a crowded spot, but yes, he knows he has infuriated me." Dominic was known for keeping his cool in all situations.

"If he was willing to cast aside his customary *modus operandi* to court a young innocent, then who knows what lengths he will go to," Rotham continued.

"Precisely. And I further forced his hand by refusing my consent. Therefore, we must discover what he is about and quickly."

"It has to be deep for him to risk getting his neck caught in a matrimonial noose," Carew said.

"I agree, which is why I need all your help."

"Shall we divide up each of the sisters so as to keep better watch?" Montford suggested.

"That will draw more attention to the situation. But perhaps, if we remain unobtrusive, it would be for the best."

"I also think it worth warning Lady Westwood about him and his set."

"Yes. I think it involves besting me somehow, or ruining the ladies."

"What did you do to anger him? Is there any history between the two of you?" Rotham asked.

"Nothing that I can recall. We have never been chums, but I have never gone out of my way to cause him bother."

"Do you think it involves all of us?" Montford asked.

"It sounds as though he would have a perfect opportunity to exact revenge."

Dominic shook his head. "When you play deep, you should expect deep repercussions, but I do not know Sir Julian well, and if he's badly dipped, he may well be reckless. I will have my secretary look into it."

"He was always a little sapskull at school. I admit, I drew his cork a time or two," Carew said.

"My horse beat one of his last year at Newmarket," Rotham remarked as he considered.

"Do you think he is rolled up?" Dominic asked. "I had always thought him to be pretty flush in the pocket."

"Perhaps not. He wagers deep," Freddy added.

"Then if he is desperate, he would be willing to do anything, which makes this more dangerous than I had supposed."

Freddy slapped his hand on the table and sat up straight. "I know! You voted him down for the Four-Horse Club."

Dominic pursed his lips. "So I did. I would do it again."

"But his pride, Dom. That would give him a reason to despise you. He thinks himself a mean whip," Freddy said knowingly.

"He can't point his leaders...perhaps you are right."

"I confess even I have a history with him," Montford admitted. "I turned him in for a cheat at Cambridge. He was sent down for it."

They all looked at Freddy, whom everyone liked. He did not have a malicious bone in his body. "Have you had any quarrels with Sir Julian?" Dominic prodded.

Freddy shrugged. "Beat him once or twice at cards, but I can't think that would set his bristles up."

Dominic choked back his laughter. Freddy never beat anyone at cards, bless his soul.

"What were the stakes?" Carew asked.

"A little seaside estate in Kent."

"The devil you say!" Rotham burst into laughter.

"Good for you, Freddy!" Montford slapped him on the back.

"If he has reason to bear a grudge against all of us, then his cronies will be wary to let slip aught which might blow the gab."

"Then we will have to be very cunning." Carew had a gleam in his eyes.

"Best to be discreet," Montford warned unnecessarily, although perhaps more for Freddy's sake than the others.

"If you can discover the Whitford ladies' movements from Lady Westwood, then we shall divide and conquer."

Dominic raised his glass. "I knew I could count on you."

"Always," Rotham remarked.

"Still, it may grow tedious to play nursemaid, but hopefully we can smoke Sir Julian out in quick measure. Certainly faster than if I was working on my own."

"Even if it did not potentially involve all of us, of course we would help. Besides, I rather like the Whitford ladies," Montford added.

"Pluck to the backbone!" Freddy agreed.

"Who shall take whom? Freddy, you already have a rapport with Joy, though I should not think her a likely target."

"I have a good rapport with Miss Hope," Rotham offered.

"As does my brother appear to have with Miss Patience. He had military duties this evening, but will be glad to help. I think it would be less obvious were I to guard Miss Whitford, and she is most likely to offer opposition to being shadowed. That leaves Grace."

"I will take Grace," Carew offered. "Though she seems the shy one and like to recoil from me," he added with a wicked grin.

"Grace will not be one to venture out on her own and pose much risk."

The plan agreed upon, they moved on to debating which horse was favoured for the upcoming races at Newmarket, where three of them had horses running.

CHAPTER 12

*M*eanwhile, the Whitford ladies were oblivious to the undercurrents surrounding their being in London. They thought it perfectly natural that their new gentlemen friends were always around to escort them wherever they went, not knowing what a dubious honour was being bestowed upon them.

Neither did they realize what a miracle had occurred when five of London's most eligible bachelors escorted them to Almack's, causing shock and palpitations in the hearts of the hardened matrons, and false hope in less fortunate but hopeful mamas.

Moreover, a more singular cause for a remark amongst the *ton* was the fact that the bachelors each took turns dancing with the five Whitford ladies present.

However, Faith was beginning to suspect something was wrong when Sir Julian approached and asked her to dance the waltz. Why did he persist? Yet, she still had a nagging curiosity to know what he was about.

"I have not been granted permission yet, Sir Julian." Neither had she been granted permission from Westwood, but there was no point in bringing that up again. However, within seconds, his lordship was at her side and guiding her to the other side of the room. It was as if he were watching and waiting to do anything to prevent their further acquaintance.

Before she could question him further, he stopped before Lady Jersey.

"Good evening, Miss Whitford, Westwood. I suppose you've come for permission?"

"Do you object?" Westwood asked.

"Not at all. In fact, I am inclined to grant permission to all of your wards for accomplishing what no one else this past decade has been able to do."

Faith looked up at Lord Westwood, who was wearing an amused smirk.

"Perhaps the five of us will even darken your doors again."

"Oh, I live to see the day! Go, with my blessing. And if you send your other wards my way, they may be granted permission as well."

Faith curtsied and Westwood made her a bow.

"I do not think it will hurt your sisters at all to sit this one out. Perhaps for the next waltz I will tell them."

Faith was still contemplating how to upbraid him for his high-handedness, yet when his hand touched her waist, all rational thought ceased to function. Even though she had practiced with him, this felt different with others watching.

Part of her wished he would keep his distance, as she had thought he was going to before that day in the park with Sir Julian. Something about Lord Westwood disturbed her equilibrium and made her wish for things that could never be. The other part of her wanted to follow those thoughts and dreams to their conclusion, but she knew it to be impossible. She was not even certain she liked him. *Later*, she told herself. *Do not think, just feel. Just enjoy being in his arms.*

Why couldn't anyone else make her feel this way? Many handsome gentlemen had asked her to dance, yet she had felt nothing. Had she never danced with Lord Westwood, would she have realized? Still, he was not for her. She was determined not to settle for less, even if she ever became free to marry.

"Penny for your thoughts, or are you minding your steps and you wish me to hush?" he asked with the mischievous glimmer she knew meant he was teasing.

She dared to look up with a smile. "Actually, I was lost in thought."

"I do not know if that is a compliment or not," he reflected.

"A compliment, certainly. You taught me the steps."

"Are you concerned for your sisters?"

"Not particularly. Should I be?"

"I was only trying to discern what was consuming your thoughts." He led her through a series of turns which almost left her breathless.

"Do you expect me to think after that?"

A knowing twinkle lit his eyes.

"I do wish you would tell me what this is about."

"Whatever do you mean?" he asked with an air of innocence.

"There is no need to play coy with me. I hardly believe you are here out of benevolence or concern for me and my sisters' welfare."

"You wound me gravely," Miss Whitford.

"I do not believe that either. It has something to do with Sir Julian, does it not?" She could see by the anger in his eyes that it did. "I wish you would tell me."

She could tell he intended no such thing. But why? Perhaps she would see Sir Julian herself and try to discern what was happening. Lord Westwood would not confront him in the middle of Almack's. If he meant to be autocratic and overbearing and keep things from her, it would serve him right.

"There is nothing to concern you at this point. As I told you before, I am only trying to prevent mischief."

Faith seethed at his dismissal, but she held her tongue. As he escorted her back to Lady Westwood, she searched to see if Sir Julian was still there.

He was at the other end of the ballroom, near the retiring rooms, but he was watching her. As soon as Lord Westwood left her side, she made her excuses to Lady Westwood and walked towards that side of the room. He stopped her as she had known he would.

"Do you dare defy your guardian and dance the next set with me?" he asked.

"Why should I? Will you tell me why he has forbidden it?" Suddenly, it did not seem like such a good idea, but still, she felt the need to know more.

"I cannot imagine, unless it stems from jealousy. I am a perfectly respectable member of Society. With five girls to fire off, you would think he would be pleased."

"I would think so, too."

"So will you do me the honour of dancing the next set with me?" She looked up to see Lord Carew standing before her.

"Unfortunately, Sir Julian, the next set is mine." He took her arm and led her out to the floor before she could protest.

"That would not have been a good idea, Miss Whitford."

"So, it would seem all of Lord Westwood's friends are as high-handed as he is," she said coolly.

"If not more so in my case," he agreed cheerfully.

"And will you do me the honour of explaining why Sir Julian is to be avoided at all costs, when the rest of Society accepts him?"

"Your guardian will not tell you?" Carew seemed to cogitate that fact as the music began.

"Have you not discovered that he is an ogre?" she asked.

"Most certainly. However, I will tell you if you promise not to tell him I told you."

"That will prove no difficulty. In fact, I will relish knowing that he thinks me ignorant!"

Carew laughed. "I rather think I am going to enjoy this," he said as they turned.

She had to wait patiently until it was her turn with him again.

"Well? How long will you keep me in suspense?"

"Sir Julian means either you or your guardian ill, Miss Whitford."

"How do you know this? What does he intend?"

"That, we have not yet discovered. You may or may not have heard that there are betting books in all the gentlemen's clubs. They will bet on anything—the more frivolous, the better. Many of them during the Season involve who will be matched with whom or on any sort of race."

"That is unsurprising. But if they are public, then how do you not know the nature of the wager?"

"That is the catch. Apparently, Sir Julian has begun his own private betting book. We know there is a wager which somehow involves you, but part of it involves remaining secret from Westwood."

"Why did he not simply tell me this instead of being odious?"

Lord Carew laughed. "I suspect there are many reasons even he does not yet understand."

Faith was obliged to take a turn with another partner while contemplating that enigmatic statement.

"How do you know he means us ill?"

"For one, Sir Julian avoids young maidens like the plague. He is never to be found at Almack's for instance."

"And you and Westwood are?"

"Touché, my dear. We are here to protect you from him and his cronies."

Her ire was piqued. She pulled back. "Then I hereby release you from your guard duties, my lord."

"Sheathe your claws, my dear. I would rather you consider us concerned friends. You are hardly up to snuff when it comes to London ways. Would you ever have thought someone unknown to you would create a wager involving your ruination or loss of virtue?'

She gasped. "Do you think it is as wicked as that?"

"I've no doubt. Sir Julian does not play for simple stakes. He wagers estates or thousands of pounds."

Faith gasped again.

"And there is a good chance it involves your guardian, and possibly the rest of us, so it behoves us to protect you from Wright and his ilk."

Faith pondered this. She had truly thought it was some silly game —not her or her sisters' possible ruin. Why oh why had he insisted they come to London?

"You may not feel as though you need protection, but you cannot guard your sisters on your own. Neither can Westwood, which is why he has enlisted our help."

"Very well. Thank you for enlightening me." She still could not understand why Westwood would keep such a thing from her.

~

AFTER WALTZING WITH MISS WHITFORD, Dominic knew he needed to distance himself from her, or he was as good as making a declaration. He signalled to Carew that he was going to the card room and to keep an eye on things. Dominic needed to make sense of Sir Julian, for if he was at Almack's, he would do anything to win.

Small stakes only were permitted in the card room at the Assembly Rooms, but the ruse he'd thought of was worth a try.

He looked around for familiar faces, but there was no one there under the age of sixty, so Dominic greeted a few people and then abandoned that idea. It was highly unlikely this crowd was privy to Sir Julian's wagers. He remained for the length of the set, then decided to return to the ballroom to help watch over his charges.

His mind was in a whirl. What would someone bet high stakes against Dominic for? To trap him into marriage, or force him into a compromising situation?

Or was the game more malicious, and intended to ruin the girls with no hope of marriage? In no way could Dominic be convinced that Sir Julian meant to court and marry Miss Whitford honourably, lovely though she be.

He returned to the ballroom and found his mother beside her friends.

"Will you honour me with a dance, Mother?"

One of her friends gasped while another gasped and tittered.

"Run out of Whitford sisters, have you?" Mrs. Drummond-Burrell asked.

"I thought it might be nice to dance with the most handsome woman in the room."

"Odious boy. There are plenty of other eligible ladies to dance with. And a waltz, too! It's not done!"

"Is it a written rule, Mrs. Drummond-Burrell?"

She shook her head and waved them on their way.

"Stop acting like you are an aged dowager, Mother. You dance better than most of the chits just out of the schoolroom!"

"Very well, there is no need to flatter me. I assume you want something?"

"I need to speak to you without a thousand ears listening."

"Did Sir Julian do something? I saw Carew intervene when he attempted to speak with Miss Whitford."

"Did he? I only stepped into the card room for one dance."

"Oh, yes. He attempted to waylay her on the way to the retiring room."

"There must be a way to discover what he is about. We have already made utter cakes of ourselves by coming to Almack's!"

"I would not go that far. You have made it clear to him you will protect them at all costs."

"All costs?" Dominic was afraid that was what Sir Julian was counting on. "Perhaps I should have him followed."

"It is not a terrible idea. Perhaps a discreet footman or two? Sadly, most servants can be bribed."

"I cannot believe he is going to such lengths to begin secret wagers involving innocent young girls. You will keep an eye on them, I know."

"I do not need a second warning, Dominic. I want no harm to come to those girls any more than you do. They have certainly alleviated any boredom you might have felt."

"Did I say I was bored?"

She gave him a look that only a mother could.

Once the Whitford ladies were safely ensconced in a carriage on the way home, Dominic and his friends decided to stop by their clubs to check the betting books in hopes they would give them a clue as to the nature of the affair to be dealt with.

When they reached White's, the book was surrounded.

"Perhaps it would be best if you go to earth, so to speak, Dom," Rotham suggested.

"I will go look. I am the least likely to be associated with you," Carew said.

"I'll go with you. I want to check the odds on some of my horses," Freddy added.

Dominic, Montford, and Rotham found some chairs to sit in and ordered drinks while they waited.

"I see some pointed looks in our direction. Hopefully, they will not close their budgets before Carew gets over there."

"Hopefully, someone will be too far gone to be careful."

It took some time before Carew returned. "Freddy is still looking for the races. No one wanted to give it up to him."

"Well?"

"There were several bets as you would imagine, but the usual fare —which sister will be offered for first, will all of them be fired off in one Season, who is most likely to succumb to the parson's mousetrap, et cetera, et cetera."

"Dare I hope our names are not on the list?" Dominic asked.

"No. The stakes are highest if you fall first, I am afraid."

Dominic cursed. Would that be the least of his worries, however.

"He can only be offering high stakes for ruining them," Rotham said. "Nothing else would require secrecy."

"I agree."

"However, who would be willing to ruin them and face your wrath?"

"Someone with a desire to die, to be sure."

"Precisely. So is the payout for compromising them into matrimony or worse?"

They all contemplated that over sips of brandy.

"What can we do but continue to guard them?"

"Nothing, but I am afraid it will frighten away real suitors when we are sitting in their pockets."

They finished their drinks, then moved on to the next club, which revealed more of the same. They ended their evening at Dom's house, where his brother was waiting for them in the study.

"Ashley! What brings you here at this hour?"

"I've been here for quite some time. I was about to give up."

"I gather you've heard something?"

"Rumour only, but it is much as you suspected. The wager involves seeing who can ruin the sisters, but without marriage."

"Good God! An exorbitant sum must be involved. Whoever did such a thing would never be able to show their face in Town again," Montford said.

"It must be personal, for what has Sir Julian against the sisters? He cannot have been acquainted with them, or Lady Halbury buried in the country," Rotham added.

"You know good and well there is little that set would not do for a lark," Carew said with disgust. "But harming innocents is a new level of depravity."

"We are going to need more help," Dominic admitted. "Is there anyone you can trust, Ashley?"

"One or two of my fellow officers I would trust with my life. I may need to speak with my commander if this will take much time away from our guard duties, however."

"I am happy to send word to him if needed. I consider this a serious matter."

Ashley nodded. "It cannot hurt my cause."

Dominic stood and went to his desk, where he penned a note to Ashley's colonel.

"What is their itinerary for the next few days?" Rotham asked.

"I promised Joy that I would take her to Astley's tomorrow," Freddy said.

All of them swung their heads around.

"What? I like Astley's."

"I suppose that is a safe enough venture," Dominic reflected.

"I have not been to Astley's before," Carew admitted. "I would not mind seeing what it is all about."

Rotham looked up to the ceiling. "If you told me I'd be spending my Season doing this, I would have said you were mad."

"I, for one, am happy to be of service. Those girls are orphans, and have no one else to look out for them!" Montford announced.

"Yes, yes, Sir Galahad. None of us intend to abandon our virtues," Carew drawled.

When Dominic had finished the note, he folded it and handed it to Ashley.

"I must be going if I am to arrange for a friend to help. Do we meet at Astley's tomorrow or at Westwood House?"

"I think Astley's will suffice. I will see that they arrive safely," Dominic answered. "See if you can discover what else Sir Julian may have planned. Perhaps people's tongues will be looser around you. Not everyone will associate you with us."

"True enough. I have some gamesters in my regiment, much to my chagrin. If they know anything, you can be sure I will wring it out of them."

Ashley took his leave and it was near dawn before the rest of them struggled off to their own beds.

CHAPTER 13

*S*ecretly, Faith had to admit that she was excited to see Astley's even though it had been Joy who had prompted the excursion. After days and nights full of balls and routs, and even a Venetian breakfast, she was looking forward to an informal afternoon.

After being one of Joy's constant companions, Faith missed her and was looking forward to her being included again.

It was quickly apparent that while Mr. Cunningham had agreed to the outing, it was Lord Westwood who had actually arranged everything. Faith knew not what to expect, but as they rode across the Westminster Bridge to the other side of the river, Joy was full of excitement and speculation.

"What kind of tricks do the horses perform?" she asked their guardian, who was driving them while their sisters were being transported in the carriage behind.

"As best as I can recall, the horses dance to music and perform tricks."

"You don't say!" Joy exclaimed.

"Not all of the tricks are performed by the horses, mind you," he warned. "There are some acrobats involved in part of the act."

"That is to be expected, I suppose," Joy replied, though she looked a bit disappointed.

"I have only been to the Amphitheatre once, though I did see a drama called The Blood-Red Knight, but it was quite different from the performance we will see today."

They arrived and made their way through the mêlée to a box which had been reserved for them. The audience was quite a mixture of people from all walks of life—much more akin to that attending a village fair in the country.

At their box, they were greeted by Lord Rotham, Mr. Cunningham, Lord Montford, Major Stuart, and another soldier who was introduced to them as Captain Fielding. He was another well-formed, distinguished-looking gentleman with full blond whiskers and piercing blue eyes. Faith had a little doubt that Patience was in raptures of ecstasy at having not one, but two soldiers present.

Lord Carew smiled at her and led her to the seat beside him. It was difficult not to like the suave Irishman, but she was suspicious of anyone handsome with a devilish twinkle in his eyes. Nevertheless, it was flattering to receive his attentions, although she suspected Grace would prefer to have them all to herself. Joy was on her other side with Mr. Cunningham and once the act began, Faith was caught up in the performance every bit as much as Joy.

When the first performer rode out bareback, that was nothing to impress notable horsewomen such as themselves. However, when he tossed a handkerchief in the air then rode around and fetched it from the ground at a canter, that made the crowd gasp then roar with applause. This was soon followed by riding two horses at once while playing some sort of piped instrument and doing headstands on the horse's back!

When there was a brief intermission, Faith finally looked around only to find Carew's eyes watching her, full of amusement.

Faith felt warm and uncomfortable at the depth of his stare. "Are you enjoying yourself, Lord Carew?"

"Surprisingly, I am," he said in a deep voice, eyes hooded.

Faith was unused to being flirted with, but there was no mistaking his tone.

"Do you ever return to Ireland?" she asked, hopelessly trying to change the subject.

His smile would have melted a block of ice. "Aye, I breed horses, and I prefer to oversee most of it myself. You seem to appreciate good cattle. I'd be obliged to take you there sometime."

"I've heard Ireland is very beautiful," she said weakly to his bold invitation.

"A beautiful land to match a beautiful lady."

Faith was out of her depth.

A throat cleared behind them. "Miss Whitford, would you care for some refreshment? Perhaps Carew would accompany me?"

Carew grinned up at Lord Westwood, then winked at her. "I do believe I've just been warned off," he said amiably, but excused himself and went along.

The two men left together with some of the others, and Faith revelled in her sisters' happiness.

"What an unexpected treat!" Hope exclaimed.

"And that is only half the show," Joy beamed, her eyes alight with pleasure.

"What do you think will be next?"

"I cannot even fathom. I hope the horses themselves do tricks!"

The next act was followed by acrobats doing flips and twists that defied gravity; rope-walkers that had the entire crowd silent with their daring; contortionists that caused many a spectator to look away in pain and disbelief, followed by clowns and a pig doing sums.

"I thought the horses could do tricks!" Joy protested a little too loudly when she believed the performance over before the encore.

"Patience, imp," Lord Westwood said, as he returned with Carew bearing fresh lemonade for them.

For the finale, there was a horse that could perform card tricks and make a cup of tea. Faith looked at Joy, who exclaimed this to be, "The best day of my life!"

No sooner were they seated back in the vehicle than Joy began, "Lord Westwood, may we go for a ride?"

"Today, imp?"

"Of course!"

"This is not because you want to try performing any of those tricks yourself, is it?"

"Well," she prevaricated. "Perhaps one or two. I am certain I could snatch a handkerchief from the ground while riding. That cannot be so difficult."

"Joy! I forbid it!" Faith was appalled.

Lord Westwood was giving her a look of disapproval over Joy's head. She scowled back at him.

"Not the way to discourage her," he muttered. "The performers have special stirrups with which to secure their leg while learning such tricks," he explained. "Otherwise, you would be certain to fall under the horse. You will not try such a thing under my guardianship, understood?"

"But if I have such a harness fashioned, what would be the harm?" Joy persisted.

"I will have your word, young lady," Westwood said in a calm but firm voice.

"But...oh, very well, sir."

Faith was impressed with his ability to deal with the headstrong Joy, but she was still vexed with him and would not say so.

"May we at least ride this afternoon?"

"It is too late in the day for a proper ride, and we are promised to the theatre, but I will take you first thing in the morning."

Faith shook her head, knowing her sister was unlikely to sleep that night, dreaming of ways she could keep her promise to Westwood but still try some other trick.

LATER THAT EVENING, they were obliged to dance attendance on the Whitford ladies once again. *Henry IV* was playing at Drury Lane, and they had yet to see a play. A Shakespearean drama was not his ideal, but anything besides the opera would do.

At Astley's, Dominic had thought Carew was flirting with Miss Whitford in order to vex him—it had always been their way to compete over ladies—not that Dominic was trying to win Miss Whitford—but it seemed Carew was intent on repeating the performance.

"What is he about?" Dominic muttered to himself as he entered his mother's drawing room and saw Miss Whitford smiling up at Carew.

"Good evening." He made his bow to them both.

He looked on Miss Whitford's toilette with approval. No longer dressed in dowdy country clothes, she would do any man of fashion credit in a robe of silver net over white satin, with short, plaited sleeves, and trimmed with pearls.

Dominic raised his brows at Carew, who smiled knowingly. "There seems to be a surplus of protectors tonight." He looked over towards Patience and Grace, who were laughing at his brother and Captain Fielding.

"I suppose there are."

"If you would prefer other entertainment tonight, it does not appear your presence is necessary."

"Trying to be rid of me, are you? If it's all the same to you, I think I'll stay," Carew remarked casually.

Dominic inclined his head while Miss Whitford looked back and forth between them as though sensing some undercurrent.

Carew might be surprised to know that Dominic had no intention of playing such games over his wards. If Miss Whitford preferred Carew, then the Irish rogue would have to toe the line. It was just as well if Dominic was not always seen with Miss Whitford on his arm.

HE LOOKED AROUND and appreciated the others in their evening finery —there was little doubt all eyes and lorgnettes would be on the Westwood box. Currently, however, they were gathered around little Freddy Tiger, watching him as he chased a feather that had been tied to a string. Joy pulled the cord tauntingly, and the kitten would pounce on its prey.

"Who would have thought Freddy would make such ado about a cat?" Rotham asked as Dominic approached the gathering.

"Not I. But apparently, his namesake is more entertaining than a play. Would that I had known, we could have been saved the bother. I've little fancy for Shakespearean drama tonight."

"I wish to try it!" Grace exclaimed, then took the string and laughed as the kitten sprang on the feather.

Not to be outdone, Freddy held out his hand for a turn. "By Jove! Look at him go!" However, Freddy was not content to drag the feather along the floor. He began to wave it in the air.

The little tiger lived up to his origins, attacking and jumping—straight onto Freddy's evening coat.

Instead of the horror with which the vision instilled in his friends, Freddy only laughed and peeled the little monster off, leaving behind claw marks and a puff of yellow fur on the exquisite silk.

"Oh, dear! Please let me see if I can repair your coat, or I am afraid you will be obliged to change," Miss Whitford said.

"No time to change," Freddy responded with a careless shrug. "I will miss the play. Not fond of Shakespeare, myself."

"Excellent! You may stay here and keep us company for a while," Joy decided.

"Don't mind if I do," Freddy said as he resumed his frolics with the string and feather and delighting in the cat's antics.

Dominic, Rotham, Carew, and Montford could only look on with disbelief.

Carew slapped him on the back. "Are you not now glad that I stayed on?" he teased.

"I am unconcerned either way," Dominic said coolly.

Soon, Lady Westwood, the sisters, and gentlemen were loaded into three carriages and on their way to the theatre. By this point, they were late and the crowd had already settled into their boxes. Chance could not have timed it more perfectly.

The sisters, of course, did not realize there was any disturbance at all about their appearance, but many heads swivelled their way, speech was halted and given a new direction, and the young bucks in the pit were straining their necks to see if the rumours about Dominic's wards were true.

The farce on stage had begun, and the Whitford ladies were every bit as enraptured with the scene as they had been at Astley's. Dominic settled in for boredom until the intermission, only taking note of where Sir Julian and his friends were in a box just around a bend in the tier, but with a clear view of theirs. He fully expected another move by the blackguard soon.

He looked at Rotham and Carew, who nodded that they had also seen and noted the enemy's position. Dominic had no doubt his brother and Fielding had as well, but he did not turn his head to look behind him.

When the intermission came, the gentlemen positioned themselves around the ladies, waiting for the results from the onslaught of gentlemen who would wish for introductions. Dominic was not opposed to the sisters meeting respectable gentlemen, but he had not seen any there that night who he would place in such a category.

The guard tactics appeared to have worked through the intermission. Sir Julian and his friends had not had the opportunity, or had not made the effort against the sea of admirers. Many vied for entrance to the box, but only a few were successful. There was no sign of Sir Julian. However, Dominic was not fooled into thinking Sir Julian would give up on the affair.

"One hurdle down," Rotham remarked.

"It will be necessary to remain ever vigilant since Dominic has forbidden any associations. He will have to use more drastic means," Ashley warned.

As the second act was about to begin, the theatre quieted to dull murmurs as everyone made their way back to their seats. A voice cried out in Shakespeare's most famous Romeo:

WHAT LADY IS THAT, *which doth enrich the hand*

Of yonder knight?
O, she doth teach the torches to burn bright!
It seems she hangs upon the cheek of night
Like a rich jewel in an Ethiope's ear;
Beauty too rich for use, for earth too dear!
So shows a snowy dove trooping with crows,
As yonder lady o'er her fellows shows.
The measure done, I'll watch her place of stand,
And, touching hers, make blessed my rude hand.
Did my heart love till now? Forswear it, sight!
For I ne'er saw true beauty till this night!

As DOMINIC REALIZED what Sir Julian was doing, he had to give the rogue credit for creativity. On the other hand, drawing such attention to Miss Whitford and her sisters in such a fashion, while not ruinous, was undesirable.

"Is he speaking to me?" she leaned over and asked as Sir Julian quoted the Bard and waved a red rose towards her.

"Indeed, he shows his desperation." Dominic tried to mask the anger he felt. How dare he?

"How romantic!" Hope exclaimed as the crowd cheered loudly and hailed Miss Whitford for a response.

"You are welcome to his attention," Miss Whitford retorted to Miss Hope.

"Incline your head and smile, Miss Whitford. Everyone is looking at you," Dominic commanded. "He is the one that looks like a fool."

She did as he said in a graceful manner.

"Very good. Now turn your gaze to the stage and do not look at him again."

Thankfully, the manager decided to take back command of the performance. "Unfortunately, sir, you have the wrong play tonight! But if you fail to capture yon maiden's hand, I am always looking for new talent!"

The crowd guffawed at this insult, and Dominic was thankful to have the attention diverted successfully away from his ward.

As he sat through the next act, he knew he needed to find a way to expose Sir Julian's wager since he was prepared to be outrageous for the sake of winning. He who cared for reputation and status above all else had just made an utter fool of himself before an entire theatre. As the stakes grew higher and higher, so did the threat to Miss Whitford's reputation.

CHAPTER 14

*T*rue to his word, Lord Westwood arrived with their horses and his entourage following closely behind. Instead of heading for the park, Lord Westwood directed them south-east towards the city.

"Where are we going?" Faith asked.

"Somewhere we will not be seen and instantly recognized," he replied with a sardonic twist to his lips.

Faith could not deny the appeal in that. She had noticed how very conspicuous they had become in their short time in London—made even more so by their handsome protectors.

However silly and unnecessary she had thought this protection before, after events at the theatre last night, she was grateful for it. In fact, she had been rather shaken by the public declaration Sir Julian had made and the spectacle he had tried to create. Without Lord Westwood's calm guidance, who knows what she might have done?

It was slow going through the city's bustle of carts and pedestrians, but when they reached the Dover Road and passed the toll gate, they were able to pick up speed.

The air was fresh, the rolling hills and meadows green, and Faith felt the constraints of Town blow away with the wind in her face.

Once they had put a few miles between them and Town and the horses had enjoyed a good gallop, Westwood slowed their pace to a canter before directing them on to a country lane.

"Where are we going?" Joy asked.

"To Taywards," Westwood answered. "Not much further now."

They followed, and turned into a set of open cast-iron gates with lions on them. This must be one of his properties, Faith mused. It was similar in size to Halbury Hall—a sprawling Jacobean mansion with a pleasing mixture of red brick and symmetrical windows surrounded by a large park. Instead of stopping at the house, Westwood led them around to the stables. Perhaps he only kept a small household there.

However, she realized she was mistaken when they reached the stables. Halbury Hall had a large stable, but this was on a different plane altogether. These stables were at least thrice the size, with a large paddock and a circular ride where at least four dozen horses appeared to be grazing or actively training.

For a moment, the sisters looked around as if surprised.

Westwood dismounted, handing his gelding to one of the numerous grooms who had rushed to help. He smiled up at her and held out a hand to assist her. "This seems a much more appropriate place for Joy to try her tricks, does it not?"

"Is this your property?" she asked appreciatively.

"The estate is. This," he waved his hand towards the stables and training grounds, "is a joint venture. Carew breeds the horses and brings them here when they are ready for sale. It is a location convenient to London and boasts a nearby pier where the boats may bring them from Ireland."

"Is this your country seat?"

"I daresay you might call it that. I also have a lovely residence in Cumberland. This is home to my grandmother and two of my aunts. You're to meet them for breakfast in due course. They consider anything before noon an abomination."

"Is this not grand, Faith?" Joy asked, eyes brimming with excitement.

Hope, Patience, and Grace all looked to be in equally high spirits.

Before them was a course created for jumping and training. "Dare I ask if all of you can clear obstacles while hunting?"

"As well as we can walk, my lord," Faith replied with an answering grin.

"Very well. I will put you on some of our more seasoned horses to give yours a rest."

The next two hours were some of the most pleasurable Faith could remember. They leaped obstacles to their hearts' content, and put some excellent horseflesh through its paces across several acres of pasture. It was exactly what they had been missing without knowing it, and precisely the thing to keep Joy out of mischief.

They were heartily exhausted and famished by the time they gained the house, where they were provided chambers in which to wash their hands and faces before being presented to Lord West-wood's grandmother and aunts.

They were first shown into an elegant drawing room, where three elder ladies sat. One appeared to be in a wheeled chair. Faith was drawn to her immediately.

She was very handsome, with elegant silver hair and knowing blue eyes that looked as though they had seen many years of humour.

"Grandmama, may I present to you Miss Whitford?" Lord West-wood said. "Miss Whitford, this is my father's mother."

"This is the young lady I have heard so much about."

Faith could not imagine what she may have heard, but she smiled and took the hand offered to her.

"You may leave us, Dominic."

He bowed with an ironic smile, and then began to introduce his friends and her sisters to his aunts.

"You may wonder what I have heard, and I will confess to reading the Society pages. Dreadful, is it not? But when one is confined to the house, one must rely on correspondence and newspapers. My grandson is an excellent letter writer."

Faith did not know precisely what that meant, other than that he must dote on the dowager. For one who made an art out of appearing to care little for others, this was at odds with his self-proclaimed profligacy.

"He has written a great deal about you."

Faith evidenced her surprise.

"He has never before done such a thing, I assure you."

"I suppose it is only natural since he has suddenly inherited five wards of the opposite sex."

"Perhaps, but he has written little of your sisters, who all appear to be as beautiful and charming as you."

"I am sure it is only because I am the eldest, ma'am." Faith could see where her thoughts were leading, but she knew that Lord West-wood was not doing this in order to catch a bride—far from it. Could he go back in time, he would surely let them return to Bath and wash his hands of them as soon as possible. If not for Sir Julian's threats, he would probably still be amused by thrusting them upon the *ton*.

"I do not think so. His mother thinks you are the one to bring him to heel, and I am inclined to agree with her."

That put Faith to the blush. "Please, my lady, I wish you would not put any store by that. I assure you there is nothing more to that than his duties as our guardian occupying much more of his time than he bargained for!" Faith laughed.

"Perhaps," the dowager said, but Faith could tell she was determined in her thinking.

"Are you teasing Miss Whitford, Grandmama? She looks as though she needs rescuing," Lord Westwood said, meeting her gaze.

"I have said what I needed to say," the lady said primly.

"I imagine you have. Shall we go into the breakfast room? These ladies might not confess to ravishing hunger, but I will. I cannot remember the last time I had so much exercise in one morning."

He stood behind the wheeled chair and escorted his grandmother. Despite the embarrassment she felt at the lady's words, Faith could understand that the dowager would like to see her grandson settled with his own family. Why she should think Lord Westwood would choose her was another matter. He'd shown her and her sisters courtesy and civility, to be sure, but in the matter of preferring Faith? He was nothing but indifferent, as evidenced by his flirtation with the widow Taylor. Besides, he could look as high as he wished for a wife, should he wish for one.

Breakfast was a lavish affair to Faith, though it might be common enough amongst the nobility. Lady Halbury had not fed them extravagantly—they had broken their fast in the schoolroom with eggs and toast. Neither did Lady Westwood hold a formal breakfast, preferring a tray in her room. They had become used to eating together in their chambers whilst in London.

The sideboard was covered with kippers, sliced beef, eggs, bacon, sausages, and an array of rolls and toast and side dishes—a veritable feast. However, Faith and her sisters had worked up a hearty appetite and did justice to the meal.

"Must you leave directly?" the dowager asked.

Lord Westwood looked up at Faith. "Have you any engagements this evening that I have forgotten?"

"No, my lord."

"Then we need not hurry."

"Perhaps you may show those who wish to see them around the house or the estate. There is more to Taywards than the stables."

"Of course, Grandmama."

"I could spend all day in the stables," Joy remarked.

After they had breakfasted, everyone first played lawn bowls, but they were all much too competitive and chose to split into other activities from lawn chess to rowing across the lake.

Faith did not think she'd ever had a more agreeable day. For the day, she allowed her worries about their futures to escape her. There was tomorrow for that.

"May I interest you in a turn about the lake?" Lord Westwood asked. "Or was your excursion with Carew enough to turn you from the sport for good?"

That notable sportsman from the rowing team at Cambridge scoffed.

"As poor Carew was so good as not to overturn the boat, I think I could manage another turn," she answered, amused by the competitive nature of the two gentlemen.

Once they were out on the lake, Faith wondered why Lord Westwood had invited her out. He had already rowed Hope around and must be tired. However, Carew was now rowing Grace, so perhaps it was not such a fatiguing endeavour as it appeared.

"Are you enjoying yourself, Miss Whitford?" he asked.

"How could I not? Taywards feels like heaven to me."

"I feel the same. However, I am supremely biased."

"You have the luxury of an estate so close to London."

"The best of both worlds, is it not? My other estate in Cumberland overlooks one of the lakes, with a mountain as a background."

"I could be happy with a small cottage with a prospect of water to gaze at from a window or porch. Even a pond would do."

"Do you picture that as your future?"

"Why not?"

He did not answer her with words, but a certain look she was unable to decipher. When next she noticed, he had directed the boat to the far shore, where he began to tie the vessel to a small pier.

"Where are we at?" she asked.

"There is somewhere I thought you might like to see, given your affinity for water."

He assisted her from the small craft and they walked upward some hundred feet to where a small waterfall flowed downward under a bridge.

She gasped in appreciation.

"This was always my favourite spot as a boy. That bridge has been my deepest confidante."

Faith nodded, understanding. "I had a similar spot at Halbury. It was not a watering spot, but there was a beautiful cliff overlooking Bath and the valley where it seemed I was closer to my parents—to God. There was a time when no one understood what it felt like to be orphaned and left with four younger sisters."

They passed some time in companionable silence before Lord Westwood broke the peaceful reverence.

"I suppose we should be returning to London soon." His voice almost sounded regretful.

Faith was in no hurry to leave the ideal of the country. However, they returned to the boat and he rowed them back across the lake. It was the first she could remember they had not crossed swords for an entire day.

When the horses were brought around, the dowager was there to bid them adieu.

She held out her hand to Faith and pulled her close to kiss her cheek. "I see you have enjoyed yourself today. Consider him, my dear," she whispered in Faith's ear and patted her on the cheek, leaving Faith to her uncomfortable thoughts on the ride back to London—on the one hand, flattered that his grandmother considered her worthy, and on the other, that she very much doubted Lord Westwood was of the same mind.

ON THIS SHE ERRED. Faith was on Lord Westwood's mind a great deal, along with the rest of Society. A flock of men awaited outside Westwood House each day to ascertain whether to attend his mother's drawing room or to follow the ladies like a gaggle of geese, as Joy referred to them. Every morning, there was some mention of them in the Society pages—which was no great thing—except when it was. This morning, as Dominic read his morning paper over the coffee cups, there was much of interest.

WHATEVER WAS London like before the Whitford ladies descended upon us? Seeing their beauty each morning as they ride along Rotten Row, walking their kitten on a lead in the park, or stealing the thunder from all of the other young ladies at Almack's?

But rumour has it, not all of the ladies are, shall we say, ladylike, as one was reportedly seen attempting to stand on her head atop her horse in the park. Do we have a future Astley's acrobat in our midst?

Dominic groaned. "Joy!"

IN OTHER NEWS, not wholly unrelated to the Whitford sisters, Sir Julian has reportedly left Town for the Martingale house party. But was it a planned event or has he gone to lick his wounds after so public a rebuff from the Season's Incomparable?

DOMINIC MULLED OVER THIS INFORMATION. His first thought was this was a trick. Sir Julian would only be more determined in his plan to ruin Faith, and what better way than to make Dominic let down his guard? Perhaps he would allow the ladies to attend the Knighton masquerade after all. It had been deemed too risky to protect them with Sir Julian lurking about, but it might be a useful place to beat him at his own game. If Sir Julian were truly gone, then the ladies could simply enjoy themselves.

Dominic dashed off a note to Westwood House and sent it with the footman before he went for his morning ride, informing the girls that he would call on them after breakfast.

Having placed his hat atop his head and taken his horsewhip in his hand, no sooner had Dominic walked down his front steps than he was accosted by a caller trying to solicit Miss Whitford's hand.

"Lord Westwood! I was just about to call on you. A moment of your time, I beg of you!" Mr. Dankworth proclaimed.

Dominic pulled out his quizzing glass and stared at the fop before him. Instead, he looked down upon him with his frostiest stare and summoned his chilliest voice. "Anyone wishing to be taken seriously by me will not accost me as I leave my house, nor will he be so rude as to come at an hour which is preserved for activities other than calls." He turned to his horse, which the groom was patiently holding. Maximus, responding to his master's tone, whinnied and pawed at the ground. "Just so, Max."

"My lord, I have tried at the appointed hour, and your butler will not admit me," Dankworth pleaded.

Dominic swung up onto his horse. "Just so." He clicked his tongue to send Max onward, wondering at the inability of youth to take a hint.

As per their usual custom, the gentlemen put the horses through their paces before any serious topics were broached, but as soon as they had slowed to a pace where speech was possible, he spoke.

"Did any of you read the Society pages this morning?"

Freddy had the grace to blush. "I swear I did not know what she was about!"

"I wondered if you were her partner in mischief, but I thought to ask before accusing."

"I had no idea what she was about when she asked to ride. I had only stopped at the house to pet the kitten when she asked to ride. I like to ride myself, so I did not see the harm. We were nowhere near the strut, nor the fashionable hour for that matter!" Freddy defended himself and his charge.

"Someone is always watching in London," Rotham remarked.

"Well, if I had known she was going to turn upside down on her horse, I would not have agreed."

"No wonder someone took notice if she was upside down in skirts!" Montford exclaimed.

"Well, the thing is, she wasn't."

"Do you mean she was in breeches?" Montford was shocked to the core.

"No, no. She had fashioned her skirt to somehow split in the middle, then tied them about her ankles. Dashed clever, I thought."

"At least she troubled to disguise it as a skirt," Carew offered.

"Of course, she did." Dominic shook his head. "I will deal with her later. What I had been referring to was the information that Sir Julian had gone to Martingale's. I was going to allow the ladies to attend the masquerade."

"I suspect a hoax," Rotham warned.

"Indeed. If he thinks me slow enough to swallow that tale, then I intend to be ready for him. However, it would be best to be prepared."

"I can ask at the Albany to see if he announced his trip. He has rooms there as well," Montford offered.

"My valet is acquainted with his man. I will ask him," Rotham said.

"I have no objection to escorting them to the masquerade," Carew said with a smile lurking in his eyes.

"Do not tell me you wish to make a declaration as well? I have already been accosted this morning on my front steps, as well as at Jackson' Saloon, and at White's this week alone."

"Do not tell me you were thinking of the parson's noose?" Freddy asked.

"You never know. I will eventually need an heir, and who's to say when another like her will come along?"

"Since there are five of them, I can say with a great deal of certainty!" Dominic retorted.

"It's too devilish early for this kind of talk. I will see you tonight. I will send word when I ask my man," Rotham said, as they all parted until later that night, and Dominic rode on to Westwood House.

"Good day, my lord," Hartley greeted him.

"Is anyone down yet?" It sounded awfully quiet to Dominic's ears. He did not think the ladies were late sleepers since they often met him for a ride in the mornings.

"I believe they partake of breakfast together in their chambers, my lord. Shall I inform them of your arrival?"

"It is Miss Joy in particular I wish to speak with. If Miss Whitford or the governess would care to accompany her, I will see them in the study."

"Very good, my lord. Shall I send in a tray?"

"No, I will not be here long."

Joy came in shortly thereafter with a look of defiance on her face. Miss Whitford was not far behind, but stopped just inside the door and curtsied.

Dominic inclined his head. "Well, child?" He set the paper down before her, turned to the appropriate column.

He watched her read, biting her lower lip when she came to the part referencing her behaviour.

Miss Whitford looked at him inquiringly, and, as soon as Joy had finished, he handed the paper to her. She scanned it quickly. "Joy, tell me this is a fabrication!"

"We were hidden! I took good care that no one saw me!"

"Apparently not enough care. You will ruin yourself before you even come out," she said with dismay.

Joy's expression had not changed from defiance. She was watching his face. "Are you going to rage at me?" she finally asked.

"You do not deny it?"

"Why should I? I did nothing wrong."

"Except expressly break your word to me," he replied quietly.

"Joy!" Miss Whitford replied with horror.

"A very cool response when Society has proclaimed you a hoyden, Miss Joy. You may leave us."

The look of shock on Joy's face satisfied Dominic, as did the click of the door when she left the room.

"That is it?" Miss Whitford asked with a perplexed look that contorted her face adorably. "Not even a good scold?"

"What would it serve, except to make her rebellious and resolved to do more?" he answered. "No doubt she thinks hoyden to be an epitaph of praise."

"I see your point. But surely there is a way to prevent her from exposing herself—all of us to such censure?"

"Of course. She shall not have the privilege of riding her horse in London again without my escort."

Dominic left his mother's abode feeling satisfied that Miss Whitford would keep her younger sister in check henceforth. Meanwhile, he was met at his entry into his own house with news that it did seem Sir Julian had left Town. The landlord of the Albany had said he saw Sir Julian leave and his valet with him. Dominic scrawled off another note to his mother, indicating their attendance to the masquerade.

CHAPTER 15

*W*ell, I for one am happy to know the costumes I ordered will not go to waste! But why do you think he changed his mind?" Lady Westwood asked as she finished reading the note from her son.

"The papers mentioned Sir Julian has left Town for a house party," Faith answered, though she was a bit worried about Lord Westwood's decision to attend the masquerade—Lady Halbury having proclaimed them to be dens of iniquity and masks to be an excuse to sin. However, Lady Westwood said this one was considered above reproach and acceptable even for those just making their come out.

Watching her sisters' excitement as they dressed in their various costumes helped to alleviate some of Faith's worry, but did not change the feeling inside that something ill would happen.

Lord Westwood must have been assured, because he had been very punctilious in his protection of them thus far. He arrived to escort them and looked over each of them from head to toe.

"Is something amiss?" Faith asked.

"Not at all. I am trying to memorize who is whom so I will be able to keep track of everyone."

"You think Sir Julian is playing a trick?"

"If there are thousands of pounds at stake, I expect it."

"Are my sisters in danger from him?"

He turned from his surveillance of her sisters and looked directly at her. "Thus far, it seems only to be you. However, having been unable to discover the exact terms of the wager, I cannot say with certainty."

"I see. So it may not be safe to go tonight."

"My friends and I remain vigilant, but it does seem an excellent time to force his hand. I want you to remain with me or one of us at all times. Understood?"

She nodded, though felt a great deal of misgiving.

"All of us are wearing identical dominoes, so Sir Julian will not know who we are. We will all arrive separately and take hacks to minimize the likelihood of being recognized." He held out his domino for them to see. It was black with a silver stripe around the hood.

"You seem to have thought of everything."

"That is impossible, but I do wish to minimize the risks. I think we should have a word so you know it is me."

"Like a signal?"

"Precisely. A secret word between the two of us you can ask if you are unsure."

She thought about that, and the word that was so obvious to her might not be to him. Laughter threatened, and she struggled to keep her face impassive.

"What is it, minx? Don't hold your tongue on my account!"

"Well, ogre seems to be the most obvious choice that no one else would think of."

"I see I've made no progress in your esteem at all, but very well," he bantered.

"That is not what I meant, my lord."

"No, no, do not withdraw now!" He flicked her on the cheek. "I will meet you there."

Faith rubbed her cheek in wonderment after Lord Westwood had left. Sometimes he seemed pompous and self-centred, then his actions would say otherwise. It would be foolish, however, to put any store by his little flirtations. She had seen him do such with some of the beautiful widows about—but never with any marriageable young ladies. Perhaps their frequent proximity lowered his normal guard and his flirtatious habits that were second nature surfaced with her. It would be dangerous to think he meant anything by them, so she warned herself to guard her heart as she put the mask of her costume firmly in place.

They arrived to find the ballroom dimly lit and decorated as a grotto. It was not as elaborate as Lady Westwood's ball had been, but it was enchanting nevertheless. There were some very elaborate costumes, but many people had opted for simple dominos.

Despite the costumes and masks, it would have been silly to think anyone would not know who the four Whitford ladies were, even though they wore different colours than they had at their ball to intentionally confuse people.

Each of the sisters' costumes consisted of a domino over their gowns, but each was designed to look like an animal or being.

Faith was a butterfly, Hope had chosen a swan. Patience was a colourful bird, and Grace a fairy.

They were besieged with requests for dances as soon as they arrived. Faith and her sisters had decided to give away only one dance at a time that evening since they did not know who anyone was.

There was some excitement in trying to discover who their partners were. There was a much more flirtatious undercurrent than was usual when people showed their faces. Yet there was never the ability to completely relax, knowing that Sir Julian was likely to be hiding in plain sight.

Most of the gentlemen were in plain black dominoes, which was what Lord Westwood and his friends would wear. How then was she supposed to tell them from the others?

As soon as her first partner in a green domino had led her onto the dance floor and had begun to speak, it was easy to determine it was Mr. Dankworth. He was a persistent suitor, though he was young and liked to write bad poetry.

Her second partner was much more mysterious. He donned the

black domino she looked for, hoping it was one of their friends. It even bore the silver stripe around the hood. Yet there was something about him that put her ill at ease.

Were Lord Westwood or Rotham or Carew or Mr. Cunningham or Major Stuart or Captain Fielding even there? She had become so accustomed to these gentlemen's protection! How she had taken it for granted!

"Are we to speak at all, sir? Or am I to remain in ignorance?"

"Is that not the allure of a masquerade?" he answered in a low voice.

"I assume you have the advantage of me."

He inclined his head. "I knew I could dance with you no other way, but I will take what I can get, even if it is by desperate means."

Had she knowingly walked right into Sir Julian's arms? If this black domino was indeed he, then he spoke with a disguised voice.

"Please," he pleaded. "Do not become rigid. I intend you no harm."

"That is not what rumour tells," she answered curtly.

"You have no reason to trust me, I am aware of that. And it is true I have never courted a young lady before, but do you not believe that a gentleman could be moved by beauty and grace? That there comes a time when a man is ready to become settled?"

"You hardly know me, to make such declarations, sir."

"I do not need to know more," he insisted.

"All I know of your character is your insinuation into my life by less than respectable means, Sir Julian. If my guardian does not approve, how can I refute that?"

"Then what choice am I left with but to try to convince you of my good intentions by whatever means I may? Yes, perhaps, addressing you at the theatre was not the best choice, but I meant it honourably, I assure you—as a romantic gesture of the highest order. May I be forgiven for my lapse in judgement?"

"Do you swear to me the rumours about the wager are untrue?" Not that she could trust a word he said, but she wanted to hear it all the same.

"I swear it." He placed his hand over his heart. His voice certainly sounded sincere, but she knew him so little.

"In fact, I am prepared to offer you my name."

"You know me as little as I know you," she answered, trying not to let the fear she felt betray herself in her voice.

"I assure you I have never made such an offer before. My lineage goes back hundreds of years and my estate and wealth are not to be balked at. You would want for nothing and know the prestige of being Lady Wright."

"While I am flattered by your offer, you know my guardian would never consent." Faith had no interest in Sir Julian, but neither did she wish to insult him.

"I understand. You do not know me well enough to understand what a flattering offer I have made you."

"Sir Julian, please. I beg of you do not continue. If it is as you say, then you may know me better and court me properly, when I am of age and no longer under the constraints of my guardian."

A flare of frustration flickered in his eyes. Though it was dim, and the mask hid his face, she had no doubt of what she had seen. There was danger lurking beneath this façade he presented, and she was afraid of him.

"I will say no more, but I will continue trying to change your mind." He bowed when the set ended and escorted her back to her sisters.

Breathing a heavy sigh of relief, her sisters sensed her anxiety.

"Who was that?" Hope asked.

"Sir Julian," she told them quietly.

Patience gasped. "He is wearing the costume Lord Westwood described as his own!"

Faith nodded. "Precisely. I had hoped it was one of our friends."

"Did he impose upon you?" Grace asked.

"Only with words. He asked for my hand. I suggest you avoid the costume, unless you know it to be one of our friends for certain."

A touch on her shoulder made her jump.

"What is the matter?"

Faith relaxed. How had she thought she would not know Lord Westwood anywhere?

"Has something happened?"

"Faith has just danced with Sir Julian," Patience explained. "He was wearing your costume."

Lord Westwood held up his hands in some type of signal, and five other men came towards them, surrounding them and sending away the other gentlemen who were approaching for dances. "The next set is spoken for," Westwood announced and the others scattered, grumbling.

Westwood led her out to the floor. "Tell me everything."

DOMINIC HAD WATCHED her dancing and had immediately known it was not one of his friends. He strongly suspected the man was Sir Julian, but with masks in place, he was not confident enough to make a scene and pull them apart in the middle of the dance floor. He could not think it a coincidence that Sir Julian had the identical domino with a stripe. Someone in his employ had much to answer for, but he would deal with them later.

He could feel Faith trembling in his arms, so she must have been more disturbed than she'd revealed when she was talking to her sisters. He gave her a few moments to settle her nerves before he spoke again. "I would not have let him take you. I was watching the whole time."

She nodded and swallowed hard, then forced a tremulous smile at him.

"Did he threaten you?' Dominic searched her eyes as best he could.

"No. In fact, he was the perfect gentleman. He even made me an offer of marriage."

"I would hardly call that respectable without first obtaining your guardian's consent."

"Yes, and so I told him, but he argued that since you would not allow it, what alternative did he have?"

Dominic scoffed. "I hope you are not taken in?"

"Of course not, but knowing he would go to such lengths to seek an audience with me troubles me more than I anticipated, even though I expected a trick."

"Perhaps you were right after all, Miss Whitford."

"How do you mean?"

"Perhaps I was wrong to make you leave Bath."

"I cannot be the judge of that, but it is done. Even in your wish for amusement, I do not think you would have wished this upon us."

"Thank you," he said dryly then spun her into a turn. "If only we could discover when the wager expires. I trust there is a time limit on it."

"Goodness, I should hope so!"

He watched her as they danced in silence. "What is it?"

"It occurs to me that I should hate to punish my sisters if I am Sir Julian's object. They are enjoying themselves enormously, you see."

"Ah, so therein lies another argument for London."

He saw a little twitch of appreciation in her lips, but he wished he could see her whole face. "What is the solution, then?"

"I do not know. If only Sir Julian would cease and desist with this outrageous wager."

"Cease to exist? It might cause a slight upheaval, but perhaps that would be the solution."

"Stop being ridiculous! You know that is not what I meant."

"If you change your mind, I am at your service." He made her a bow as the dance ended and they joined the others at the side of the ballroom. Hope immediately began tugging at Faith's domino. "You will never guess what I just heard!"

Dominic held up a finger and indicated for Hope and Faith to follow him to a more secluded spot. "Now what did you hear, Hope?" he asked.

"Well, I did not know who my partner was, you understand, but even I could tell he was a bit..." She waved her hand.

"Bosky? In his cups? Inebriated? Drunk?" Dominic suggested.

"Well, yes."

Dominic imagined she was blushing beneath her mask. "Do go on."

"He asked me which sister I was, because Sir Julian was trying to find Miss Whitford in order to win his wager."

"When I said he had already found her, he said. 'Hell and...'"

"Yes, yes, he cursed," Faith supplied. "What else did he say?"

"He said he'd be obliged if we kept you from Sir Julian because he had a great deal placed against him."

"Then I said how I didn't approve of wagering about my sister."

"'Well, everybody does it,' he snapped back at me, and then he said he wished he could see my face to see if I was as pretty close to as everyone said."

Dominic noticed Miss Faith tapping her foot with impatience as she waited for her sister to tell the story.

"Since he was being so forthcoming, I decided to question him a bit more."

Faith and Dominic glanced at each other hopefully.

"I asked if it was true that Sir Julian was trying to ruin Faith, and he asked how I knew such a thing."

"That confirms what my brother heard. At least there do not seem to be any additional riders on the bet."

"If only we knew how much longer this is to go on!" Faith exclaimed in frustration.

"Oh, he did mention there was only a fortnight to go, so he expected Sir Julian to try anything."

"Thank you, Hope. Can you think of anything else he might have said that would help? Anything at all?" Dominic prodded.

"No. I believe that was everything."

Dominic turned towards Faith. "Perhaps if there are only two more weeks, it would be better to spend them in the country, where it would be very difficult for Sir Julian to do you any mischief."

"Do not make us leave before Vauxhall!" Hope cried.

Dominic sighed. That was about the least safe place he could think of to take the sisters. "When is Vauxhall?"

"Tomorrow evening."

"It would surprise me not at all if he were to do something out of desperation there if he gets wind of your intention to go. Especially since he may feel he has tried being gentlemanly."

"Is it unsafe for Faith? Perhaps she should not go," Hope said, and thought better of it. "That's hardly fair, is it? I am sorry, Faith."

"I think it best if we make an early departure. This is hardly a safe place for discussion. We will escort you to Westwood House. Stay together while I inform my mother to have my brother escort her home."

Soon the sisters were returning to Westwood House. It was hardly inconspicuous for all the sisters to leave at once, but it could not be helped. Knowing how short of time remained made Sir Julian a lit fuse.

"We did not even get to see the unmasking," Grace complained.

"Or dance more than three sets," Patience commiserated.

"Sir Julian found Faith tonight. He was in the disguise our guardian was wearing. You can understand that she is not comfortable remaining when she is unable to discern who is who," Hope explained.

"Of course. Forgive me, Faith," Grace said.

"Believe me, I want this over with as much as the rest of you. I hate being forced from London and yes, I did say that." She cast a knowing glance at their guardian.

"If we leave, it will only be temporary, ladies. You seemed to enjoy yourself at Taywards. I had thought to send at least Faith there to keep her safe."

Once back at Westwood House, the sisters climbed the stairs towards their chambers, but Dominic stopped Faith. "May I have a moment?"

"Of course."

He led her into the study and realized she was still wearing her mask. "Would you not be more comfortable without your mask?"

"Of course, but the tie became knotted in my hair. The maid can help me later after we have spoken."

Dominic frowned, then stepped behind her. "Nonsense. I know these are not comfortable, and I prefer to see your face when we talk."

As he worked, however, he found such a simple task to be terribly intimate. The feel of her silky hair through his fingers and the scent of her soap intoxicated his senses. Disturbed by the domestic image, he released the knot and stepped away.

"Thank you," she said, pulling the mask away and turning to face him. "What did you wish to speak to me about?"

"I wished to know your opinion about Vauxhall before I consult with my friends. Is it widely known that you intend to be there?"

"I could not say. I believe your brother arranged it."

"Ashley is not one to prattle, and he would have consulted my mother." He wrinkled his brow in thought. "Perhaps I should consult him. He will be bringing my mother home soon. On the one hand, it galls me to think of rearranging anything for the sake of Sir Julian, and drawing more attention to the situation. On the other hand, I wish to protect you and your sisters from harm, and there is little doubt left in my mind that is what is intended."

"Surely your credit will see us through?"

Poor innocent. She did not understand that more than his credit would be necessary to redeem her if Sir Julian succeeded. "The only thing that redeems a ruined lady is marriage."

She nodded, but he could see her fighting some emotion. "Why is he doing this to me? And how could someone be so full of malice?"

Dominic hated to disillusion her, but the world—London, at least —was full of people who had no conscience at all. He stepped closer and tilted her chin up. "It has little to do with you."

"The consequences certainly do!"

"Undeniably, they will affect us both," he murmured, wondering what he was about.

CHAPTER 16

Faith had difficulty sleeping that night for the troubling thoughts she could not banish from disturbing her peace.

Sir Julian's desire to ruin her was deeply upsetting when she had done nothing to deserve to be the centre of such cruelty. Her leaving would also affect her sisters by turning them away from their first Season when they were enjoying it so much.

What her thoughts kept returning to was her reaction to Lord Westwood. He meant nothing by it, but the simple gesture of removing her mask had upset her equilibrium greatly.

It had made her feel things—had even made her a trifle warm and dizzy, truth be told—and stirred her thoughts in a direction they had no right to go. Why was his touch so different from a sister's or a maid's?

Westwood was a determined bachelor and flirt, and she needed to distance herself from him before she lost her heart to someone who could not reciprocate the feeling. Becoming his latest flirt would be the nadir of humiliation.

Faith needed to remove from London for more than one reason, and perhaps it would be best if only she and Joy went away. There would be less talk than if all of the sisters went at once. Especially since the wager only seemed to involve her.

But she wished there were somewhere else she could go besides one of Westwood's properties. She loathed being beholden to him and completely at his mercy. Hopefully, at least being distanced from his person would help her regain her equilibrium. The worst thing would be if he knew how he affected her. She'd never been good at disguising her feelings, and that would be the most lowering thing of all.

She threw back her covers and walked to the dressing table, then absently picked up a brush and began to run it through the tangles she'd formed in her restless night.

A knock on her door interrupted her maudlin thoughts.

"Enter," she called, expecting one of her sisters.

Lady Westwood looked inside. "I hope I did not wake you."

"Not at all. Is something wrong?"

Lady Westwood looked much younger in her dressing gown with her hair in a plait, and was still very beautiful.

"I do not think so. I have just received a note from Dominic. He says the gentlemen will still escort your party to Vauxhall tonight."

"Oh?" Faith frowned. It was not at all what she had expected him to decide and was concerned.

"We will put it out you are taking your sister to the country to recover from some ailment. Not everyone will believe it, of course, but no one will be able to say otherwise without looking peevish."

"How will I be kept safe?"

Lady Westwood took the brush from Faith and began to stroke her hair softly.

"You will be surrounded by me, your sisters, and your magnificent cadre of gentlemen. Many ladies would promise their first-born to be surrounded by such a crew!" She laughed.

Faith hoped it would be as safe as Lady Westwood seemed to think.

"I never had a daughter to do this for," she mused.

"That is one of my best memories of my mama. She used to brush my hair every night," Faith said wistfully. It did feel divine.

"Everything is going to work out, you know. When Dominic told me he was bringing the five of you to London. I questioned his motives, but I do think it has been good for him."

Faith swallowed her retort about his motives being absolutely selfish. "He has certainly inherited more than he bargained for." Faith would call it his just deserts if she were not the desert in question. "He did not send us to the country as soon as he realized how much trouble we caused."

"One thing I will say, my son would not do this if he did not wish to. Everyone caters to him horribly. The men envy his sporting abilities, and the ladies want his looks, title, and wealth, and that has made him rather selfish."

Faith could not refute the point. All evidence to her eyes agreed with the viscountess.

"This has been good for him—for all of them to have a purpose other than themselves. That is not to say Dominic is not a conscientious landlord. He cares very deeply for his land and his tenants. And he positively dotes on me and his grandmother."

"I had noticed he is a very attentive son."

"Yet he is also very attentive to you and your sisters," she said with a smirk that Faith saw in the mirror.

"I beg you will not have expectations of anything between your son and I, ma'am. I assure you he is only fulfilling his duty as our guardian. He has shown no partiality for me in that way."

"My child, I must beg to differ. His grandmother and I both noticed it."

Hopefully, the dowager would not go on and on about how she thought Faith would be his perfect bride. Faith could hardly call them liars. "Be that as it may, I had not thought to marry, at least before my sisters are fired off. My primary responsibility is to them."

The viscountess smiled indulgently, but did not press her any further, for which Faith was grateful.

By the time they were ready for Vauxhall later that evening, the excitement from her sisters was palpable.

While the evening was not a masquerade, they had decided to wear almost identical gowns. They wished to make it more difficult to distinguish between the sisters—especially in the darkness. Moreover, they had determined never to be separated from either another sister, Lady Westwood, or one of their gentleman protectors. Personally, Faith had no wish to leave the box for the evening as another measure of safety.

Lord Westwood had arranged for them to arrive by river boat, which was a special treat. None of them had ever done such a thing. The closest they had ever come was being rowed on the lake at Taywards.

They had loaded onto a luxurious barge covered with a canopy and seats beneath, with men in livery posted about to guide them through the water.

"Oh, the memories this recalls," Lady Westwood said wistfully. "However did you come by this?"

"Freddy's father keeps it docked at his house, just off the river. He still prefers to travel by boat. He was happy to lend it and his men in this cause."

"We always came by the river in my youth."

"You also wore dreadful wigs and hoops, and the men had ridiculous heels," Lord Westwood retorted dryly.

"Yes, it was glorious! The men were beautiful. It was something to behold." She beamed, causing all of the sisters to laugh. "I should have powdered my hair and worn a beauty mark!"

"Perhaps that can be the theme of your next ball," Hope suggested. "I would love to dress like your portrait in the gallery."

"A child after my own heart!" she said warmly to Hope.

"I can see I will need to plan a grand tour for next Season," Lord Westwood murmured.

When they pulled up to the gates of Vauxhall, they were not the only ones arriving by boat, but the others were in hired wherries.

"Look!" Hope exclaimed. "It's magical."

Thousands of colourful lanterns twinkled throughout the trees of the park, and music wafted seemingly from the trees as they wandered away through the dim paths towards the grove. This was no *ton* event, as commoners mixed with Society on neutral ground.

"Remember, never go anywhere without one of us," Westwood warned. "As you can see, the rules of the beau monde do not apply here. The women are not all ladies and the men will not behave as gentlemen. And under no circumstances take to the dark walk—even together! There are no rules at all there."

"You fill me with such confidence," Faith muttered.

"I want you to carry this. It is only a precaution." He slipped a muff pistol into her hand. Faith looked at it as though it were poison, but slipped it into her pocket, wondering why they had come after all. However, her sisters' faces were full of delight, and had she not been afraid of what Sir Julian would try next, perhaps she would have been excited as well.

THUS FAR, the evening was going as planned. The Whitford ladies seemed delighted by Vauxhall—even Dominic had to admit it was enchanting. The weather was warm with a slight breeze coming off the river. The music was superb, and so far, the audience was well behaved. Often the more raucous crowds did not venture out until later at night, and Dominic hoped to have the ladies safely tucked up in their beds by then.

At the end of the performance, the music changed for dancing and a light supper was served. An array of chicken, thinly sliced ham, bread, and fruits were served them, along with the rack punch that the gardens was known for.

Friends and acquaintances passed by to greet them, and Dominic thought Miss Whitford had relaxed enough to enjoy herself.

Lady Sefton, one of Lady Westwood's close friends, stopped by the box with her husband. "We just came from watching the acrobats and they were walking across ropes over our heads!" she marvelled.

"There are acrobats here? Where?"

"On the path to the rotunda," she answered.

"May we go see? Surely it would be safe if we all go together?" Hope asked.

"I think if ten of us go, there could be no harm," Rotham offered.

"Very well," Dominic conceded. It was still not late, and none of the walks were considered dangerous. The paths were crowded, however, and they were jostled about as people moved in either direction.

"Take my arm," Dominic said to Miss Whitford, as he was already placing her hand through his elbow. It was a firmer grip than if they'd been on promenade.

Carew was on her other side escorting Grace. For some reason he did not care to examine, Dominic was grateful to have her to himself.

"Look!" Hope said as she pointed.

There, strung above the paths were ropes, and men in very tight breeches were walking across, a couple of them even twirling batons with fire on either end.

As the group made to walk underneath, Dominic halted them. "Perhaps here would be safer," he remarked. "And more decent," he muttered.

The acrobats continued to put on a display, twirling and tossing the batons back-and-forth between each other. They scurried across the ropes and, occasionally, one of them would perform a leap and a twirl on the thin rope.

"You find this a dead bore, I imagine," Miss Whitford said in his ear.

"What does that matter? You and your sisters are delighted."

She laughed. "It takes very little for those who have been sheltered in the country. I imagine if they had been of the female variety, it might have been a bit more attractive to you."

He looked down and smiled at her. "But of course."

"Shall we walk on to the rotunda? It is much too crowded here for my liking." He signalled over the ladies' heads to his brother and Rotham, and they indicated to the others to move along.

Rotham was at the far end with his brother and Fielding, and they began to push their way through the mass of people. However, someone took exception to being forced to move and turned around and threw a punch. It connected with Rotham's shoulder, and he thrust out an elbow to protect Miss Hope.

"Mill!" someone shouted, and that was all it took for the scene to erupt into chaos.

Arms were swinging everywhere whether they connected with flesh or not; the ladies were shrieking with displeasure and horror—although, a time or two, he saw one of them put out a well-placed leg to trip someone or shove someone in the back when they came too close.

Dominic's only thought was to protect Faith, and he could see the others trying to usher the ladies to safety as well.

Before they could reach the edge, someone grabbed him by his collar and tried to pull him backwards. Every instinct in Dominic wanted to turn around and fight back, but he held tight to Faith, having to wrap his arms around her to ensure she did not get pulled away from him.

Every effort to forward progress was halted by bodies fighting. Dominic could only hope and pray that the other men were able to protect the sisters, but he could no more see or look around him for fending off the wild mob intent on fighting.

When someone pulled him by his hair looking for a partner to brawl with, he was obliged to partially release Faith in order to land a right hook and a kick to the groin in order to be released. This was no leisurely bout at Jackson's boxing parlour. This was street fighting with no honour.

When he turned, he registered her battle cry as someone made a grab for her.

"Keep your back against mine!" he called as he continued to fight strangers off, even while he felt her kicking and shoving behind him.

Dominic knew they had to get out of there. These brawls became notoriously nasty and would progress from a drunken mill into more dangerous fighting with weapons.

He saw an opening and pulled her up against him.

"Towards the boat!" he yelled at Rotham, hoping his friend had heard him.

Pulling Faith along behind, he shoved, hopped over bodies, and barrelled his way through the mob, holding her arm and trusting her to keep up. They ran until they reached safety, where they stopped, breathing hard.

"Are you harmed?" he asked, searching her up and down. Her dress was torn and her hair was tumbling down her back. She shook her head.

"No...are you?" she asked, as he noticed his own dishevelment. His neckcloth was unravelled, he tasted blood on his lip, and he felt the tell-tale ache of bruises forming all over his body.

Gently, she took a handkerchief and reached up to blot his lip.

She was so close he could feel her breaths that were coming shorter and shorter as she traded the rush of fear for that of desire. How he wanted to lean slightly forward and taste her, but he dared not. Once he let his control snap, he was not sure if he could find it again. His hands still grasped her arms and they stood far too close for his sanity.

Desperate to control himself from further intimacy, yet not ready to pull himself away, he made an attempt at humour.

"See? Nothing happened...with Sir Julian."

Faith burst into nervous laughter. It was always unsettling to be in a situation like that, and the terror mixed with euphoria afterwards wanted release. Most likely she had never witnessed anything like it before and didn't understand what she was feeling. Dominic felt it all too well and the urge to pull her into his arms and kiss her senseless was alarming.

Becoming aware that they were in a public place where anyone might recognize them, and before he did something unforgivable, he slowly separated himself from her and took stock of his surroundings. It looked as though the sisters and gentlemen were making their way towards them, though looking as dishevelled as they.

"Whatever did you do to start the brawl, Rotham?" Montford asked.

Rotham glared icily at him. "I? The other fellow knocked into me."

"Come, let us get away from here. If we stay, it could only grow more violent," Dominic interrupted the pointless banter.

"But we will miss the fireworks!" Dominic did not know which sister protested.

"You may watch them from the barge," he answered as he began to move them along. He sent one of his men back for Lady Westwood, then waited while the sisters exclaimed at the fireworks.

CHAPTER 17

$\mathcal{T}$he next morning, Faith and Joy were to travel to Taywards. Faith had mixed emotions about leaving her sisters in London, but for now, she could only leave and hope that the trouble with Sir Julian would go away in her absence. How ironic that the threat at Vauxhall had not been from him!

In actuality, she was looking forward to visiting the estate again. But she wished there was not so much at stake, and that Taywards did not belong to Westwood.

The truth was, last evening had awoken the undeniable certainty that she wanted him. It had felt natural to be by his side in danger, and he had protected her—would have protected her with his life had it been necessary. Unfortunately, though she knew he might desire her —she could have sworn he'd thought about kissing her—there was little doubt he was interested in nothing more.

With that melancholy thought, she finished dressing. Then her maid finished packing her trunks while she went downstairs.

There, she found Lord Westwood drinking coffee and reading a paper. He stood at her entrance, and she noticed a bruise near his lip and one near his eye.

Instinctively, she stepped forward and reached out her hand. She barely stopped herself before she touched him. "Do they hurt?"

"They look worse than they feel, I assure you. And how do you fare this morning?"

"I suffered little more than a few scratches, my lord. It was certainly an unexpected adventure."

"Yes, an adventure." He searched her face with a questioning look, and she was hard-pressed to maintain her composure under the scrutiny, unsure of what it meant and afraid her newfound feelings would be as transparent as glass.

"Will you join me for coffee while we wait for Mr. Cunningham to join us? He wishes to accompany us."

"Of course." She sat down, and Lord Westwood signalled to a footman.

"Would you care to read the paper? There is enough to share."

He pulled out part of the paper and handed it to her. As she sipped her coffee, she read through the Society pages. Lady Halbury would be appalled if she knew her wards not only read gossip but also featured as some of the more prominent fixtures in the column.

She scanned the lines quickly, hoping that no one had caught wind of their involvement in last night's brawl. A slight giggle escaped her when she thought of it. It was easy to laugh now, but she had felt real fear when in the middle of it.

"What is it?" Lord Westwood asked.

"Oh, I was just thinking about last night. It seems quite fantastical that we were caught up in a fight last night."

He smiled his understanding. "The evidence is on my face. I am only grateful that nothing serious happened."

They both went back to reading, then another alarmed cry rose from Faith's throat.

"No! No, no, no!"

Westwood was instantly at her side. She handed him the page with the offending words as she cast her hand to her mouth to keep from sobbing.

· · ·

Could it be true? Rumour has it that Miss Whitford eloped with Sir Julian Wright after being caught in a compromising situation at the Knighton masquerade. It is hard for this writer to imagine how they slipped past the guard dogs her guardian put in place around the sisters, seemingly at all times. Yet reliable sources inform me that it is true.

A STRING of curses erupted from his lordship's mouth. Were she not a lady, she might have joined him, for it was precisely how she felt.

"What are we to do?"

Lord Westwood began to pace about the room. She thought she would never like to be on the wrong side of his temper. He looked ferocious, like a lion on the prowl about to decimate his prey.

He called to the footman. "Send for Rotham, Montford, and Carew immediately. Tell the stables not to put to the horses until I say."

"Yes, my lord."

Finally, he looked at her and his expression softened when he saw her obvious fear.

"I will admit he has caught me unawares. I had not expected this, but he will pay. I will send a retraction immediately, but I am sure it will take more than that to undo the gossip it will cause."

"Am I ruined? Has he won?"

Westwood shook his head. "It cannot be that simple or he would have done so sooner. He has no proof." He banged his fist on the table. "What am I missing?"

"I do not know," she whispered.

He held out his hand. "Come with me to the study."

His hand rested on her back to guide her, which was reassuring but also unnerving. She began to tremble inside and was furious that she was letting Sir Julian affect her so. She could not be forced to marry him, so she knew his intention was to ruin her.

Lord Westwood led her to a comfortable leather armchair, then pressed a glass of brandy into her hands.

"Small sips, my dear. It will soothe your nerves."

She obeyed, but was surprised by the burning sensation which was followed shortly by a relaxing warmth.

He sat at his desk and began to write furiously—the scrawl of the pen scratching against the paper the only noise in the room.

Mr. Cunningham was the first to arrive, followed shortly by the others. Apparently, dispatching the footmen had not been necessary as they had already read the announcement in the papers.

Rotham marched into the study in barely leashed fury. "Shall we hunt him down? This is no act of a gentleman and therefore does not warrant gentlemanly rules."

"I assume you have already sent the retraction?" Carew asked, entering on Rotham's heels.

Lord Westwood nodded.

Carew came immediately to Faith's side and kneeled before her. "I know the circumstances are less than ideal, but would you be willing to accept me, lass? Even my tarnished name would be better than nothing."

"I beg your pardon?" Westwood asked angrily. "We are not in such dire straits yet!"

Lord Westwood's anger startled Faith. She looked down at Lord Carew and could see the flicker of annoyance in his eyes. His offer was made in earnest. But how could she admit that her feelings for him were of nothing more than friendship? Could she bear to marry him when she had feelings for Lord Westwood? She strongly suspected Grace had a tendre for the Irishman yet Faith might have no alternative to save her good name and that of her sisters. What a pickle!

"That is very generous of you to offer. I do not know what to think at the moment." She tried to muster a gracious smile.

Carew flicked her on the chin. "You need not decide now, lass. But I think we would get on well together."

"We can allow Miss Whitford to choose her fate later. First, we must deal with Sir Julian," Westwood interrupted savagely.

"What do you intend for him?" Faith asked.

"Being drawn and quartered is too good for him," Westwood snapped.

"Please do not call him out. I do not want him killed," she said, firmly. "Promise me." She looked steadily into his eyes.

He looked at her for a long, hard moment. "Very well. But it is no more than he deserves."

"Surely there are other ways to torture him?" Rotham suggested.

"Indeed there are, but we must find him first," Montford snarled.

"Knowing him, he's at the club, preening like a peacock. He will think he's won," Freddy suggested.

"But how? The elopement is a sham. It is impossible for them to have gone to Gretna Green and back already. It is easily refuted. Besides, he requires my permission since she is not of age."

"Not for an elopement. It is possible everyone will consider her ruined anyway."

"This is ridiculous! She has not left London!" he almost shouted.

"Even without proof, rumour is often enough."

"It is his word against mine. Not to mention the witnesses at Vauxhall."

"Is that enough?"

"Perhaps not, unless she marries someone else. Hence my offer," Carew defended himself.

"He will have gone to hide on the Continent if he knows what's good for him," Lord Westwood growled.

"How can he think to win with this antic?" Montford shook his head.

Faith listened to this discussion, feeling herself sinking into despair. Now her choices were limited, and what choices she did make would affect her sisters' chances of good marriages. It was pointless to wish she'd never come to London or heard of Sir Julian. She could not even be angry with Lord Westwood, for how could he have known what would happen?

"I will go to White's and see what the word is," Rotham offered.

"I will join you," Freddy said.

"Perhaps spreading it about that the notice was false will limit the damage," Lord Westwood suggested.

"If it will help, then we will."

"Montford and I can check at Boodle's," Carew offered, and Montford agreed with a nod.

"Perhaps you should have a word with your solicitor and the bishop," Rotham recommended to Westwood on his way out.

Faith was in shock. She stood but did not know where to go. She did not even realize Lord Westwood had moved next to her.

"There has to be something we can do." Much to her dismay, her eyes filled with tears. She was pulled into his arms and laid her head on his shoulder as if there were no gross impropriety in such a thing. "What do I do now?"

"How you must hate me."

She shook her head and pulled away, feeling embarrassed at losing control and wiping her eyes with her knuckles. "How could you have known what he would do?"

He took her chin in his hands and gently lifted it so she was looking into his eyes. "I will make things right."

DOMINIC ACHED FOR MISS WOODFORD. It was an entirely new sensation to be concerned by the sensibilities of a female, but then again, he had brought her into this situation. How the devil had his innocent wish for amusement, and thrusting them onto the *ton*, turned into this malicious evil?

Moreover, was Sir Julian so deluded as to think he would be able to maintain his way of life in England? Because one thing was for certain: when Dominic was finished with Sir Julian, he would wish he'd never heard the name Westwood nor be able to show his face in respectable circles again.

After seeing Faith into his mother's capable care, he dashed off a note to his solicitor to investigate the matter and advise him on what was advised should the marriage look authentic.

Secondly, he also wrote to the bishop, who had been a school friend of his father's and explained the situation to him.

As he made his way to White's, he mulled over the situation in his mind.

Dominic had little doubt the false announcement could be dealt with, but it was Faith's reputation that perturbed him. Carew had been correct, devil take him, that marriage would solve everything, but Dominic chafed at the idea of Carew being the one to save her. He certainly had not expected him to offer for her right then and there!

Dominic knew he'd been 'hoist by his own petard.' Had this been his fate from the moment Miss Whitford and her sister had burst into his hunting box and charmed him?

However, he loathed the idea of being forced into anything in such a fashion.

Despite being known for his determination in bachelorhood, he had always suspected he would marry one day, but in his own way and in his own time. Yet his hands were tied to act immediately by the guardianship. These were extenuating circumstances, but still it was not the done thing to marry one's ward.

He could not even say that Miss Whitford would have him. It was lowering to think she might choose Carew over him! However, he did not think Carew's feelings were engaged, nor Miss Whitford's. Over the past week or so, he had detected a spark of interest in her, but that could be no more than the awakening of human nature.

He'd wanted to know his own mind better before deciding, though for weeks he'd been suspicious of developing a decided tendre for her. At least, he found that he was having to restrain himself from seeking her out and bringing more attention to her—which was why he felt the need to distance himself to be certain. Fate seemed to have its own ideas.

Dominic entered the club and began to hand his hat and cape to the major-domo when Rotham and Freddy met him on their way out.

"Walk with us," Rotham, said, clearly not wanting to have the discussion where other ears might hear. They turned down St. James's before Rotham spoke. "I do not have good news, I am afraid."

"Was he there?" Dominic asked. He had no intention of leaving the weasel at the club to do more damage.

"No, but he was earlier, waving a marriage certificate around that looked authentic to all who saw it."

Dominic cursed. "And what was his story? Surely he cannot think to pass off a whopper about Gretna Green."

"No. He says he compromised her at the masquerade, then obtained a special licence at Doctors' Commons."

"That is easy enough to confirm," Freddy suggested.

"Buying the license does not mean a ceremony took place, nor that I consented," Dominic pointed out.

"Saying she was compromised is as good as ruining her, let alone having the marriage annulled," Freddy remarked.

"*False* marriage," Dominic growled. "Did either of you say anything?"

"No, we only pretended to be surprised and said this was news to us."

"I said I did not know how that would have been possible because there was not a time when she was not accompanied by one of us or Lady Westwood."

Dominic thought. "That will at least plant a seed of doubt when we must openly call him to account. We need to find him. He must have another trick up his sleeve. He cannot hope to think he wins with this and that I will not retaliate."

"You do not mean to keep your promise to Miss Whitford?" Rotham asked.

"She did not exhort me not to duel—only not to call him out. And I will not intentionally kill him, perhaps, but he will meet me or leave England in shame."

"You mean to force him into it," Rotham remarked.

"He has feathers in his cock-loft," Freddy remarked.

By this point, they had arrived at Boodle's. If Montford and Carew had found Sir Julian, Dominic hoped he was gagged and bound in a dark room by now.

"Are Lords Carew and Montford here?" Rotham enquired of the porter.

"Indeed, my lord."

They handed over their capes and hats and proceeded into the club. They finally found their friends at the back entrance, looking out of breath.

"What happened?" Dominic asked.

"He was here, but he escaped, the snake. We have chased him this past half-hour, but he had help," Carew answered.

"Were you able to discover anything else?"

"Only that he was boasting of having compromised Miss Whitford and that was why they'd married clandestinely. He ran off when he saw us."

"Not quite the same story as at White's, but close enough," Rotham remarked. "I think it is time to dispel Sir Julian's story. He cannot have claimed his prize if he is still about trying to convince people of its truth."

"What are we missing?" Dominic paced back and forth. "There has to be more to it."

"Two can play the game of ruination," Rotham said, with a wicked gleam in his eyes that Dominic recognized all too well. However, since they were not playing by gentlemen's rules…

"What do you have in mind?"

"A few well-placed whispers about his finances will do the trick."

"They would instantly be suspected to have come from one of us," Carew pointed out.

"I have no intention of them coming from one of us."

"Servants?" Montford asked knowingly.

"Precisely. It will only be what they've heard, mind you. Sir Julian can be left to prove whether it's true or not, just as he's left Miss Whitford to do."

"Ruthless. I approve. I will send my man down to the local tavern. It should not take long for that to send him to ground," Carew offered.

"Maybe he can find some sympathy with Brummell in France," Dominic said wryly.

"I suppose we have nothing left to do here for now."

They began walking back through the club, but Mr. Sackford-James, another crony of Dominic's father, stopped him. "Devilish careless with your wards, Westwood."

"On the contrary, sir, every one of my wards has been under my, or my mother's, direct supervision at all times."

"You mean Sir Julian is lying?"

"That is precisely what I am saying. My ward is innocent of all wrong-doing. Did you not see how he made his escape as soon as he saw me coming?"

"He has much to answer for in trying to ruin an innocent lady, all for a wager." Sackford-James shook his head. "A very bad business."

"I'd be much obliged if you would dispel the rumours should you hear anything further." Dominic knew well that people wanted his support on various political matters. He was not above calling in favours at this juncture to save Faith.

"You can be certain I will!" the man said with a humph that imparted his thoughts on such havey-cavey happenings and caused his thick whiskers to shake.

"Well, that was a fortunate meeting," Montford said as they left the club.

"Let us hope he's in the mood to spread the word."

They parted, all with the intention of sending their valets to their favourite haunts to gossip while Dominic returned home, thinking there was one person whose support would keep the *ton* from speaking openly against Faith. Failing that, he hoped his solicitor or the bishop had returned helpful words. It was difficult for Dominic to wait for anything. He wanted to hunt Sir Julian like a fox and attack him like the vermin he was.

With no news awaiting him from either, he sent off a note to his most powerful ally, then found his mother and Faith in her sitting room, discussing what was to be done.

"Dominic, at last. Please help me convince Faith she needs to stay in Town. She must face this with her head held high and prove that the rumour is untrue. If she leaves for the country as he expects her to do, then it will make proving the truth that much harder."

Faith shook her head. "I do not care what anyone thinks. In time, it will become apparent that we did not marry."

"But will it dispel the rumour that you were compromised?" Dominic asked, knowing it was likely to be something she had not considered.

"How can I dispel it now?" A warm blush had risen to her cheeks, showing she had understood.

"Mother is right, you know. If you continue on as before, it will become very obvious that he played you false."

"I am thinking of your sisters as well," Lady Westwood said gently.

"Guilt by association? The sins of the fathers are to be visited upon the children? Or sisters, in my case," Faith said bitterly.

"Unfortunately, it is often the case."

"What about Joy? She had her heart set on removing to Taywards."

"I never should have tempted her with my jumping course," Dominic said dryly. "I daresay, if she were willing to agree to supervision by my head groom, Chauncy, then I know my grandmama would love to have her there."

Faith nodded. She could not bear to continue disappointing everyone. Joy needed to be free in the country or who knew what other mischief she would get into. "Very well. I will stay, but only long enough to prove this wretch is lying."

"That's my girl."

CHAPTER 18

*S*tay and fight, they said. Did they not understand that Faith felt defeated? Humiliated? That she did not give a fig for the *ton* or their false opinions? All she wanted to do was to be alone where no one could find her. She needed time to think.

With Joy and Miss Hillier on their way to Taywards, Faith struggled not to feel jealousy that her sister was leaving Town. How she longed to be fifteen and free of all cares with no responsibility for her sisters!

She heaved a heavy sigh as she made her way upstairs to steel herself for what she felt sure was to be the worst night of her life.

Dressed in her favourite gown of cerulean blue netting over a matching satin slip, with the bottom of the skirt ornamented with tiny roses. The bodice fitted snugly, with short, full sleeves to accentuate her shape.

Her maid styled her hair, pulled elegantly back from the sides with loose curls falling from the back. She pulled on her gloves like armour, then turned as there was a knock on the door.

It was Lady Westwood. "You look perfect, my dear. I want you to wear these tonight." She held out a box that she was certain contained jewels.

"I do not understand." Faith stared at the stunning sapphires surrounded by diamonds.

"These are well-known Westwood heirlooms. If you are seen wearing these, it will make a statement that you could not be wed to Sir Julian."

"But will it not also make it look as if I am betrothed to Lord Westwood?"

"Only if we say it is so, and he is a much better prospect, my dear. However, you are his ward, and it is unexceptionable for you to wear my jewels. I think it's far more important to dispel the rumours about Sir Julian at this juncture."

Faith gasped when the heavy jewels were placed about her neck and on her ears. They were a brilliant counterpoint to the blue of her eyes and the gown.

Lady Westwood smiled with approval. "They look made just for you. Remember, you have done nothing wrong. Smile and whatever you do, do not behave as though you are guilty. Dominic and I will do the rest."

"How are you to do that?"

"A few well-timed comments, in addition to dancing with the right people. Trust me, we will weather the storm. Are you ready?"

Faith shook her head in dismay. "Not particularly, but I do not see any other choice."

"When people stare and whisper, hold your chin up with indifference. Nothing else impresses the stuffy matrons and crotchety patriarchs more."

That drew a slight laugh from Faith.

They made their way downstairs to where her sisters and the gentlemen were already waiting. Thank God for their protection. Faith could not have done this without knowing they would be by her side. As she looked at her sisters, her heart overflowed with affection, and she steeled her nerves to be courageous for a few hours. She could wilt later.

Lord Westwood came straight to her and bowed over her hand,

continuing to hold it as he spoke to her. "Mother dressed you in full battle armour, I see."

Faith tried not to blush under his approving gaze, but it filled her with confidence to perform the farce necessary to survive the evening.

"Marking your territory, Dom?" Lord Carew drawled as he approached and flashed a glance at her necklace. He bent over Faith's hand and boldly kissed the air above it. "My offer stands if you'd rather be announced as my betrothed this evening."

Something in his devilish gleam made Faith wonder if he actually wanted her, or was more interested in besting Westwood.

Faith shook her head with a shy smile. The hard part was, she really liked Carew, she just did not want to be married to him. "You are a true gentleman for offering, but you do not really want to be married to me."

He placed his hand over his heart. "Give me time and I will convince you."

"Thank you," she answered softly. "You are a good friend."

"More damning words were never spoken." He chuckled.

After greeting the others, they filed into the carriages and made their way to the Jersey residence. Waiting was more agonizing than the act, Faith decided, as it took over an hour for them to reach the front of the mansion. Once they had at last climbed the stairs and were announced, it was a relief.

"Ah, Miss Whitford. I wondered if the rumour could be true," Lady Jersey said. "I would not think you'd have willingly chosen Sir Julian over your other choices." She smiled knowingly, and Faith fought a blush.

"I may trust you to help us dispel the rumours, my lady?" Lord Westwood asked the *ton's* greatest gossip with his most handsome smile.

"Of course. Go on with you," she said as she turned to greet Faith's sisters.

There were stares and whispers just as expected, and Faith was immensely grateful for the support of Lord Westwood's arm. The ballroom glittered in the candlelight, with swathes of colour dotting the room, but Faith barely registered any of that.

"I will dance the opening set with you," he said. She nodded, grateful again to have that decision made for her.

However, afterwards, she wished she had been prepared ahead of time for what would happen. Their minuet was interrupted by an arrival, and the music changed abruptly to *God Save the King*.

"The Prince is here," she heard someone nearby saying. The dancers fell apart into an aisle of sorts in the middle of the ballroom floor, and everyone bowed or curtsied as the Prince Regent entered and walked down the floor, greeting people.

Faith had never thought to see royalty. Drawing rooms and presentations had not yet resumed since the death of the nation's beloved Princess Charlotte, and even the Regent rarely made social appearances. Given his reputation as an extravagant wastrel, Faith thought his genuine grief over his daughter did him much credit.

She felt Westwood's arm pull her back up to standing as she noticed the Prince stop directly before them.

"Westwood. Who is this lovely creature?"

"Your Royal Highness, this is my ward, Miss Whitford."

Faith blushed as the Regent held out his hand to her. It was so unexpected, Faith was unsure of what to do.

"Take his hand, my dear," Westwood said in her ear with a chuckle.

Faith looked apologetically at the Prince and gracefully extended her arm. He bowed over it and kissed her knuckles in a scandalous way that was no longer the fashion. He did not let go of her hand, but proceeded to pull it to his elbow.

"A waltz," he proclaimed quietly, but it seemed even the orchestra was at his command.

He was every bit as rotund as she'd heard rumoured, but could see the remnants of a handsome youth left in his visage along with the remnants of grief. Her heart ached for him.

He drew her into the waltz. Despite his size, he was a graceful dancer.

"Are you enjoying London, Miss Whitford?" he asked politely.

"Yes, Your Royal Highness."

"I heard there has been some difficulty."

Faith wondered at the remark and who could have told him.

"Matters shall soon be set to rights," he said with calm assurance.

A nagging suspicion occurred to Faith. Had Westwood implored the Prince to come on her behalf? Surely her guardian did not have so much power? She looked up to see the Regent smiling down at her. Faith's throat began to burn with the threat of tears.

"You must smile, my dear," he said. His kindness overwhelmed her. "You have four sisters, I hear?"

She was grateful for the distraction. "Yes, Sir."

"Perhaps you could introduce me when the dance is over. I hear they are all as beautiful as you, and perhaps even a trifle hoydenish?" His eyes were twinkling.

"Only the youngest, Sir," Faith replied, in awe of his knowledge. Though she had heard he was a great flirt, she felt in no danger from him. She was almost of an age with his daughter who had died. It was a sobering realization.

"I have a fondness for a bit of playfulness." His gaze moved to her shoulder and he looked lost in a memory for some time as emotions from happiness to sadness crossed his features. Her heart ached for him. "Forgive me. I am not very good company these days, but hopefully this dance will do enough good."

"I am most grateful to you, Sir."

When the set ended, Faith noticed more people staring as he led her from the floor towards Lady Westwood and her sisters.

"Thank you, Your Highness." She curtsied deeply.

"It was my pleasure. If Westwood fails to come up to scratch..."

"Your Highness," Westwood interrupted before he could finish the sentence. Instead of taking offence, the Prince grinned at the Viscount before turning to be introduced to Faith's sisters.

He left directly after that, making it clear to all why he'd come.

"Did you ask him here?" Faith asked Westwood.

"Of course. I had a small favour to call in, but he would have come anyway."

"Why?" She could not fathom his reasoning.

"He can never resist a damsel in distress. Especially not one with your beauty and four sisters to match!" he answered sardonically.

WHEN THE BALL ended without disaster, Dominic was pleased. He ushered the girls and his mother into two carriages and took the place beside Faith.

"I would call that a success," he said to her, while her sisters sat across from them and chattered about their evening.

"No one turned their back on me, if that is your measure."

"You may jest, but I have seen it more than once."

"What is this favour you were owed?" she asked, still apparently awestruck from meeting the heir to the throne.

"He most certainly would not wish me to share it," he clarified before she delved deeper.

"An answer which only makes me more curious," she remarked.

He chuckled.

"I wonder that you wasted a favour on me!"

"You shouldn't," he answered softly, wanting to give her cause to consider, yet warring with saying too much.

When they arrived at Westwood House, Dominic handed the sisters down from the carriage first, then Faith.

"Are you coming in, my lord?"

"Not tonight. It is a lovely evening. I believe I will walk." He sent the carriages back to the stables. When he turned back, she was waiting for him.

He raised his brows in question, but she stepped forward and kissed him lightly on the cheek. "Thank you." She turned away and hurried into the house, leaving him to hope all was not lost.

As he walked, Dominic reflected on the success of the evening. He'd known there was no other sure way to prove Faith's innocence short of marriage to someone else. He'd appealed to Prinny's chivalrous nature and was grateful he bestirred himself. Even though much of the nation did not approve of Prinny, no one would speak out against him. At the moment their sympathy was still with him over the loss of Princess Charlotte and her son.

He'd known Faith's beauty would also appeal to the Prince, but thankfully she was not in his normal style, so Dominic had no need to worry about the royal gallant taking a fancy to her.

Dominic had skirted the edge of the ballroom after the waltz, indolently greeting acquaintances, and was pleased with what he had overheard.

Obviously, she cannot be married to Sir Julian or he would be here with her!

Then why would he say he compromised her?

Perhaps the Westwoods are just covering up from their own negligence?

I cannot think so. I heard a rumour that it is all a bit of mischief by Sir Julian.

Lady Westwood said it was impossible for the girl to have been compromised. The girls had not been out of either her supervision or that of Lord Westwood.

In the card room, he had even heard whispers about Sir Julian being under the hatches, and that is why he was trying this desperate wager.

Dominic would not be fully satisfied until all his wards were married, but Sir Julian was going to have to pay. It was one thing to strike against Dominic personally, but another thing entirely to go after his ward, who was innocent of any wrong-doing. Not that Dominic could believe Sir Julian would still want revenge over his denial to a whip club.

No sooner had Dominic entered his house and taken off his coat and poured himself a brandy, than someone was at his door.

He'd just sent the footman to bed for the night so he answered it himself.

"Come! We've got him!" Rotham exclaimed.

179

Dominic didn't need to be told twice. He reached for his hat and coat and hurried out the door after his friend.

"Where?" he asked as they hurried back out into Berkeley Square.

"At Cheatham's. Apparently he arrived before the ball, drinking heavily and bragging about winning. Fortunately for us, Fielding and your brother happened to be there and kept an eye on him. Then Brosner wandered in and told of how Prinny came and danced solely with Miss Whitford, giving the lie to all of Sir Julian's proclamations that he had won. Not to mention the whispers about him being badly dipped."

"He certainly will be now, having lost this wager! I still want to know the terms of it! It makes no sense that he thinks he can get away with ruining a young lady!"

"He was not counting on her appearing in public again, nor your connection to the Prince. Most ladies would have left Town with their tail between their legs."

They arrived at Cheatham's, Dominic's ire settled somewhat by the fact that Sir Julian had already been exposed. It did not mean that he did not wish to beat him to a pulp. He flexed his fingers in anticipation.

Cheatham's was a gaming hell known for deep—and often dirty—play, which was where those not welcomed or without deep enough pockets for Watier's went to satiate their need. It occupied the ground floor of Chuffy Cheatham's town house in St. James's.

The room was a fog of smoke and darkness when they entered, and it took a moment for Dominic's eyes to adjust. The sound of clicking dice, along with that of shuffling cards, mixed with the dull murmur of conversation and the odour of smoke and spirits. A crowd was gathered in one corner, and Dominic spotted his brother's fair hair above the gathering. He tapped Rotham's sleeve and inclined his head towards Ashley.

As Dominic and Rotham approached, the sea of onlookers parted slowly when they realized who had arrived. Those on the edge strained closer to hear. Dominic had little doubt bets had already been exchanged on the outcome. He wished this could occur in private, but he was not about to let the weasel escape again, and frankly, it would do to have witnesses. Sir Julian was looking like a fox cornered by a pack of hounds, guarded by Ashley and his friends. He was exactly as he'd imagined him: cowering like the coward he was. The room became eerily silent as they awaited the confrontation.

"This is unexpected." Sir Julian's voice cracked.

"Indeed? This is precisely what I expected of you," Dominic drawled. "I would call you out, but that honour is reserved for those who hold claim to the name gentleman."

A low murmur greeted this proclamation.

"I have no intention of fighting you, Westwood. It would imply that I have done something wrong."

"Attempting to ruin innocents is hardly right. Especially for the sake of a wager," Dominic countered.

"I was trying to salvage her reputation."

"By instigating a wager meant solely to ruin her? By lying about having compromised her? By putting a false announcement in the papers? By waving about a false marriage certificate? I will have satisfaction here and now. You will answer for this." Dominic removed his jacket and waistcoat, untied his neckcloth, and rolled up his shirt-sleeves with deliberate slowness while Sir Julian stood and watched.

"The wager was not about ruining her," his shaking voice said as he watched Dominic strip.

Dominic stepped closer as the crowd parted to watch the fight. Sir Julian attempted to withdraw but was met by the wall.

"Pray tell, then. What was it about?"

Sir Julian smirked. "Telling would compromise the wager, but I have not yet lost."

"That is a pity. However, I am still going to enjoy destroying you on behalf of the lady's honour. You can stand up and fight or remain in the corner like a coward. It makes little difference to me."

The crowd began to egg on Sir Julian. Dominic saw the moment he realized he had no choice but to fight or be labelled a coward. He was a man-milliner with falsely padded shoulders and buckram wadding and was very likely debating what was worse: to strip or ruin his coat, Dominic thought acidly.

"If you wish to fight, we should do it properly with an arranged time and place with seconds." He tried to delay matters. The crowd did not approve. They began to jeer and taunt him.

"No." Dominic cracked his knuckles and took a fighter's stance, though he knew it would hardly be a fight.

"Very well." He stood forward like a martyr. "You will pay for this later. Ruining a lady is only the beginning."

"You are a coward," Dominic growled as blind rage overtook his body. Whatever concessions to a fair fight he had intended to make disintegrated. He slammed Sir Julian up against the wall, then he brought his arm back and slammed his fist into the blackguard's jaw.

Shouts of approval roared in the background, but Dominic did not register any of it. He punched with a bent elbow into Sir Julian's stomach, eliciting a groan from his opponent.

"Westwood." Rotham's voice registered faintly. "The cur isn't fighting back."

Dominic let out a curse and stepped back.

"I am not sure he can," Rotham amended.

Sir Julian was slumped over, holding his side. Dominic shook his head. "Unbelievable." He stepped forward and hauled Sir Julian up by his coat. The man winced. "Do not for a moment believe this is over. I will make certain you are never welcomed anywhere but Hell ever again."

"We will see about that," he responded weakly.

"You do not know when to fold, do you?" Dominic slammed another fist into his face then dropped him as he slid to the floor. He did not look back to see if the scoundrel was conscious, but he stopped in front of one of his friends. "See that he leaves the country, or I will not show restraint next time."

CHAPTER 19

The next morning, Faith awoke feeling that somehow things had changed between Lord Westwood and herself. Yet she had been warned so many times about how he was a hardened flirt and determined bachelor that she did not want to delude herself and become one of his victims.

However, she knew she would be devastated were she to lose his friendship, so she was determined not to let his attentions go to her head.

He called on the sisters late into the morning and found them in the small parlour that had been set aside for them. Hope and Grace were reading while Patience was sewing.

"Good morning, ladies," he said as he bowed on the threshold. "'Tis quite a picture you paint, all in repose."

"Good morning," they all replied.

"I think everyone is a little weary," Faith said.

"The Season can be wearisome in many ways." He smiled boyishly. "Are you too fatigued to take a turn about the garden with me, Miss Whitford?" he asked. "If I am not disturbing you, that is?"

"Oh, no indeed, sir. I was only writing to Joy about Vauxhall." She stood and smoothed down her skirts before following him from the room. Suddenly, she felt nervous about being alone with him.

It was a warm spring morning and the daffodils were giving way to fresh blooms of tulips.

"I wanted to apprise you that I do not think Sir Julian will be troubling you again."

"Did something happen?"

"You could say that. Last night, I was able to confront him."

Faith narrowed her eyes. "After you left here, sir?"

"Indeed. My brother and his friends happened upon him and… kept him occupied, shall we say…until I could speak with him."

"You did more than speak, however, did you not?"

"I did not break any promises to you. I neither called him out nor killed him."

She considered him for a moment. "What, precisely, did you do, my lord?" Did she imagine the sheepish twist of his lips before he answered?

"Very little, as he was an exceptionally reluctant opponent."

"Did you hurt him?"

"Do you mean hurt as in maimed for life, or hurt as in I caused him pain?"

"Are those rhetorical questions? Did you engage in fisticuffs with him?"

"Engaged is not the precise word I would choose."

Faith was becoming exasperated with his evasiveness. "Did you fight?"

"A few hits were made."

She stepped forward, concerned. There were no noticeable cuts or bruises on his face.

"Is everything to your satisfaction?" He looked down at her with amusement.

Not entirely, she answered him silently. If he was hurt, he was hiding it well. She longed to run her hands over his face to see or remove his gloves and examine his hands. He was so close…she stepped back, appalled at her thoughts. "How are you convinced he will leave me alone?"

"The confrontation was rather public. He as good as confessed to his falsehoods, and I made it very clear that you will be protected by me."

She raised her brows at him. "What, precisely, does that mean?"

"Simply that he was not worthy of a duel, and he was made to pay for slandering you. And, hopefully, no one else will attempt any such sort of wager involving you or your sisters or they will also answer to me...and that you need not marry Carew." The last was so quiet she barely made it out.

"I should think you would be delighted to have me off your hands." She was deliberately poking the beast, but she could not help herself. She wanted him to want her as much as she did him.

He opened his mouth, no doubt on a crushing retort about to be delivered. "That is what you think, is it?" Instead of remonstrance, his head descended to hers, and their lips had barely touched when one of the grooms burst into the garden.

"Chauncy?" Westwood asked in confusion.

Faith's heart began to race. She recognized the groom from Taywards.

"You must come quickly. The little mite's been hurt. I sent for the doctor and he is on his way to her, then I came directly here."

"What happened?"

"She fell from her horse and was kicked in the head."

Faith's hand flew to her mouth and she barely held back a cry of anguish.

"Have the best available horse saddled," he ordered.

"Ready a mount for me as well, if you please!" Faith called after the groom as he hurried off to do his master's bidding.

Westwood turned and looked at her. She thought he would protest, but said, "We leave in ten minutes. I will inform my mother and she can do as she thinks best with your sisters."

Faith heard him, but she was already running to change into her habit.

She was downstairs in less than ten minutes. Her sisters had heard the commotion and poured out into the entrance hall to see what was going forward.

"What's wrong?" Hope asked.

"Joy has had an accident."

"What kind of accident?"

Reacting as one, her sisters drew together and grabbed each other's hands.

"She fell off her horse and was kicked in the head. Westwood and I are setting out now. Do whatever Lady Westwood thinks best, and I will send word as soon as we get there and have judged the situation."

Her sisters' faces reflected the fear she felt inside. They all crushed each other in a hug when Faith heard Westwood call to her.

"The horses are ready."

Faith nodded, gave her sisters one last squeeze and hurried out of the front door to the waiting horses.

Westwood boosted her up into the saddle and as soon as she had hooked her leg over the pommel and arranged her skirts, she nodded to him, and they set off.

The ride would forever be a blur in her mind, as thoughts about what could have happened and what state Joy would be in when she found her whirled about in her mind. It was hard not to think the worst, just as it was impossible not to blame herself for letting her sister go to Taywards alone. She knew better than any what Joy was capable of, with her insatiable curiosity and energy.

Grooms ran outside to take the horses from them upon their arrival, and Lord Westwood threw himself from his horse to help her from hers. It was so tempting to collapse in his arms, but that would never do. A reassuring squeeze of her hand from Lord Westwood helped her to maintain her dignity.

"Come, my dear," he said.

She nodded and let him take her arm to lead her into the house and up the stairs to where Joy was.

It was hard not to cry out when she saw her sister looking tiny and lifeless in the large canopied bed. Words could not express the emotions coursing through her mind and heart as she rushed to Joy's side and took her hand. She was pale with a large bandage around her head and swelling distorting her face. A housekeeper Faith remembered from their previous visit was at her other side. Freddy Tiger was curled up beside her and let out a little meow when Faith scratched his ears. She needed to do something with her hands and she was afraid to touch Joy.

"He won't leave her side, poor thing," the housekeeper told them.

"Where is the doctor?" Lord Westwood asked.

"He is waiting to speak with you in your study, my lord. He said to keep her still and quiet for several days. She is dosed with laudanum so she does not move," she answered in a hushed voice.

Faith listened, but was looking her sister over. Her head was heavily bandaged around the top and one side. Bruising was already spreading to the other side of her eye.

"Do you wish to stay with Joy or would you care to speak with the doctor?" he asked Faith quietly.

Faith reached over and kissed Joy's cheek. "I am here now, Sister. Everything is going to be well," she whispered, as much to herself as to Joy. "I would like to hear what the doctor has to say."

He nodded to Mrs. Armstrong, and they went back down the stairs.

Lord Westwood immediately went to shake the doctor's hand. "Thank you for coming, sir. We have just arrived. What can you tell us?"

The physician introduced himself as Dr. Harvey, and he bowed to Faith before beginning his explanations. Faith was grateful Lord Westwood had returned to her side. She wasn't used to having anyone to lean on and she found she needed him very much.

"From what I can ascertain, the young lady was trying to perform some trick when her foot was caught in the stirrup and she was unable to kick free. Subsequently, due to the manner of her fall, the horse was unable to refrain from kicking her in the head." He pointed to his temple. "I do not detect any other injuries at present, other than some bruising, but if there are fractures, none of them are displaced. She needs to remain sedated with her head elevated to allow the swelling in her head to reduce. I have cleaned and stitched the wound at her temple, but it will need to be watched for infection."

"How long until we know…" Faith's voice broke before she could finish the question.

"Not before the swelling reduces. It could take days or weeks. And often patients with these injuries do not recover. She was not awake when I arrived. I believe she had a few minutes of consciousness immediately after the unfortunate event."

"What can we do?" Lord Westwood asked.

"Keep her still and quiet. Spoon barley water into her mouth several times a day for nourishment. She will not swallow well, but 'Better half a loaf than no bread' as the proverb has it. I will call again tomorrow, but summon me at once if there is any change in her condition."

Faith bit her lip to hold back the tears. How unfeeling doctors seemed, but they must have to be so to deal with such matters. She thanked the doctor and Lord Westwood saw him out. Then Faith sank down on the couch, unable to keep the tears from falling.

A warm pair of arms came around her and pressed her head to a muscular shoulder as a hand with a large linen handkerchief began to dab gently at her eyes.

She could not remember the last time she'd been held. If only the circumstances were different.

DOMINIC WAS UNUSED TO INACTION. There was so little he could do. He stood at the window, hands in his pockets, looking out over his vast estate. The stables and circular ride were visible in the distance, the site of the unthinkable tragedy.

The little hell-cat had put them all in a pucker. Dominic had received the story from his head groom. Joy had been determined to try some of the tricks she'd seen at Astley's. Dominic had thought Chauncy would be able to curtail her flights of fancy, but she had found a way to slip his charge, it seemed. She'd fashioned a harness to prevent falling, but it had failed and she'd been unable to kick free.

Dominic shook his head. It was more disturbing than he'd imagined to see the little imp, once so full of life, now limp and lifeless. If she did not recover…

If he was thinking these thoughts, how must Faith be feeling? The weight of his responsibility was crushing, yet this was her sister, who she'd brought up practically as her own. There must be some way he could help beyond sending the doctor in every day.

Faith had refused to leave Joy's side since they'd arrived. Dominic could understand her reluctance, but she was going to fret herself into exhaustion.

He had to admit to himself he had been denying from the beginning that he cared for the sisters, but in a very different fashion from the way he felt about Faith.

Dominic realized he would move heaven and earth to erase these burdens from her. When he thought how he must have added to them by almost kissing her…no, he thought with unaccustomed humility, it was likely she had not given him a second thought since Joy's accident. What a humbling thought! Although he'd not thought her indifferent to him, or he would not have taken such a liberty. Was he twisting the memory to suit his own desires? Would she somehow blame him for sending Joy away and be disgusted by him?

Perhaps that was coming it too strong and merely his own self-recrimination clouding his reason. Yet now was hardly the time to pursue the matter, especially when he was undecided and had not fully made up his mind on the subject. However, almost kissing her had been as good as committing himself. But their lips had touched, hadn't they? Had Chauncy not interrupted them, the kiss would have been a declaration. Perhaps it was inevitable, for he was coming to see that he did not mind the idea as much as he would have imagined.

Now was hardly the time for exploring these feelings. Yet how could he help Faith?

"You can stand there fretting about your incompetence, or you can go and be useful." His grandmother appeared inside his study, her chair being pushed by one of the footmen. "You may wait for me outside," she said to the man over her shoulder.

The footman made a slight bow, then closed the door behind him.

Dominic went over and kissed the dowager's cheek.

"I can hardly force her from her sister's side," he said helplessly.

"Why not? When have you ever allowed anyone to tell you what to do?"

"She is not my blood. Miss Whitford has been like a mother to Joy."

"Yes, but from whatever trick of fate, you are her guardian. Faith will be of no use to Joy if she burns herself to the socket. At least make her sleep on a truckle-bed in the dressing room while you keep watch. Perhaps one of her sisters could have convinced her to take herself off and sleep, but they are not here and you are."

"You are saying I should bully her?"

"You have never been stupid, Dominic. Of course that is what I am saying!"

"I suppose it is worth a try."

"Take your feelings for her and use them to the good."

"My feelings?" Was he so obvious? Thankfully, she did not push him further on what he was not yet prepared to discuss.

"You must help her through this ordeal. She is not accustomed to leaning on anyone, you know. Lady Halbury may have taken them in, but had very little maternal instinct, if I know anything from our Season together. Not but what it was good of her to give them a home. What Faith needs now is someone to lean on. Someone masterful who knows what she needs for herself when she is too distraught to see or even know what she needs."

Could his grandmother be right?

"Go to her. I've already directed the bed to be made ready for her. All you have to do is convince her to lie upon it. And send that footman in on your way out." She waved her hand before he could protest.

Dominic walked slowly up the stairs and down the hall to Joy's chamber, pausing in contemplation before the door. He tapped lightly and opened the door when there was no answer.

Faith was sitting next to the bed, staring at Joy, looking like a ghost of herself. She had not even noticed him enter.

He walked quietly towards her and put his hand on her shoulder, causing her to start.

"I did not see you there," she said apologetically.

"It is no wonder. You are worn to the bone. Please let me sit with her for a while so you may sleep."

She bit her lip and shook her head. "I cannot leave her. What if she wakes and I am not here? Or worse, what if she…" A tear rolled down her cheek. Dominic reached up to wipe it away.

"You will not be leaving her. Come and see."

Reluctantly, she stood and took the hand he held out to her. He walked her to a door across the room and opened it. "You will only be as far as this. The moment she stirs I will wake you."

He saw her look with longing at the bed inside the dressing room.

"You must let me help you, Faith. You will do Joy no good if you are exhausted."

"I know it, but it is impossible to make myself leave her."

"You will not be leaving her. I would have had them put the bed inside the room for you, but I think this is a better solution. Then I may watch over her while you sleep."

Faith nodded acquiescence, and Dominic felt guilty. He should have thought of this sooner. He wanted to pull her into his arms, but she was already halfway to the bed.

"Shall I send a maid to you?"

"No, thank you. I can do for myself."

"Very well. I will let you know if she stirs."

Faith nodded, and Dominic wondered if she would remember to remove her shoes before she fell asleep.

Dominic closed the door behind him and went to begin his vigil over the patient.

"Well, imp. You are saddled with me, I am afraid. I recommend you sleep because I have no intention of waking your sister."

He decided to ring for some coffee and a book.

CHAPTER 20

Faith awoke and could not recall where she was or what day it was. She stretched and blinked and looked around, but she recognized nothing about her. Daylight was coming in through the small window of what appeared to be a dressing room. She sat straight up in the bed as she immediately remembered what had happened.

She still wore her clothes from the night before. Lord Westwood had ordered her to sleep and she knew he'd been right.

She stood and made an attempt to wipe the creases from her gown, but it was of no use. Looking around, she saw a dressing table and set to work, trying to make herself presentable. After brushing and replaiting her hair then winding it into a simple coil, she splashed her face with water and used the toothbrush and powder set out for her.

Gingerly, she turned the handle to the chamber where Joy was, and saw to her relief that Lord Westwood still sat beside her sister, who appeared to be sleeping.

"Good morning. How do you feel?" he asked. He stood as he came to her in his shirtsleeves and his hair slightly dishevelled.

"Almost human." She had not been as quiet as she thought.

"I am glad to hear it."

"What time is it?"

"Thirty minutes past seven," he said, consulting his pocket watch and looking terribly handsome in his disarray.

"I have slept for fourteen hours?"

"I should say it was well deserved. Why do you not have a bath and break your fast? I can remain a while longer."

"I would not impose so! I have already slept much longer than I should have. You should have woken me."

"Nonsense. I am quite used to being awake until dawn. I will rest when you are ready. I will not take no for an answer," he said, with a look she was certain he meant to be stern, but instead was rather endearing. To be taken care of was a new sensation she could grow accustomed to.

"Very well, but I shall not be long."

He rang for a servant and directed them to have a bath drawn for her, followed by breakfast.

"Did she give you any trouble last night? I missed giving her the next dose of medicine," Faith declared in sudden realization and began to hurry to the table littered with vials and draughts.

"I managed to administer it," he confessed, placing a gentle hand on her arm to stop her. "The directions were well written."

Faith turned back and looked up at him. "Thank you." So much was encompassed in those two words that she could not seem to express. She reached out her hand as if it would explain. He took it and brought it to his lips as if to say he understood.

"I will take my bath now, then." She stepped back and left the room before she turned into a puddle in his arms as she longed to do.

The one thing she'd reflected on over and over whilst keeping vigil beside Joy was when Lord Westwood had almost begun to kiss her that day in the garden. Had it only been a few days? Perhaps she should not be thinking of such things at a time like this, but what else could she think on besides that which would certainly send her into madness?

When she reached her chamber, a maid was there to help her into the bath. She could not deny the relief she felt at sinking into the warm lavender-scented water. It was a guilty pleasure indeed.

It only served to turn her thoughts again to Lord Westwood. Was she a fool to think anything might come of it? Of course she was when he had discarded hearts all over England. Why would she be any different? And now he was only performing his duties as guardian. Nevertheless, he was unexpectedly attentive to her every need; arranging everything—from ensuring that she ate to passing time with her in easy conversation to ordering her to sleep—thus it was only natural that in such circumstances she should come to lean upon him and feel an affinity and comfort from such a saviour. It would surely pass once she was away from Taywards. With this in mind, she said a fervent prayer for Joy's hasty recovery for both their sakes.

The maid helped her to towel herself off and dress again, then told her she would escort her to the breakfast room.

"Oh, no, a tray in my sister's room will do very well."

"The dowager has requested you to breakfast with her, miss," the maid said as though it were an order, so Faith followed, knowing it was useless to argue.

The maid took her down a flight of stairs to the main floor, where the dowager's apartments were, and led her inside.

Faith curtsied. "Good morning, my lady. I thought you did not rise before noon."

The older lady cackled. "Not normally. Certainly I do not leave my apartment before noon, but I wanted a chance to speak with you."

Faith could not imagine what there was to say, but she sat down as the dowager pointed her to a chair.

"How is your sister?"

"Unchanged, my lady."

"That is most unfortunate, but I am glad you followed my grandson's advice to rest. He is quite capable of sharing your burden."

"It is quite unnecessary for him to do so, but I cannot deny I feel better for it."

"He is pleased to do it. He would do more would you allow it."

Faith tried not to let her embarrassment show, but she felt her cheeks warm.

"You are unused to plain speaking, I can see. In my day, we were not so mealy-mouthed."

A maid brought in a tray and set it on a table between them. The dowager paused in her speaking while she was served a cup of chocolate. The maid then turned and also poured one for Faith.

"Eat as you please," the dowager said as she waved to the tray which held an array of rolls and scones. Faith's stomach turned, for she did not know how to react to this verbal assault.

"Well? Have you made progress with my grandson? My feelings on the matter are unchanged."

"Ma'am, at the moment, my thoughts are wholly reserved for my sister and her future."

"Balderdash! I do not mean to disrespect your feelings towards your sister, but there is little to be done until Dr. Harvey says so. You have little else to think about all day as you sit there. Have you not considered my grandson as a match? I assure you he is quite eligible."

As if Faith were unaware of that! "Ma'am, he is my guardian. Such thoughts would be highly improper."

"Not with me, they are not. You should encourage him. Gentlemen always need a little help to see the proper path clearly."

Faith took a sip of the warm, rich chocolate. She had no idea how to reply. None of her upbringing had prepared her for such a one as the dowager, and she knew quite well that what the lady proposed was outrageous.

"On the other hand, perhaps you have the right of it," the old lady said thoughtfully as she tapped one gnarled finger on the table. "Perhaps it is your indifference to him that has sparked his interest."

"My indifference?" Faith was utterly lost.

"Indeed, I believe he suggested as much. Yet with one such as Dominic, who has come to see the opposite sex as vessels of fawning and simpering, you are a novelty. However, if he has no encouragement, will he miss his chance?"

The dowager seemed to be carrying on a conversation with herself.

"What do you wish me to do?"

"Do not fawn and simper."

"No."

"However, do not discourage his attentions should he make them."

Faith could only shake her head. It was not so simple as the dowager inferred and her interactions with Lord Westwood were limited to the times he visited her at Joy's sickbed. They would be even less so if they were to take alternate watches, as he would be sleeping when she was awake. Faith nibbled on a roll, wishing she could excuse herself and return to her sister's side. She may have slept a little, but her thoughts were hardly clear—especially on this matter.

It was one thing to consider the viscount herself, but another to hear his grandmother plot coldly against him. Did Faith want him? Yes, if she knew his affections to be true, but she wanted him to decide for himself—not because his grandmother wished for the union.

Faith finished her chocolate and her roll while the lady continued to pour unwanted advice into Faith's ears. Granted, the anecdotes about Dominic in his youth were amusing, but she did not feel she had the right to them as his mere ward.

"My lady, forgive me, but I must return to my sister. Lord Westwood has been with her for over sixteen hours now.

"Pooh. It does him good to exert himself, but I have prated long enough. Thank you for humouring an old lady. And heed well my words, miss."

How could Faith possibly forget them? She made her escape while she could.

DOMINIC HAD SLEPT for a few hours and had just finished breaking his fast when the door opened and Freddy burst inside. Dominic had not even heard him approach.

"I have but just heard! I was at Newmarket and when you were not, I sent a groom to your house. What happened? How is she?" he asked, out of breath.

Here was yet another who would be devastated by Joy's demise, Dominic reflected. Freddy had become uncommonly attached to the girl.

"She was trying her tricks," he answered. "She somehow managed to slip away when my groom's back was turned."

"I've never met a more determined girl," Freddy said, and slumping into a chair, repeated, "How is she?"

"It is too soon to tell. The doctor has given her a draught to make her sleep. He says it may be several days before we know how grievous are her injuries."

"So, she can't even wake up?"

Dominic shook his head. "Only enough to enable us to force more medicine and water into her. He says that while her brain is swollen it would be dangerous for her to wake up and be agitated."

"Good God." Freddy put his head in his hands and did not look up.

Dominic understood. The palpable fear was almost overwhelming, and the helplessness, when all one could do was to sit about, unable to command her healing, was untenable.

"Little Freddy will barely leave her side. He gets angry when we force him to go out twice a day."

Freddy chuckled, half-heartedly. "Loyal little devil."

Desperate to lighten the uncomfortable heaviness, Dominic changed the subject.

"The horses were running well?"

"Seemed to be," Freddy replied, wholly distracted and uninterested. "How are things in Town? I know it has only been a few days."

"The girls are upset, of course. Mother is of a mind to keep them there and occupied. Miss Whitford sent a letter assuring them there was nothing they could do here—although I believe she might have allowed her sisters to take turns watching over Miss Joy. Thus far, she has refused anyone's help but mine," Dominic replied.

Freddy shook his head. "You cannot allow that. She will become fagged to death."

"I agree, but it is not a matter of allowing," Dominic retorted.

"You've met your match, have you? I thought so all along, but I suspect if you did not give her a choice in the matter, she would allow you to share nursing duties."

"All I am allowed to do is to take watch at night so that she may sleep for a few hours, but she will only go as far as a cot in the adjoining dressing room."

"You may have to force her to take the air and get away from the sickroom. Can't have her falling ill, too."

Dominic supposed it was as simple as that. Thus far, he had not wanted to test Faith. "Do you have any news of Sir Julian?" he asked. They had drifted back to Joy.

"Actually, my valet said he heard he had fled to the Continent," Freddy replied.

"How reliable are the sources? We heard he'd left Town once before."

"Servants are usually more knowing, though it was in the Society pages, too."

"We all know the remarkable accuracy of those," Dominic said acidly.

"But this time, they reported he was forced to flee because he has extended his credit so far he's in the basket after losing the wager."

"We can but hope it is true. He deserves everything that comes to him. Miss Whitford should be safe enough here for the nonce. Has there been any talk about her absence? Or mine?"

Freddy shook his head. "Only that you are tending to her sister. May I see Joy? I promise to be quiet. I just need to see..." His normally placid friend spoke rapidly, clearly tormented.

Dominic understood. Sometimes things did not feel real when they were only told to you.

"I think that can be arranged," he said, motioning for his friend to join him.

Dominic stopped at the door and turned about. "I say, did you really leave with Windrunner running at Newmarket?"

"Who can think of a horse while Joy is fighting for her life?"

Dominic agreed, but horses were everything to Freddy. It was a testament to his regard for Joy. Many would find it hard to believe that Dominic himself would not be at Newmarket.

They climbed the stairs and Dominic gently pushed the door open wide enough to look inside. Joy had not changed from her supine immobility in the bed, but Faith looked distressed.

"What is it?" He went directly to her side, but then he saw what concerned her. Blood had eased through the dressing. "When was the last time it was changed?"

"I am not certain." She shook her head. "The hours and days seem to merge together."

Suddenly, Little Freddy let out a howl and leapt from the bed.

"Oh! Mr. Cunningham!" Faith exclaimed.

He lifted the kitten up to his cheek, and it was difficult to say which of them was more pleased to see the other. "Forgive my intrusion, Miss Whitford, but I could not stay away without seeing for myself how she goes on."

"It is hard to say. She stirs when her sedative wears off, but she has not yet said anything or seemed to recognize me."

"Do you wish for me to send for Dr. Harvey?" Dominic asked.

"I assume he will visit soon. He has not yet attended upon her today, but the bleeding worries me."

Dominic noticed Freddy standing there, looking upset. "Would you mind taking little Freddy outside, Freddy? He hasn't been out in several hours."

A look of relief passed across his face. "I would be happy to."

With another sad look at Joy, he left the room.

"Mr. Cunningham looked like he was going to be ill. The sight of blood does not agree with everyone. How prudent of you to have sent him on an errand."

"He seems deeply affected."

"My lord, I think the dressing needs to be changed. The bleeding seems to be worsening."

"Are there spare bandages? I confess, I have little experience in the sick room." He looked at the stack of medicines and towels on the table.

"Yes, but some boiled water would not go amiss," she said, frowning at the basin of cold water.

He reached for the bell-pull and requested the water and fresh towelling and to have someone send for the doctor.

Faith washed her hands as soon as there was fresh water and Dominic removed his jacket and waistcoat before washing his own hands.

"How may I help?" he asked.

"If you would hold up her head while I unravel the bandage."

Dominic gingerly lifted the uninjured side.

"I have nursed my sisters through any number of illnesses, from measles to chicken pox to sore throats, and cleaned and bandaged any number of cuts and scrapes, but this is entirely beyond my experience," she revealed nervously.

"You are doing well. I do know, if it bleeds heavily, we will need to put pressure upon it," he said. "I remember that from watching someone who had been shot."

Faith gave him a look of shock.

"I will tell you about it another time," he murmured.

Slowly, he lifted Joy's head as she unwound the bandage. Parts of it were stuck to Joy's matted hair and Faith peeled them away, then uttered an exclamation at what she saw.

Dominic lowered Joy's head and came around to look. He muttered an unintelligible curse. Joy's temple bore a large cut, half the size of a horseshoe, which had been stitched and now looked like a side of raw beef from all of the swelling and bruising, the more so due to the trickling blood.

"How is she alive?" Faith whispered. She had not been present when the doctor had dressed the wound. It would leave an ugly scar on Joy's beautiful face.

"All that matters now is that she is alive," Dominic said, putting his arm around Faith. She nodded into his shoulder, and he heard her sniff back tears.

He somehow knew she had not allowed herself to cry, so he waited while she composed herself, marvelling at the rightness of the feel of her in his arms.

"What do you wish to do?" Dominic asked once her sobs eased. The wound did not seem to be bleeding too much, just a small oozing from one of the sutures.

She took a deep breath. "I believe the best course is to clean it gently and reapply the bandage. Thankfully, it does not appear to be infected."

Dominic held Joy's head again while Faith washed away the blood and reapplied fresh strips of linen, then he tenderly lowered her to the pillow again. When Faith had finished bandaging, Westwood took her hand and gently pulled her from the room.

CHAPTER 21

*H*aving an occupation had helped Faith's state of mind. If only the task had lasted longer. The endless hours of watching Joy's still body were exhausting. Lord Westwood directed her into the hallway, where she resisted going further.

"You need to be away from here for a while."

Faith shook her head, even though she knew it was true.

Mr. Cunningham returned with the little cat, jumping along in front of him as though it was trying to pounce on something every step of the way.

"I could not keep him out long. He wanted to come back straight away," Mr. Cunningham said apologetically.

Faith could not help but smile a little even though the kitten's energy was a pointed reminder of what Joy's had been.

"Freddy, I am going to take Miss Whitford outside for a walk. We have changed the bandage, so Miss Joy should not need anything for a few minutes, and hopefully the doctor will be here soon. Would you be able to sit with her?"

Faith began to protest, but Lord Westwood's hand on her arm stayed her.

"Of course. Be glad to. Fresh air will do you good, Miss Whitford."

"And remember, call for someone should there be any need."

Faith followed blindly as she was led down the stairs and out into the garden.

"I am not certain Mr. Cunningham has the constitution for the sickroom," she protested.

"He will be well enough now that he cannot see blood. In fact, I think it will do him good to be useful."

"I wish I could be useful. I feel so helpless."

"Being at her side is everything of the most importance. Hopefully, Dr. Harvey will allow her to wake up soon. I doubt we will have much peace until we know."

He sat her down on a bench and, thankfully, remained quiet, allowing her some time to breathe the fresh air and enjoy the sunshine.

When a vehicle sounded on the gravel drive in the distance, he stood up.

"That will be the doctor," he said quietly, and held out his hand, knowing she would want to be present.

She said nothing as he guided her back to the house and then to the entrance hall.

They waited as Armstrong opened the door for the guest, her emotions strong with impatience, wanting to know if Joy would live and if she would be herself again.

"Faith?"

"Hope?" Faith did not remonstrate with her sister for coming. She was too glad to see her. They met and embraced, and Faith struggled to hold back the ready tears.

"Has there been any change?" Hope asked.

Faith shook her head. "The wound was bleeding a little and we are waiting on the doctor now. I hope he will let her wake up. Did you come alone?" she asked, taking stock of her surroundings.

"No, Lord Rotham escorted me in his curricle. It is no farther than Richmond and it is an open vehicle, with his tiger behind. Lady Westwood did not want everyone to come at once for fear it would be too much for you and Joy."

Faith nodded. She would be lying to say she was not relieved. Lord Westwood was doing his best, and had been unbelievably kind, but she could not lean on him for support as she could her sisters. She had not the right to do so.

"I will take you to see her. Mr. Cunningham is with her now."

"I will bring Dr. Harvey up as soon as he arrives," Westwood said.

As they climbed the stairs to where the bedchambers were, Faith prayed Hope could keep her countenance.

"Remember to stay calm and quiet in there. The doctor says we must not upset her."

"Do you think she can hear us?" Hope questioned.

"I do not know, but it is best to be on the safe side, just in case."

When they entered the room, Mr. Cunningham was standing by the bed, stroking the kitten with one hand and holding Joy's hand with the other. Her head was thrashing back and forth.

"Thank goodness," he declared fervently. "She started to wake up a few moments ago. I have just rung the bell to alert you." Mr. Cunningham stepped aside and took the kitten.

Both Faith and Hope went to Joy's side and took her hands.

Faith began to whisper reassuring words to Joy, and she stilled her thrashing.

"Faith?" she whispered.

"Yes, and Hope is here, too. Try to stay calm."

Faith was so relieved that Joy recognized her, but she wondered if she should be sedated again. If only the doctor would arrive!

"I did not mean to do it," Joy said tearfully.

"Hush, I know."

"Do not distress yourself," Hope told her. "We are not angry with you."

"Thirsty," Joy croaked.

Quickly, Faith reached for the barley water on the table next to the bed and spooned some into Joy's mouth.

"More," she begged and finished an entire glass before closing her eyes again. "My head...hurts...so badly," she whispered, then drifted off.

Once they were assured she was asleep, they sat next to each other on the chairs beside the bed. Faith did not want to give Joy the sedative again.

"That is the first time she has fully awakened. I cannot tell you my relief. I did not know if she would be herself again."

"I remember the same thing happened to a neighbour's groom and he was never the same afterwards," Hope recalled unhelpfully.

It was another hour before Dr. Harvey arrived, and Lord Westwood escorted him upstairs. He looked inside the room and on seeing him, Faith rose and went to the door.

The doctor made her a bow.

"Mr. Cunningham said Miss Joy wakened?" he asked.

"Indeed, she did, sir, if but briefly. I hope we did no wrong by allowing her to, but I stepped out to take some air and failed to give Mr. Cunningham instructions."

"I understand. How did she seem?"

"She recognized me, sir! She seemed to have all of her wits about her. She drank a glass of barley water, then went back to sleep."

"It is sooner than I would have wished, but this is a good sign indeed. Lord Westwood mentioned she has had some bleeding from her wound. I will examine her now to make certain there is no infection."

"Will she have to be sedated again?"

"I will not know for certain until I examine her, but I suspect she will sleep a great deal and need something to ease the pain, but not the heavy sedation as before."

The doctor went into the room where Hope was sitting with Joy, and Faith began to sag with relief. "Thank God!" Westwood's warm arm wrapped around her, and she placed her head on his shoulder, too near to be resisted. It was too easy to let herself depend on him, but she knew that when they went back to Town, things would not be the same.

Reluctantly, she left his arms and went back to Joy.

⁓

DOMINIC LEFT FAITH with her sister after the doctor had left. Dr. Harvey had been encouraged by Joy's progress, but said she would be under strict physical restrictions until they were sure the swelling in the brain was gone. Dominic knew as soon as the little imp was feeling better there would be no holding her down, but they would deal with that problem when it arose.

For now, he had other things on his mind, but he needed to greet Rotham first.

He was in one of the salons with Freddy, Dominic's grandmother, and his two aunts, charming them with well-practiced ease.

Cackling with laughter, his grandmother flirtatiously rapped Rotham on the knuckles, as if she were five decades younger.

Dominic smiled as he entered the green and gold room as he thought of it. Freddy was sitting on a sofa in between Aunt Flora and Aunt Rosemary, showing them the kitten.

"Dominic," his grandmother greeted when she finally looked up and saw him.

"I have been in here five minutes. It took you as long as that to take your eyes from Rotham," he teased.

"I may be old, but I am not dead," she answered with a mischievous grin.

"How is Miss Joy faring?" Freddy asked.

"She has woken and recognized her sisters. Dr. Harvey is optimistic about her full recovery."

"That is very good news," Aunt Flora said.

"Keeping her in bed to recover will be the challenge, I predict," Rotham remarked as he rose to his feet. "I must be returning. I promised my mother I would be back in time for her dinner party."

"Are you taking Miss Hope back to Town?" Dominic asked.

"That was the intention, although she might have decided to stay."

That was not the case. Hope was satisfied by having seen Joy awake and was willing to return to London. Freddy decided he would return with them.

Dominic saw them off and was about to go upstairs to see how Faith went on when his grandmother stopped him.

"A word, if you please, Westwood." She beckoned to him.

"Is it not time for your repose?" He was prevaricating, and they both knew it. She was going to ask him questions he did not want to answer to her before he'd answer them to himself. At least consciously.

"I will not wilt if my nap is delayed by a few minutes!"

He could not help but smile at her. "Would you care to go into the garden?"

"You know I would," she snapped. He took her chair and rolled it out through the door with the ramp built just for such occasions.

He wheeled her down the path towards the rose garden, which she'd planted as a new bride there at Taywards. It was still her favourite place. They stopped near a bench, and he sat down on it next to her chair.

"What do you mean to do now?" she asked without preamble.

"Should one not taste the meal before adding salt, Grandmama?"

"Food always needs salt, and I would think you've had plenty of time to sample!" she retorted. "Enough with your ridiculous metaphors. Well?"

"I can hardly make love and woo a lady whilst she is caring for an invalid sister."

"Ha! I knew it"! Her tone and the gleam in her eyes were full of satisfaction.

"And besides, you can hardly expect me to make a declaration while she is still under my guardianship."

"Pooh!" She waved her hand dismissively. "A few days here and there matter not. Do you think the day the conservatorship ends no one will know you've been wanting her? Even you are not that stupid, my boy!"

"It is a matter of honour, Grandmama," he said, restraining his voice from the growl he'd rather use.

"I am too old to wait for your niceties and notions of honour!"

"At this juncture, I cannot even say whether she would accept me. She's had other offers."

His grandmother began to laugh and cackled herself into a

coughing fit. She beat her hand against her chest, then ended with a contented sigh. "You really believe that, do you?"

"Miss Whitford is very reserved with me," he found himself confessing. "Occasionally, she leans on me for support, but that is only because she needs the comfort of a broad shoulder from time to time. She has shown no more affection for me than she might an elder brother, had she one. I do not know how she managed for so long by herself. She could not have been more than a girl when their parents died."

"One becomes accustomed by taking things day by day."

Her gaze became distant, and he knew she was speaking from personal experience. The dowager's lot had not been an easy one despite her privileged position.

Dominic stood and went over to examine a yellow rose to give her a few moments. He twisted one from its stem and brought it to his nose. She would not thank him if he saw her become emotional.

He waited until she cleared her throat. "If she's reserved with you, then you must convince her to be otherwise. Perhaps your reputation precedes you."

"My reputation?" He turned back and looked at her with his brows raised.

"Don't get on your high horse with me, Westwood. I am telling you no more than the truth."

Dominic was well aware of his reputation, but he never toyed with innocents. Those he flirted with knew exactly what he was about and had no expectations. It still made him cross to hear that his own grandmother thought he was no better than he ought to be.

Then he could not repress the guilt he felt when he thought of Jemima Taylor. He had deliberately flirted with her in full view of the *ton*—and Faith—the night of their ball. It had been as much to fool himself as to fool the *ton*. But had that ruined his chances with Faith?

He ran a frustrated finger around the edge of his neckcloth, which suddenly felt as if it were squeezing the life out of him. How odd that marriage was referred to as the parson's noose when it was the thoughts of losing Faith that made him break out in a cold sweat.

Knowing his grandmother was watching him with immense satisfaction, he forced his thoughts back to the present. "What would you have me do? I can hardly propose to her in such a situation!"

"No, but you can make it clear to her how she is very different from one of your flirts."

"I have never treated her like one of my flirts, as you so vulgarly put it!"

She scoffed at him. "You most certainly have not. One of your flirts at least expects…"

"Enough!" he commanded before she could finish. He was tempted to cover his ears. He treated Faith with honour and respect, and perhaps a little flirtation, but only because he enjoyed bantering with her. Was he really no better than that? "I am doing what I can to make myself pleasing within the confines of being responsible for her." It had been devilishly difficult, at that. Frankly, he felt he was deserving of sainthood.

CHAPTER 22

$\mathcal{W}$ ith Joy out of immediate danger, Faith continued to sleep in the dressing room at night with the door open, but she allowed others to remain with Joy for short intervals during the day. Thus far, Joy still slept a great and was not her usual ebullient self. When Faith presented her concerns, the doctor proclaimed this to be in the normal way of healing from a kick to the head and having been immobile in a bed for over a week.

Lord Westwood had been all that was good and kind during this time of trial. Had she not experienced it for herself, she might not have believed him to be capable of such kindness. Their friendship had grown into comfortable camaraderie, yet there had been no more moments where she thought his feelings to be no more than that of a sister. He coaxed her from the sick room for an hour or two each day for walks or rides; but no hints of love or flirtation accompanied them. Faith could not but wonder why Lord Westwood remained at Taywards when he could return to Town and all his entertainments— and flirts.

For her sanity, she wished he would go. Every moment, every day, he was near she felt it would be that much harder to be away from him. Perhaps if he left now, she could bear it.

It was time to write to her sisters to inform them of Joy's progress that day, and she went to her chamber to do so. When she returned, she overheard voices.

She stepped to the door, but did not go inside. Lady Halbury would have rung a peal over her had she witnessed her eavesdropping, but Faith could not seem to help herself.

Lord Westwood was with Joy, gently scolding her about her antics.

"Dr. Harvey has informed me that you may now take the air for a few minutes each day, but you will follow his orders and mine to the letter from this moment forward. Is that understood?"

"Yes, my lord. I am sorry for causing so much trouble."

"You have put your sister through a great deal of distress. Before you awoke, she would leave your side only under duress and then merely to the adjoining dressing room."

Faith heard Joy sniff.

"I say this not only because you will ruin yourself, or possibly even not survive the next time, but because you will also ruin your sisters' chances in Society," he said in a gentler tone.

Faith moved to the open doorway to see Joy's face. She was looking away from Lord Westwood, who also faced away.

"This foolishness has to stop now, Joy. Will you promise?"

Faith appreciated what he was saying and doing. Nevertheless, she did not wish for Joy to become agitated.

"I have no desire to repeat what happened, my lord."

Faith stepped inside and walked towards the bed. "How are you feeling today, my dear?"

"I would like to go outside. I am beginning to feel confined," Joy replied.

Little Freddy meowed his agreement.

"Dr. Harvey gave permission for you to enjoy a short airing today, so I will arrange it," Lord Westwood said. "Would you like to go to the garden or by the lake?"

"The lake." Joy smiled.

"Then I will see to it whilst your sister helps you prepare."

Half an hour later, Joy was dressed and carrying a big floppy straw hat for her outing.

She was still unsteady on her legs, and while dressing had tired her, she nevertheless wanted to walk.

"I think not," Lord Westwood said, and scooped her into his arms. "One thing at a time."

Faith followed along behind them, carrying Little Freddy.

When they reached the entrance hall, one of the wheeled chairs used by the dowager was sitting ready and Dominic lowered Joy into it.

"For me?" Upon Westwood's nod, Joy exclaimed, "Capital!"

"If the ride does not jostle your head too much," he warned.

It was a beautiful late spring day, and as they reached the lake, Faith saw that an area had been prepared for them under an old chestnut tree that looked as though it had many good stories to tell with its large trunk, winding limbs, and gnarled roots. A blanket and some chairs were underneath with a glorious view of the lake.

Joy sat and played with little Freddy, and Lord Westwood even found a goose feather for the kitten, the miniature tiger delighting in leaping and jumping at it.

It was unbelievably refreshing to hear Joy laugh again. It brought tears to Faith's eyes, because less than a week ago, she had not known if her sister would live.

"I believe we have company," Lord Westwood said, interrupting Faith's thoughts. She looked towards the house and saw her three sisters coming towards them.

"Joy!" Patience and Grace exclaimed as they ran to her side. They had not yet seen her. "We did not expect to find you up and about!" Patience said.

"What a relief it is to see you at last!" Grace added.

Lord Westwood greeted each of them. "Do you come alone?"

"Lady Westwood accompanied us, my lord," Hope answered. "She has remained at the house."

"I will go and greet her while the five of you reacquaint yourselves with the goings-on. However, I will be back in half an hour to return Joy to the house. She must not overdo it on her first outing."

"I am sitting still whether I do it here or in my bedchamber," she said with her mischievous smile.

"Do not try me, imp," Lord Westwood said with a flick of his finger on her chin.

As he left, the sisters sat on the blanket surrounding Joy.

"I hope you do not mind our visit, but we could not stay away any longer. Once Hope told us Joy had awakened, we simply had to see her for ourselves."

"Not at all. We only kept you in Town to provide you with distraction."

"I would ask how Joy is, but I can see that she is very well. What does the doctor say about her recovery?" Patience asked.

"You should see under the bandage," Joy said with zeal. "The doctor says I will have a scar for life!"

Faith supposed if one of her sisters had to bear a scar, at least Joy would mind the least.

"You have no objection?" Grace asked.

"Not at all. It gives me a good story to tell."

The sisters laughed and shook their heads.

"I am surprised you do not have your guards accompanying you," Faith remarked.

"They have been continuing to escort us to events," Hope explained. "But now that the threat posed by Sir Julian seems past, their vigil is not quite so pronounced."

"You are still enjoying yourselves?"

"Yes, dearest, although we have not attended as many functions as before."

"Are your suitors still too numerous to count? Or have you managed to scare some away?" Faith asked with amusement.

"There are still too many," Grace remarked and they all laughed.

Faith reached out and gathered her sisters to her for an embrace. "I am so happy you are here."

~

DOMINIC HAD BEEN to visit one of his tenant farms that morning and rode into the stables with one thing on his mind.

With Joy healing, and all of the sisters at Taywards, Faith was spending her time with them, and Dominic found that he did not like it. He had begun to cherish the hours they had spent together when he'd had her to himself. Soon, they would all return to London and where would that leave him? There were still three months left until Faith reached her majority, but something told him he should not wait to make his feelings known, because once they returned to London, it would be far more difficult to enjoy the freedoms and intimacy they had shared at Taywards.

Many enquiries had been made as to Dominic's whereabouts and why he had yet to return to Town. He could not explain to them that Town held no allure without Miss Whitford's presence. He could no more enlighten himself as to why it was so with her and none other, but it was so.

He was perfectly content to spend his life shielding her from all adversity, and could see no other replacing her in his esteem or as his companion, wife and mother of his children.

He no longer had any doubt in his mind that Faith was the one for him. Never before had he given any thought to a permanent relationship with any female of his acquaintance. Yet he still could not be certain she reciprocated his feelings and desired anything more than friendship.

Was he simply like an elder brother to her? Did she regard him with any more emotion than fondness? How his friends would laugh when they knew how low he had been brought!

The one time he had exerted himself, Joy had been hurt and they had since behaved as though that caress had never happened.

He kept trying to think of some way to lure her away from his sisters, but what would tempt her and not make him seem ridiculous?

Would rowing on the lake be enough to tempt her? His memories of doing that on their first visit to Taywards, which now seemed an eon ago, were some of his fondest with her, but would she feel the same? The bridge was where he'd like to speak with her, but he was uncertain if she would even accept his invitation.

He found the sisters in the drawing room with his grandmother, mother, and aunts.

They were laughing at something the dowager had said.

"There you are, Dominic. Dr. Harvey has just left us and now we are at a stand."

"What did the good doctor have to say?"

"He has removed my sutures!" Joy said, apparently relishing this gruesome occurrence.

Her other sisters made faces of disgust. His grandmother laughed, then explained. "He is very pleased with her recovery, but he thinks she should remain in the country for a while, and Faith does not wish to leave her. Do you not think Miss Whitford should return to Town and finish the remainder of the Season?" His grandmother's keen eyes watched him for his response.

Actually, Dominic did not want Faith to return to London, but it was not his place to say so.

"Am I to have any say?" Joy interjected. "I do not see why it matters if I am in the country or in Town. There is a garden I may sit in there. I cannot ride in either place. There are only a few weeks left of the Season, after which we may return here."

"But Joy, the air is so much fresher and cleaner here," Grace explained.

"It was not my lungs that were injured," she argued.

Dominic felt his lips twitch with amusement.

"Besides, our friends are there, and I do not want to be the reason Faith misses anything more. She has already suffered enough because of me."

"Joy," Faith said with a mixture of chastisement and affection.

"There is certainly no harm in trying it if you do not think the journey to be harmful. You can certainly return here should you find the London air is not agreeable to you. We will send you in our best carriage to minimize your being jostled," his mother suggested.

"If we surrounded you with pillows and blankets, I suppose we..." Faith said hesitantly.

"Excellent!" Joy needed no further encouragement.

"Perhaps we should spend just a few more days here," Grace suggested. "Much though I have loved the Season, a little respite is very welcome."

"How about if we were to leave on Monday? Will that do?" Dominic asked.

"That will do nicely, thank you," she replied.

"Miss Whitford, I wonder if I might interest you in another turn about the lake?" he asked quietly, where he hoped only she would hear. Fortune failed him.

"'A stitch in time may save nine,' eh, Westwood?" his grandmother shouted with glee.

"In the future, I will remember that you only pretend to be hard of hearing," he murmured wryly. Turning, he noticed Faith had gone rather pale. He held out his hand to her. "Come. I think it best if we speak without an audience."

Hesitantly, she put her hand on the arm he held out for her.

"What is happening?" Joy asked as they began to walk out of the door.

"Hopefully, my dear, my grandson is about to stop kicking his proverbial heels and offer for your sister!"

Dominic bit his lips on an acid retort and refrained from speaking until he and Faith had reached the front steps.

"Forgive her. She has decided you are the proper viscountess for me. It just so happens that I feel the same, but I would not have you be uncomfortable."

"I beg your pardon?" She looked astonished.

"Come, let us stroll down to the lake, where we may speak further and without interruption."

He led her to the lake and settled her into the rowing boat before taking his own seat. He removed his coat and began to row the oars. Somehow, it was easier to speak when he was not idle.

"You need take no heed of what your grandmother says," Faith began.

"I confess, quite abominably, that I do not. I am quite capable of thinking and speaking my own mind."

"But you cannot think to marry me. As I recall, you made it very clear you had no intention of ever entering such a state."

"No, did I?" He pursed his lips. "I am quite sure I did not. Perhaps my reputation precedes me."

"Perhaps," she agreed.

"But you cannot believe my philanthropy extends so far as to injured schoolroom chits. Everything I did was for you."

She narrowed her eyes at him. "Sir, I must tell you that you speak utter rubbish! You would have helped any of us or your friends."

"I fear I never have before," he said, even though he probably would should such an eventuality become necessary. "I was attempting to be romantic."

"I wish you would not, for it confuses me."

"Are you unable to think of me in such a light, then, Faith?" He stopped rowing for a moment to look directly into her eyes.

Her blushing cheeks betrayed her, but she did not look away. "It has never entered my head that you might consider offering for me. I have told myself from the beginning to dismiss such considerations. Indeed, I thought, what could I possibly have to offer you that one of your beautiful flirts did not?"

Dominic was not one to live his life with regrets. But at that moment, he would happily remove every past female from his life because they paled in comparison before this one. He wanted not one ounce of doubt, jealousy, or sadness ever to befall his love.

"I know it may be difficult to believe, but I hope you can trust me when I say that none of them has ever moved me as you do. I have never before considered marriage with anyone else."

"I want to believe you."

They had reached the opposite shore and he tied up the boat. He stepped out first, then offered his hand to assist her.

Instead of placing her hand on his arm, he kept hers grasped within his and led her to the bridge. She did not try to remove her hand, which he took to be a good sign. The river was flowing rapidly from the spring rains and they stood in contemplative silence for a few minutes before he turned to her.

"I was going to declare myself to you here, but perhaps it is too soon. Are you not ready? I had intended to wait until you had reached your majority, as would be proper, but being here with you every day has erased any doubts I had about delaying. If you need more time or wish to consider other suitors, just say the word. I will not like it, but I will not press you. I cannot vow, however, that I will not seek to persuade you otherwise."

"No." She shook her head and then reached her hands up to his face. "My lord, I have wanted to do this since that day in the garden when we were interrupted." She stood on tiptoe and placed her lips to his. It was sweet and innocent and genuine, and Dominic knew in his heart that she was his.

He wrapped his arms about her waist and began to kiss her back, gently teaching her about the art. When he slowly withdrew, he kept her in his arms, placing her head against his chest.

"Will you be my wife, Faith? My friend, my confidante?"

"Are you quite, quite certain?" She tilted her head up to look at him.

"I have never been more certain of anything," he said, looking down at her.

"Then I would be pleased to be your wife, but you may flirt solely with me," she demanded boldly.

"Baggage," he said affectionately as he punished her impertinence with another kiss.

CHAPTER 23

A few days later, they had settled back in London. Joy seemed to be happy being back with her sisters, and the governess seemed pleased to read to Joy for entertainment since her last employer had thought novels were the devil's work.

No time had been wasted in putting the betrothal announcement in the papers, and Lady Westwood was wasting no time in making preparations for the wedding the day after Faith reached her majority.

The viscountess had wanted to hold another ball, but fortunately Lord Westwood had been able to convince her that an intimate dinner with their closest friends would be better.

Faith still could not believe she was betrothed. Everything seemed to have happened so fast and was out of her control. She cared not for a large Society wedding or her standing in the beau monde, but the change in people's behaviour and the deference with which she was treated was astonishing.

"Are you ready, my dear?" Lady Westwood asked as she entered the parlour Faith shared with her sisters.

"I believe so," Faith answered. Lady Westwood was insisting on a grand trousseau, and they were going to make fabric selections from one of the silk warehouses.

It felt very unnatural to have such a fuss made over her, but she tried to assure herself that once the wedding was over, there would be less.

The one thing she had not counted on without the necessity of being guarded every moment was seeing less of Lord Westwood than before. It seemed she was always being called away for meetings with regard to the wedding that she had little opinion about. If she were not busy, then Westwood was occupied with estate matters or some such. At least she would be able to see him that evening at their betrothal dinner.

In all honesty, she reflected with irony, had it not been for Sir Julian's wager and then Joy's injury, Faith might not have had the opportunity for the closeness with Lord Westwood that had brought about this betrothal.

However, Faith was still nervous to go out without one of the gentlemen's escort, but she knew there was no longer reason for her concern. Still, she could not stop the eerie feeling that came over her as they rode to the silk warehouse. It was as though she were being watched or that something was amiss. Perhaps she was still oversensitive from all that had happened. When they arrived, the feeling passed, and Faith resolved to humour Lady Westwood to pass the time until she could see her betrothed that evening.

"Now, my friends, the lure has been cast," Julian said, as he sent the letter off to be delivered to Westwood House. "Tonight, my revenge will be complete. Everyone remembers their role?"

"Yes, sir," the group of reprobates he'd hired answered. They loved nothing more than the prospect of kidnapping and killing someone for money.

That, with a loyal friend or two, and it would be enough to deal with the wily Viscount Westwood, especially when he'd be taken unawares. Nothing dulled a man's brains like being in love. Julian shuddered at the thought, then smiled wickedly as he realized victory was within his grasp because of it.

His original plan had not been to kill Westwood, only humiliate him by forcing him into marriage, but then he had decided to interfere and try to ruin Julian before the wager was complete. Now Julian was left running from creditors. It was not to be borne and Westwood must suffer.

"Take your places and be ready. Watch both entrances to the house and have a signal to the others, whichever door he leaves by. My carriage will be waiting for you at the end of the alley to bring him to me."

"Yes, sir."

"Do not fail, and you will be well rewarded."

His ruffians left, and Julian grimaced with repulsion. Abhorrent though they may be, they were a necessary evil to achieve his ends.

$\sim$

"A LETTER FOR YOU, MY LORD," Satterlee said, entering Dominic's study.

He looked up from where he sat reviewing reports at his desk and accepted the letter, which bore no familiar markings or script.

Satterlee left, and Dominic slid his finger under the seal and opened it. He glanced at the signature and realized he'd never before seen Faith's handwriting.

My lord,

If it is not too great an imposition, could you please come early to West-wood House so that I may have a few moments of your time? Perhaps at six o'clock?

Your affectionate,
Faith Whitford

. . .

Dominic smiled and checked the clock. He just had time to dress himself and purchase Faith a betrothal gift along the way. Several matters of business concerning his Cumberland estate had occupied his time since their return to London, and he had been remiss in choosing a gift.

Dressed in a navy blue coat, a silver embroidered waistcoat, and grey breeches, he went downstairs, pleased with the idea of spending some time alone with his betrothed. He had not intended to abandon her as soon as they had returned to Town, but fully intended to take her away again as soon as the nuptials were over.

After placing his beaver hat upon his head, he took his walking stick and left by the back door, deciding to walk to the shop to buy the gift instead of taking his carriage.

He closed the garden gate and had walked but five steps when he realized that something was wrong.

He was instantly surrounded by men in dark clothing with their faces covered and hats pulled low. The tell-tale feeling of a steel barrel was thrust into his back.

"If you cooperate, my lor', this will go easier fer you."

Dominic was many things, but stupid was not one of them. If he fought, he was vastly outnumbered and with only the sword inside his walking stick as a weapon. If he cooperated, it would buy him more time to come up with a plan for escape.

"I've no intention of fighting you," he said. "What do you want from me?"

"If your lor'ship would be so obliging as to put your hands behind your back, just fer security purposes, you see."

Dominic debated what to do with his walking stick. They would be sure to notice if he attempted to tuck it into one of his boots—not that there was room to spare.

One of them held out their hand to relieve him of it. He suppressed a sigh. That had been a gift from his father.

As his hands were pulled behind his back and tied together, he could not help but ask, "How much are you being paid for this?"

"It's no use offering us more, your lor'ship," the leader said.

223

"I was more curious what I am worth," he muttered. Was there truly honour amongst thieves? More likely Julian had some hold over them.

"If you change your mind…" Dominic began to offer as he was shoved inside a carriage. There, he was treated to a blindfold and his feet being tied together. If only they had troubled to cover his nose, he thought with some remorse, as his guards inside the carriage had not seen soap and water this side of 1800.

He tried his best to pay attention to his whereabouts, but it was difficult at best. He could tell when the city turned to countryside by the sounds and smells, but he was uncertain whether they had gone due west or northwest. He was certain they had not crossed the Thames.

He was surprised when the carriage stopped but a few minutes later. He thought for certain they were headed for the coast when they left the city. He would've thought Julian's taste ran more to dumping his body in the Channel or a dark, damp cellar.

The carriage pulled to a stop, and the door was thrust open.

"It's time fer your appoin'men', your lor'ship." A beefy hand grabbed hold of his arm and hauled him from the carriage. It was a bit of a rough landing, but for all that, the hired ruffians had not been overly rough. He was walked inside what smelled like a barn and lowered to the ground and sat when he heard a familiar voice.

"Well done. You are earlier than expected," Sir Julian said. "Send your men back in the carriage."

Dominic heard some mumbling and groaning.

"But you said there would be some action, your worship."

"There will be, but unfortunately not for you. My driver will pay your men. I want you to stay here and keep watch while I finish my dinner. His lordship can stand to stew a little while with the goats and pigs, then I will be back to carve him up piece by piece. When that is finished, I will enjoy finishing the task of ruining Miss Whitford in earnest. Then she has four other delectable sisters I may enjoy at my leisure."

Over my dead body, Dominic seethed, but he refused to react.

"You had the terms of the wager wrong, you know," he said, so close to Dominic's face that he could smell onions mixed with burgundy on the man's breath. "You fell directly into my trap, though not precisely as I planned. Nevertheless, I have won."

Sir Julian paused for a moment. "Had you not interfered, you could have married and lived a happily ever after. Yes, the wager was to bring you to heel." He laughed as though he were possessed.

Dominic heard Sir Julian walk away as the carriage rolled off. He knew the leader of the gang must be nearby. He wished he would move or say something so Dominic would know where he was.

He did not mind a few moments to get his bearings and make a plan. He worked a little on the knots behind his back, but they were so tight he'd have to displace his thumb in order to escape. If he could not loosen them a little, his arms would soon be numb and completely useless.

"Are you comfortable, your lor'ship?"

"Not precisely, but it is a new experience I shall not soon forget."

The man laughed. "I like that about you. You're not quite what I expected."

"Nor is Sir Julian, I suspect." Dominic tried to incite a little enmity.

"Is that his name? Seems like I've heard it afore."

"I hope he paid you beforehand. The reason he wants revenge on me is because he lost a very large wager against me and the creditors are after him."

Dominic could hear the man chewing what sounded like a piece of straw, hopefully in contemplation.

"Will you tell me how many other men he has with him?"

"Aye, at least two."

Dominic gave a grateful nod and pulled his knees up to his face to try to displace the blindfold enough to orient himself. Sir Julian would only give him so much time.

∽

"WHERE COULD HE BE? It is not at all like him to be late!" Lady Westwood fretted as they stood around the drawing room with thirty guests, waiting to go into dinner. Hartley had announced it almost half an hour ago.

"Major Stuart will be back soon, my lady," Rotham said, trying to reassure her. Lord Westwood's brother had decided to enquire at Berkeley Square as to what might be delaying him.

Faith was trying not to worry. There had to be a perfectly reasonable explanation. Dominic would not abandon her in such a manner and embarrass her in front of all their friends.

Hartley walked into the drawing room and whispered in Lady Westwood's ear. Faith was standing next to her and strained to hear what he said.

"There is a man here to see you, my lady. He says he has information about his lordship. I've put him in the receiving room."

"Very well, I will go to him."

She took Faith's arm and led her from the room. They were about to enter the receiving room when Major Stuart returned.

"He left hours ago," he said. "His secretary said he received a note but dressed for the evening before he left."

"Did he take his carriage?" Lady Westwood asked.

"No, he left on foot."

"Come with us, please. Someone has just arrived, saying they have information."

Faith was grateful Major Stuart had returned, but it did not fill her with any reassurance.

The visitor was a servant dressed in Sir Julian's livery, who she'd seen before on her drive with him. Something was very wrong. He bowed when they entered the room. "Your ladyship, I had to come and tell you." He fidgeted with nervousness.

"You did very right to do so. What has happened?"

"They have taken him. I was told to drive the carriage, but then he made me leave. They had your son tied up and meant him harm. I've never seen my master in such a taking—like he's possessed. He's not alone, but he sent the hired ruffians back with me, save one or two."

"Where is he?" Major Stuart asked.

"A small farm less than ten miles from here, near Kilburn."

"Can you take me there?"

The man looked hesitant.

"At least to the gates, man. If Sir Julian is determined on revenge, we have no time to lose," Major Stuart said with frustration.

The driver nodded. "I want to help."

"Let me gather some friends. We will need reinforcements."

Faith longed to go with them, but she was too afraid to ask as Lord Rotham, Lord Montford, Lord Carew, Mr. Cunningham, and Major Stuart assembled, checked their weapons, and debated how best to go about a rescue. Some would go with the driver, and some would ride horses.

Lady Westwood left to take the remaining guests in to dine, but the tenor of the evening had grown sober. "We might as well eat since there is nothing we can do in the meantime," she reasoned.

Faith refrained from joining them because the thought of food on top of what might be happening to Dominic could not be borne. She went to her chamber and paced up and down for a few minutes while she watched out of the window as the men readied themselves to leave.

"I cannot stay here," she murmured. Quickly, she changed into some simple, dark clothes and made a dash down the servants' stairs. She ordered one of the grooms to saddle a horse for her and was shocked when he did not protest. "Quickly, please!"

The others were leaving, and she feared that she would lose their trail. They were already moving down the street at a spanking pace when she came around the bend. She could barely make out the silhouettes of the riders and horses up ahead. It was a tricky business to follow along, but they were so intent on reaching Lord Westwood that hopefully they would not notice her behind them. The sun was beginning to set on the horizon, which might work to their advantage.

Thankfully, once they reached the outskirts of the city, there was an open road and she was able to keep them in her sights.

Once the carriage slowed and stopped at a gate, she watched the others dismount. She waited until they walked through the gate, then tied her own horse to a post not far away.

It was becoming difficult to see with the darkening sky, and Faith did her best to keep hidden behind the trees along the drive. However, the house and barn were not in the trees, so she was forced to wait at a distance. Noticing movement near the barn, she realized the gentlemen had surrounded it.

Even though she wished to go forward, she did not want them distracted by her. Once she saw them make their move to go inside, she rushed to the door of the barn to look inside.

What she saw made her sick.

Sir Julian was kicking Dominic, who was lying on the floor with his hands and feet tied—the former behind his back—as a few other men watched, cheering him on. The gentlemen rushed into the fray, and fists began to fly. It was mayhem and Faith wanted to retch.

She saw Carew rush to Dominic and slice the ropes from his wrists and ankles.

"Thank God," she whispered, but then gasped as she saw him stumble to his feet. The ropes must have caused his limbs to go numb.

His friends noticed and tried to shield him from the ruffians, as best they could whilst fighting, while he regained feeling. Faith could tell the moment that he did, for he went straight at Sir Julian without holding back. She would never forget the sickening sound of fists pounding against flesh and the stench of sweat and blood as it sprayed into the air.

As Dominic was fighting Julian, several of Julian's friends broke loose of their own opponents to jump Dominic from behind.

That was when Faith noticed that Sir Julian had a gun.

"Look out!" she screamed as she heard a gun fire.

Both Sir Julian and Dominic fell to the ground.

"No!" Faith ran into the barn and rolled Sir Julian off Dominic. Blood was all over Dominic's chest, and she frantically searched him over for wounds.

"Faith? What are you doing here?" he groaned.

"Where are you hurt?" she asked.

"It was not I who was shot."

She turned to see that it was, in fact, Sir Julian who had been shot and was dead.

"Ashley shot him," Dominic explained.

"So this is not your blood?"

"It is not my blood," he reassured her.

She fell on top of his chest with relief and he squeezed her tightly.

"Oh, thank God. I'm never leaving you alone again," she said.

He chuckled. "I thought you wanted to stay in Bath."

"Ogre," she said affectionately before she kissed him without regard to the scene around them.

EPILOGUE

*H*ope had watched that morning as Faith and Dominic married, and not without a little trepidation. Nothing would change, they said, but Hope was sceptical. She now sat at the wedding breakfast, watching as Dominic danced with Faith, the two of them looking as though nothing or no one else existed in the world.

Hope could not supress some jealousy towards Lord Westwood. She was not proud of this emotion, but it was difficult to think of Faith as anything other than their motherly older sister. She had not even wanted to come to London and had had no thoughts of getting married. It was not that Hope wasn't pleased for her, but she did not want everything to change. But how could it not?

She looked around the ballroom, which no longer resembled the heavens. Instead, it looked like a rose garden with tables for dining and room for dancing. Mr. Cunningham was doting on Joy and Freddy Tiger as the cat was currently taking turns jumping between their laps. Hope laughed as she thought of the cat's performance during the ceremony, when he'd leaped from Joy's pocket to pounce on Faith's train as it had snaked along behind her.

Patience was surrounded by her court of regimentals. They all looked the same to Hope except for Major Stuart. He at least resembled Lord Westwood enough that she recognized him.

Lord Montford was asking Grace to dance, and Hope stabbed her confit de canard with her fork, chewed it without tasting it, then took a long swallow of her champagne.

"May I join you?" Lord Carew asked, sliding into the seat beside her before she answered. "You look as though you are in mourning rather than celebrating."

Hope tried not to watch as Lord Rotham twirled the beautiful Virginia Cunningham around the room. She was Freddy's younger sister and every bit as beautiful. She was the complete opposite of Hope, with her blond curls, and looked ethereal next to Rotham's dangerous dark looks.

"Would it help if we danced?" Carew asked, as if reading her thoughts.

"I doubt it."

"Which sister will be next, do you think?" the dowager asked Lady Westwood none too quietly—at least from where Hope sat it seemed as though she was almost shouting.

"It is hard to say. All of them have plenty of suitors."

Hope heard a humph. "Better catch Rotham for the next one."

Her ears pricked at the name.

"He will have to want to be caught. I am not certain that will happen very soon."

"Balderdash! He will want what his friends have, mark my words."

Hope frowned at that. What a lowering thought. To be wanted only for such a reason.

"Come. You need to dance." Carew held out his hand to her, and she accepted it.

"Perhaps you are right."

"My attentions to your sister seemed to get Westwood's notice. Maybe Rotham will wake up and notice the prize before him as well."

As she was swept into his arms, Hope thought perhaps she had fallen for the wrong man.

~

"Someone doesn't look happy," Faith said as she saw Hope sitting at a table, scowling at Lord Rotham dancing with Lady Virginia.

Dominic's gaze followed Faith's to where Hope sat, looking miserable, despite Lord Carew trying to charm her. He laughed. "Do not worry. Carew knows what he is about."

"Does he?" Faith was not so certain.

"Stop worrying your beautiful self about Hope. Everything will work out as it ought."

"I only want her to be as happy as I am." She smiled up into his face, unable to mask her love.

"Everyone should be as happy as we are." He squeezed his hand on her waist.

"Everyone?" Had he already forgotten about Sir Julian? Although he was dead, and perhaps no longer counted.

"Why the wrinkled brow?" he asked as they waltzed around the ballroom floor.

"I was thinking about Sir Julian."

"I most definitely was not. He has no place in our wedding day. Although, were it not for him, it might have taken me longer to come to my senses."

Faith scowled at him and he laughed.

"I think it is time we leave, my dear wife."

"After the dance, if you please," Faith said primly.

"I was not going to carry you from the dance floor. Though it is not a bad thought…"

"What would everyone think?" She blushed furiously.

"That we are married and madly in love?" he suggested.

Faith did not want anyone thinking about them at all. Before she knew what was happening, he took her hand and led her from the floor to where the family was gathered.

"I think it is time we left for Taywards," he announced. "But please, feast and dance to your hearts' content."

The dowager and his aunts were to stay in London for a fortnight to give them time alone together. After tears and farewells with each of Faith's sisters, they were loaded into the carriage.

Faith was happy yet nervous to be alone with Dominic at last.

"Stop worrying, my love. Your sisters will be perfectly fine with my mother."

"I know, but…" He stopped her thoughts with a delicious kiss. She had not been thinking about her sisters at all.

He rapped on the ceiling of the carriage before they had gone very far at all. Faith was too distracted from the passionate kiss to even think. "Why are we stopping?"

"Taywards is too far." He almost pulled her from the carriage and led her up the steps to his town house.

She looked at him in confusion.

"Have a little faith." He picked her up and carried her across the threshold.

All she could do was laugh and do as he said.

AFTERWORD

Author's note: British spellings and grammar have been used in an effort to reflect what would have been done in the time period in which the novels are set. While I realize all words may not be exact, I hope you can appreciate the differences and effort made to be historically accurate while attempting to retain readability for the modern audience.

Thank you for reading *Leap of Faith*. I hope you enjoyed it. If you did, please help other readers find this book:

1. This ebook is lendable, so send it to a friend who you think might like it so she or he can discover me, too.

2. Help other people find this book by writing a review.

3. Sign up for my new releases at www.Elizabethjohnsauthor.com, so you can find out about the next book as soon as it's available.

4. Come like my Facebook page www.facebook.com/Eliza bethjohnsauthor or follow on Instagram @Ejohnsauthor or feel free to write me at elizabethjohnsauthor@gmail.com

ALSO BY ELIZABETH JOHNS

Surrender the Past

Seasons of Change

Seeking Redemption

Shadows of Doubt

Second Dance

Through the Fire

Melting the Ice

With the Wind

Out of the Darkness

After the Rain

Ray of Light

Moon and Stars

First Impressions

The Governess

On My Honour

Not Forgotten

An Officer Not a Gentleman

The Ones Left Behind

What Might Have Been

ACKNOWLEDGMENTS

There are many, many people who have contributed to making my books possible.

My family, who deals with the idiosyncrasies of a writer's life that do not fit into a 9 to 5 work day.

Dad, who reads every single version before and after anyone else—that alone qualifies him for sainthood.

Anj, who takes my visions and interpret them, making them into works of art people open in the first place.

To those friends who care about my stories enough to help me shape them before everyone else sees them.

Heather who helps me say what I mean to!

And to the readers who make all of this possible.

I am forever grateful to you all.

Made in the USA
Middletown, DE
12 November 2023